CHARLIE GREEN

and the
Pirate's Treasure

MARTYN BLUNDEN

This is a work of fiction. Names, characters, businesses, places, events
and incidents are either the products of the author's imagination
or used in a fictitious manner. Any resemblance to actual persons,
living or dead, or actual events is purely coincidental.

Matador
9 Priory Business Park,
Wistow Road, Kibworth Beauchamp,
Leicestershire. LE8 0RX
Tel: 0116 279 2299
Email: books@troubador.co.uk
Web: www.troubador.co.uk/matador
Twitter: @matadorbooks

ISBN 978 1785890 673

British Library Cataloguing in Publication Data.
A catalogue record for this book is available from the British Library.

Printed and bound by CPI Group (UK) Ltd, Croydon, CR0 4YY
Typeset in 12pt Aldine401 BT by Troubador Publishing Ltd, Leicester, UK

CHARLIE GREEN

and the
Pirate's Treasure

Thanks to my two daughters, Jaye and Lexie,
for inspiration and for reminding me of the imagination
that is possible when you let go of boundaries of the adult mind
and let your thoughts wander away with the fairies!

And to my partner Helen
who believed in and supported
the absurd idea of me writing a novel.

Chapter 1

"Come on, Charlie Green," shouted Laura. "Get a move on and put that back in the box." He should have realised that when his mum called him by his full name, she was beginning to lose patience. The stress in her voice had been slowly rising all day and it had been an early start for them all. Packing for the move had begun the week before, and now, as the moment they were due to leave hurtled towards them, Laura was reaching boiling point. Had she got one of those kettle whistles attached to her brain, it would certainly be starting to blow. It was a Friday afternoon in late July. Earlier in the day there had been a good amount of warmth in the air, even though the sun had still been low. Now, after midday, with the sun well up and hardly a breath of wind, the temperature topped nearly thirty degrees – truly hot for Alexander Avenue, which didn't help Laura's rising frustration at getting the kids organised.

High in the sky, wisps of cirrus cloud danced like horsetails across the blue horizon. All of the doors in the house were open, allowing a breeze and the removal men to filter through the rooms. The smell of summer was abundant, and there was the humming sound of somebody nearby mowing their lawn.

The children had recently broken up for their school summer holidays, and today the Green family were moving to the country, to a rather neglected Victorian house. It was a place in which Laura could carve out a new, completely different life with her children. The house had once been the home of Captain Oliver Bramley, who had lived there for many years until one day he had disappeared without a trace and the house had been left abandoned.

The kids, or at least the boys, were very excited about the move; their sister, Olivia – known affectionately as V – however, was not so sure. She was sad to be leaving her friends and the only house she had ever known. Laura, on the other hand, was too busy to properly think about the decision, instead making sure that the removal men knew what would be going where in the new house. She was checking and labelling boxes, and hurrying from one room to another to try and make some semblance of the disorder.

"Come on, Charlie," shouted Laura, again. "Please would you finish packing those toys and stop playing around or we'll never get there in a month of Sundays!"

How long is a month of Sundays? thought Olivia. Her mum often used words and sayings that she found hard to understand.

Olivia was nine years old and a prettier little girl would be hard to find. She had a round face with just-above-the-shoulder auburn hair that hung as straight as a stair rod. It was fine, too, and no one but her could brush it without there being screams. She was also highly inquisitive and often thought deeply about the world around her, about why things were the way they were, and she was forever asking questions. Why is that? What is that? How is that? Today was the same.

"How long is that, Mum?" she asked.

"How long is what?"

"A month of Sundays."

"Oh, just a long time, dear. The time it usually takes Charlie to do anything," replied Laura.

Seated comfortably on the stairs, Olivia was ready to go. Her favourite red shoes were poking out from beneath her long dress as she hummed a tune that she had recently learnt at school. She also had hold of Babbit. Babbit was a small, rather grubby, very soft teddy bear that went everywhere with her. He had replaced an earlier, rabbit-like soft toy that had been lost, so this Babbit rarely left Olivia's side. For no particular reason, it had always been a 'he'. The ribbon around his neck was tied in a loop so that she could hold on to him with a tight grip.

This was a friendship for life, one that meant they would never, ever have to be parted. Babbit was usually gripped by Olivia's fingers, while the thumb of the same hand was firmly located in her mouth. Her forefinger would be over the bridge of her nose and moving gently in sympathy to the sucking action she made. Olivia did this most of all when she was tired, and now was one of those times. Having been woken at seven this morning by her brothers arguing, she had not had the amount of sleep she really needed. It was now two o'clock in the afternoon and a lack of sleep and the sadness of leaving was beginning to catch up on her. Olivia's eyelids began to feel heavy, filling with tears, as she rested against the wall. Laura soon finished hoovering the lounge and moved into the hall to find Olivia crying on the stairs.

"What's wrong, darling?" she asked.

"Ben says we're never coming back."

"That's right, dear, I'm sorry. People move all the time and now it's our turn. I'm sure you'll get to like the new house just as much and you can choose how to decorate your new room."

"I don't want a new room," cried V. "I want my room."

"I'm so sorry, dear, but this is what we have to do."

Laura picked V up and gave her a big hug. V clung on tightly, flinging her arms around her mother's neck.

"Come on, darling, it will be alright," said Laura. As she did so, however, a tear began to appear in Laura's eye too. She eventually put Olivia down, wiping her tears and then her daughter's.

"Come on, let's get you three in the car."

They made their way to the front door, down the steps and along the path for the last time. Turning to look back at the house as they reached the pavement, Laura told them to say goodbye.

"Goodbye, house," they all cried, and gave it a wave too.

Ben got in first and slid across to the window

seat on the other side. Then, before they could argue about it, Laura told Charlie to sit in the middle and let Olivia sit by the window. With a long face, Charlie did as he was told.

Laura then popped back into the house to have a final word with the removers about the last bits and pieces to go on the lorry. Once done, she returned to the car and they were off.

"Well, kids," she said, "this is it. Next stop: Pegasus Ride, Rock Lane. I've packed us a picnic and we'll find somewhere to stop halfway to have it."

And so they drove out of Alexander Avenue for the last time. Olivia was still very sad, her eyes watering as she clutched Babbit very tightly and sucked her favourite thumb.

★ ★ ★

Having passed through a village, Laura continued away from the junction and pulled up at the side of the road to check the directions on a piece of paper that was lying on the front seat. She continued and soon a road appeared on the right; here a rather tatty sign could be seen in the overgrowth that announced the road to be that of Rock Lane.

Good, we're here, thought Laura. Somehow, it seemed closer to the village than before. Reaching the end of Rock Lane, she pulled up outside Pegasus Ride.

The removal lorry was already there, unloading her life into the new house. She'd noticed Ben wake up as she'd turned into Rock Lane and now she turned around to face him.

"Ben," she said, "wake Charlie and V, would you? I'm just going to see the man about the keys."

Mr Burt, from Bacon, Burt, Crook & Co estate agency, had arranged to meet the removal men at the house for Laura and let them in. There was a final bit of paperwork to sign and then the keys were handed over. Mr Burt passed the children by the side of the car, smiled and said goodbye. Excitedly, the boys ran towards the house in an attempt to be the first one in. Olivia, holding tightly onto Babbit and with her thumb in her mouth, stood at the gate, looking for a moment. Laura, by now, was standing at the front door and, once the boys had rushed past, called to Olivia: "Come on, V."

Olivia started to move more purposefully towards the house.

As she approached the front door, her mum said, "Come on, let's have a look round together." Taking hold of her daughter's hand, they made their way inside. They could hear the boys clattering around upstairs on the bare floorboards. "Let's join your brothers and have a look upstairs first."

The stairs led up from the hall to the right of the front door, first to a small landing and then turning left to go all the way upstairs. This led to a long corridor, which, in turn, led to all the bedrooms. Olivia was going to have the smaller bedroom at the front of the house that overlooked the pastures beyond the front garden. Seeing her own bed and furniture as she entered into her new room, V's face began to melt into a smile. She walked across to the window and gazed out to see several ponies grazing in the meadow beyond the lane.

"Look, Mummy," she called out, "ponies!"

Laura joined her by the window and admired the view with her daughter. "Well, if it's nice tomorrow, dear, we'll go over and have a closer look. Come on, let's go and see what those boys are up to. Charlie? Ben?"

"In here, Mum," came the joint reply. It seemed that they had already found their new room at the back of the house and were busy arguing how to arrange their stuff. Laura and Olivia walked the length of the landing, past the bathroom and the entrance to Laura's bedroom, and stood in the doorway to the boys' room. Both Charlie and Ben were now looking out of the window.

"Look, Mum, you can see the airfield from here and the pathway leading to it from our garden. I wonder what's in those old buildings?" said Ben.

There were three old, corrugated-iron-clad aircraft hangars and a crumbling concrete control tower. Laura thought back to the conversation she had had with the village shop owner on the way, when she had dropped in to pick up some bread and milk in the village store. Mr Hobbard had become quite agitated when she had asked if the old airfield was still used and whether they could go walking over there. He made it very clear that she should keep the children away from it, but without really explaining why. She thought this reaction rather odd, especially as the estate agent had said it was only used for grazing sheep and had a couple of footpaths crossing over it.

"Well, don't bother wondering because I don't want you going over there," Laura told the boys.

"But I thought you said it is disused, Mum. Can't we just have a look?"

"Yes, it's abandoned, but I still don't want you going on one of your little trips to explore it."

"Oh, Mum! Why not?" sighed Charlie.

"Because I say so; it's derelict and probably dangerous. No, absolutely not. Do you understand?" she repeated, firmly.

"What if we are careful, Mum?" asked Ben.

"What don't you two understand about no? Look, we have a big garden out there for you to play in. Just enjoy that for now."

"Okay, Mum. You're right, the garden will be great for making a camp," said Ben.

Then, a shout from downstairs beckoned Laura. It was one of the removal men. He needed to know where to put some of the lounge furniture. Laura left the three of them to carry on sorting out the boys' room, returning downstairs to supervise the placing of the last bits off the lorry.

★ ★ ★

A while later, having spent some time unpacking their toys and books, Charlie felt bored and decided it was time to do something different. The garden was looking increasingly more interesting and inviting – anything to avoid sorting his clothes into neat piles and then into the wardrobe.

"Come on, I'm bored with this," he said to Ben. "Let's go and explore the garden." With that, the two boys ran along the landing and down the stairs, shouting at V to join them as they flew past her room. Clattering down the bare wooden stairs with the noise of a herd of cattle, they whizzed past their mother and towards the back of the house.

"What are you lot up to?" Laura quizzed, as they bundled by.

"Going out to the garden."

"Well, you be careful out there, and don't leave the garden."

"Okay," they replied.

Of course they didn't really listen and spent the next hour or so darting about the garden exploring all of its corners. Charlie found suitable sticks to hit things with and Ben looked for a place to build a den amongst the trees and overgrown laurel. Laura, meanwhile, welcomed the break so that she could get to grips with the most urgent things that needed sorting. This was mainly to do with where boxes had ended up, which, as it turned out, was not always where they were supposed to be.

★ ★ ★

They continued down the garden towards the shed, which, by normal garden shed sizes was quite large. Several windows, covered in a green mould, ran down one side, with a door at the end. The roof sagged in a gentle curve to the middle, possibly due to the weight of ivy and all of the other wild climbing plants that had clawed their way over it. Many years must have passed since anyone had used the shed for its intended purpose and now nature was trying to reclaim the site. Rust ate into the metal of the hinges and lock – another sign of years of neglect. Ben hacked away at the brambles that engulfed the building, trying to clear a way to the door. Keeping Charlie out of the way while he swished and slashed at nature's growth, Ben slowly cleared it to reveal the bare wooden door. In vain, he gave a tug on the metal handle. It was not going to give up its secrets easily.

"Try having another look through the windows, Ben," Charlie said.

As well as being covered with wild tentacles, they were just too high for Charlie to see anything. Ben cut and pulled greenery away and rubbed the encrusted dust from the window. Pushing his nose against the glass, he told Charlie that it did indeed contain an awful lot of stuff. Not just normal garden things, but boxes of strange objects that Ben didn't recognise. There also looked like there was a couple of old wardrobes and a pile of hats.

"Wicked," he exclaimed.

"What can you see, Ben? What is it?" enquired an excited Charlie, as he tried to pull his little body up far enough, without success, to see through the window.

"Cool, I think we could find some great things in here, Charlie," said Ben, wiping away some more grime from the next window. Then, he muttered to himself, "But why would anyone keep all of this out here?"

"What?" asked Charlie.

"Oh, nothing really. It's just that there's a lot of weird stuff in there."

Charlie tried tugging on the door handle again and kicked it in frustration.

"We're going to have to find the key, Charlie," said Ben, stepping back from the window.

Charlie thrashed the door with his stick, but it still didn't open.

Ben then checked out the smaller shed beyond, but it was a similar story. Although it was covered in wild overgrowth, Ben could see by rubbing away the grime on a window that it looked like a well-equipped workshop. It was as though someone had been using it and then just left – as if they had walked out with no intention to return. He could see a lot of, what he thought were, expensive tools gathering dust. *Why has no one cleared it out? Must be worth a fair bit of money*, he thought. On the far wall, he could make out a drawing of something pinned to the wall. Perhaps it was a technical drawing of something being made in the workshop?

"What's in there, Ben?" Charlie asked.

Again, the windows were just a little too high for

Charlie to see in. He tried the door, but as with the first door it was secured by a rusty lock.

"Well, it looks like some sort of workshop," said Ben. "I can see a large bench and a lot of tools hanging up."

The sun glinted off the windows, which made it harder to see through the grime. Ben pressed his nose closer to the glass. He could see a row of chisels neatly hanging on the wall, but there were a few missing. Everything looked well ordered and neat.

"Someone very proud must have owned this once, Charlie."

★ ★ ★

Having explored the jungle and found no trace of unnatural wildlife – although Ben had spotted a couple of likely places for a hideout – they decided to return to the house to help unpack some more of their possessions. Ben led the way back through the elephant grass, where the merest hint of a pathway remained. Olivia now joined Ben, while Charlie brought up the rear, still thrashing away with his stick. It was when he looked up to swipe a particularly tall piece of weed that something caught his eye.

"Hey, guys, did you see that?" he said.

"See what?" asked Ben.

"In that little window." He pointed up to the back wall of the house where there was a small, square window.

The other two looked and saw nothing.

"I can't see anything," said V.

"Neither can I."

"I'm sure I saw something in the window."

"Like what?"

"I don't know. I'm just sure I saw something move away when I looked up."

"Sure, Charlie, course you did," said Ben, dismissively. "It must be a window in the attic and you need a ladder to get up there, which we don't have. And Mum is only person in the house."

As the trio made their way back to the house, Charlie couldn't help but glance up at the window a few more times.

★ ★ ★

Tramping back into the kitchen, where their mother was unpacking a box, Charlie asked her about the little window.

"Yes, Ben's right. It's a window into the loft. The estate agent assured me it had been cleared, but there was no ladder up to it for me to check. He did say, however, that it was boarded over and would be large enough to be converted into another bedroom if we wanted. "Why do you ask, Charlie?"

"He thinks he saw something at the window," said Ben.

"I did," protested Charlie.

Laura patted him on the head, saying, "Well, it must have been some sort of reflection because there's nothing up there."

★ ★ ★

With occasional help from the children throughout the rest of the day, Laura was able to make some sense of the remaining mayhem and empty more boxes. After a simple supper, they all decided to go to bed. It had been a tiring day and did not take long for them to fall asleep. Before closing her eyes, however, Laura thought through the plan for the following day. Whether or not it would actually go to plan was another matter entirely!

Chapter 2

The next day, an early morning mist hung low over the fields at the front of the house as the sun rose up from behind the garden. It shone brightly through the un-curtained kitchen window, highlighting the peeling paintwork on the bare walls. As it was so quiet and calm in the country, with just the sounds of the wildlife calling to each other, they all overslept. Usually it was the noise of traffic that woke them up, but today there was none of that.

Charlie was the first to stir, but it didn't take long for the whole family to awaken. He was not known to be a quiet child and his clattering about on the house's wooden floors did nothing to keep the others' eyes closed! He hurriedly dressed himself in the same clothes he had had on the day before and bundled downstairs. Still half asleep, Laura pulled on her dressing gown, slipped on her pink fluffy slippers and followed at a more sedate pace.

While it seemed that Ben and V were intent on having a lie-in, Laura found a wide-awake Charlie sitting at the kitchen table when she got downstairs.

"Morning, Charlie," she said, dragging herself across to the window of light. She squinted as her eyes adjusted to the bright view of her new garden, the rays of sunshine dancing on the tops of the undergrowth.

"Morning, Mum," replied Charlie with a bright smile and a hedgehog-like hairstyle.

Grabbing hold of the kettle, Laura started the breakfast ritual by clumsily spraying herself with high-pressure cold water that missed the spout. "Sod it," she exclaimed, somewhat startled.

"Mum!" Charlie shouted, in a mix of surprise and disapproval.

"Sorry, Charlie."

Laura stepped back to the tap and tried again, this time paying more attention. She was no good in the morning until a cup a tea had been downed. Charlie, meanwhile, tapped impatiently on the table with no particular rhythm.

"What's for breakfast, Mum?"

"Give me a minute, Charlie," she gently protested.

Laura opened the fridge and took out the milk that had been purchased from that odd little shop in the village. She thought back to the experience, drifting into a momentary trance.

★ ★ ★

She had stopped outside a very old, thatched shop with small windows and a white front door. It was in a row of buildings of similar vintage, the kind that graced the centre of the small village, and was fronted by a small low-walled garden. With the children still asleep in the back of the car, Laura popped inside for some groceries.

As she opened the door a bell had rung above her head, and again as she closed it. Inside, Laura found a shop completely different from anything she was used to. The layout was the same as it had been for decades and some of the wares on display looked like they had been there for as long. It seemed almost Victorian and very quaint. Covering all of the walls were wooden shelves stacked with cans and jars of all sorts. The counter itself supported two small glass display cabinets and a vintage bacon slicer. The remainder of the counter was clear apart from some daily newspapers and a sloping wooden box containing some vegetables.

The layout suggested that it was definitely not self-service. It was as if the modern age had bypassed Rosemie Common, or at least the shop. Suddenly, from behind a slatted plastic curtain of rainbow colours, a smiling, larger-than-life woman appeared. Wearing a floral apron over an ample midriff, she, with corn-coloured hair that looked as if it had been dropped from a great height straight onto her head, welcomed Laura.

"Hello, my dear," said a definitive country accent. The woman had the face of a bright red radish that had split across the middle through over-watering. Her smile didn't just make use of her lips, but her eyes and the rest of her body, too. "How can I help? What would you like, my dear?" she asked.

Laura had paused in thought, raising a hand to her mouth while still digesting the view in front of her. She hadn't been able to decide which was more surprising:

the vintage shop display or the lady with the haystack on her head. It had seemed to stick out horizontally from the top in all directions, as if were attracted by an invisible force from the four walls of the shop.

Before she had been able to reply, the rotund lady had leaned ever so slightly over the counter and said, "Guess you'll be moving into Pegasus Ride, won't you, my dear?" and then a knowing nod.

Laura, never having seen the woman before, took a slight gasp and said, "Well, actually… yes, we are. But how did you…?"

"Oh, it's quite a small village is Rosemie, my dear," interrupted the woman. Her folded arms slightly lifted her motherly bosom, like a hen rearranging her eggs in a nest.

"We've been expecting someone new for a while now. Then I heard that a woman and three children should be arriving sometime today. I was upstairs and saw you pull up in the car. We don't get many visitors from other parts these days, you see. Not since the aerodrome closed, you see, and, well, that was some time ago now. Oh yes, sometime. Back then, people often stopped to ask directions, but that was a long time ago now."

"No, not many at all these days," echoed a voice from behind through the rainbow curtain. A man had then appeared through it, saying, "It'll be nice to see someone living in that house again." He paused. "I'm sorry, my dear, my name is Hobbard, Harry Hobbard, and this is my wife, Beryl." He offered his hand across the counter.

Laura smiled and shook his hand. "Pleased to meet you. I'm Laura."

All through this exchange, Beryl had silently broadened her smile from ear to ear, as if she had slept with a coat hanger in her mouth, and continuously folded and refolded her arms.

"Of course, I haven't taken any post to Pegasus Ride for, well, quite a few years now," said Harry.

"No," his wife continued, "not since Oliver..."

"No, not since..." said Harry.

"Oh," remarked Laura, puzzled by their conversation and still rather surprised at their knowledge of her arrival.

"Yes, pity 'bout Oliver, he was such a nice man."

"Oh yes, a very nice man," confirmed Mrs Hobbard as she looked at her husband.

"I'm sorry about, well, about whatever happened," replied Laura.

"Well that's it, miss, we don't know what did happen."

"No we don't," said Beryl. "We just don't know, but we're glad somebody will be living in it again."

"Oh, yes. Yes, we are. Mind you, young miss, I'd not wander over the airfield if I were you. Not just yet anyways. No, best be on the safe side, eh," said Harry in a slightly forceful tone.

"Oh, I'd thought it might be a nice place for a walk with the children."

"Definitely not, my dear. Not good for children to go wandering about over there. You never know where they might go and those old buildings probably aren't safe."

"I'm sorry, dear, we're rabbiting on and you must have come in for something," said Mrs Hobbard.

Remembering what she had come in for, Laura replied, "Er, I just need some milk and bread for now."

"Of course, my dear," replied Mrs Hobbard. "No problem. Yes, of course we have that for you." The old woman disappeared through the multi-coloured curtain to get some milk, before returning to pluck a loaf of bread off the shelf behind the counter. "Is there anything else?"

"No, thanks, not for now."

"Well, if there is anything you want regularly, then just let us know and Harry can deliver it for you, my love. Saves you the trouble, see. That's £2.65, my dear."

"Thank you very much," said Laura as she paid for the milk and bread.

"You're very welcome, my dear – very welcome indeed. Anytime. If there is anything we can help you with, don't be afraid to ask. And if we are shut, just ring the doorbell. We won't mind," said Mrs Hobbard.

"No, we really won't mind," continued her husband.

"Thank you. Well, I had better get on. Lots to do. It was very nice to meet you," said Laura as she turned and left the shop.

As she had returned to the car she had thought how different this place was to the town they had just left. Where they had lived had been modern and cosmopolitan, with all the resources you would expect to find in a town. It had, however, been a very impersonal place and even though she had lived there for twelve years, she had not known the neighbours two doors down. Here, they seemed to know her before she had even properly arrived! The Hobbards seemed like nice people – friendly at least, but a bit odd.

What she didn't hear was the conversation Beryl and Harry had after she had left the shop.

"You should have done something before, Harry, now they're moving in," said Beryl.

"I know, I know, but I was always hoping he'd come back. I'll find an excuse to go up there and sort it. I promise."

★ ★ ★

"Mum? Mum?" shouted Charlie, loudly. "You alright?"

"Oh… yes, dear. Sorry, I was just thinking about something that happened yesterday."

She put the milk down on the table and then began to explore the cupboards. As she opened each in turn, she made a mental note that the awful pallid green colour that currently adorned them would have to go. In fact, the only fitting that wasn't green in the kitchen was the beige Aga that occupied the space along one of the walls which was the only means of heating water. There was an electric immersion heater to supply hot water, but that was broken. She had told V when they had first arrived that the kitchen 'was out of the ark'.

Ben and V moped in. V was wearing a cardigan over her nightdress, sucking her thumb and clutching Babbit tightly with her eyes barely open. Ben, too, was still in his pyjamas. They seated themselves around the kitchen table, awaiting the arrival of breakfast.

"Morning, Ben, morning, V," said Laura as she gave V a hug from behind and a kiss on the head. There was some kind of mumbled response from V, but the thumb never moved.

"Why can't you get up quietly, Charlie?" moaned Ben. "It's too early."

"Thought you'd wanna go do some more 'sploring, Ben?"

"I do, but it could wait a bit."

Charlie sat fidgeting as Laura worked her way around the room. Noting the old pantry at the side of the kitchen, Laura remembered where she'd stored away the cereal. With Ben's help, they were all soon enjoying their breakfast and holding a conversation together through mouths crunching cereal.

"So, what's the garden like?" enquired Laura. She had only looked at it from the kitchen window so far and had not ventured out herself.

"It's great, Mum," says Charlie, "and much bigger than our old place."

"Can I build a tree house?" asked Ben. "There's a

pile of old wood I could use and there may be more stuff in one of the sheds."

"What? There's more than one shed?" queried Laura.

"Yeah, there's a smaller one behind the big one," said Ben.

"Can I go to see the ponies?" Olivia asked excitedly, having only just properly woken up.

"One at a time," said Laura, raising her voice to be heard above the children.

"We tried to get in them but they were locked, and covered in brambles and weeds," said Charlie.

"Yeah, we tried to look through the windows, but couldn't see very much. There's a load of old junk in the big one, but the other looks like it might have been a workshop," said Ben.

"Well, that sounds like a good place to put your father's old tools. We've got a lot more unpacking to do today and it would help to get those out of the lounge," said Laura.

"Have you got a key to the sheds, Mum?" asked Charlie.

"I don't think so," she replied. "They only gave me these." She picked up the key ring that held the front and back door keys. "And they are just for the house."

We'll have to find another way, thought Charlie. "Maybe we could smash it with a hammer?" he said out loud. "Ben's got a hammer."

"Don't you go smashing anything!" his mother quickly replied. "You'll end up hurting yourself or someone else."

Charlie was disappointed; he quite liked the idea of bashing something with a hammer.

"There's also a gate at the end of the garden, which I think leads onto the airfield, Mum," said Ben.

"Well, definitely don't go through the gate. Goodness knows what trouble you could get into out there," insisted Laura.

Of course, this only made Charlie want to explore the airfield more. The buildings he had seen also looked inviting, and the fact that it was supposed to be deserted only added to the mystery. To Charlie, it was just another adventure to go on.

★ ★ ★

When breakfast was finished, Charlie was keen to go outside and find a way into the 'shed of mysteries'.

"Can I go now, Mum? Can I? Can I?" he requested eagerly.

"Okay, but be careful out there. It's all so overgrown – you could hurt yourself on something hidden in the long grass," warned Laura. "And please stay in the garden."

Charlie wasn't really listening as he dashed out of the kitchen into the back garden. Picking up an old garden cane as he went, he thrashed at the grass as if cutting his way through a jungle. Well, it was a jungle to him and this was like a jungle adventure. *What will I find?* he thought. And off he went, in his mind, to find tigers and elephants and explore the horizon of his world.

Laura watched this from the window and

wondered how long it would be before the box of plasters would be needed.

"He'll hurt himself somehow," she said, shaking her head. She then turned round with a resigned look on her face.

"If you've finished, Ben, can you go and keep an eye on Charlie?"

"Why do I always have to look after him?" he said with a protesting groan.

"You can still play, but just keep an eye on him," Laura pleaded. "You know what he's like."

"Okay, okay, but it's not my fault if he does hurt himself," replied Ben, grumpily.

"And I'll need you to come back in a while, anyway, to give me a hand."

Ben disappeared upstairs to get dressed, returning a few minutes later. He then strolled out into the garden, leaving the door wide open so as to let in some warm morning sunshine. Looking down the garden, a small paved area with an adjacent woodshed gave way to overgrown wasteland of tall grass and weeds. A hedge reached out halfway across the garden, near to an unseen pathway that Charlie was currently thrashing his way along. Beyond the hedge and the once cultivated part of the garden were several out-of-control laurel trees, which surrounded the intriguing huts.

Ben nosed into the woodshed to look for something to help clear the brambles and bushes. He found a likely tool hanging up – it had a curved, rusty metal blade, which was about the length of his forearm, and a slightly woodworm-full wooden handle. Removing it from its resting place of two rusty nails, he practiced a few slashing actions as he walked towards the unseen path. Had his mum seen the budding swordsman chopping the garden air, she would have had heart failure and taken it off him immediately. As it was, she was consumed with the task of clearing up the breakfast carnage.

★ ★ ★

Turning to Olivia, Laura said, "Would you help me unpack some more boxes this morning, dear? We'll make a start in here."

"Of course, Mum," she said sweetly. "But can we then go and see the ponies?"

"Of course, dear."

The two of them set about clearing away breakfast before unpacking some more of the boxes marked as 'kitchen'. There was not a lot of cupboard space in the actual kitchen, but the pantry made up for that.

Olivia was quite intrigued by the pantry. She had never seen one before; a little room just for storing food. *What a great idea*, she thought. There was even a small pair of wooden steps so that she could reach everything.

She soon busied herself unpacking, sorting and stacking the pantry goods, while her mum stocked the higher cupboards in the kitchen. Other than the occasional, "Where shall I put this, Mum?" V got on with the job on her own.

Charlie appeared in the undergrowth, wielding a stick and trashing away at the brambles.

"Oh great, that'll do the job, Ben. Can I have a go?" asked Charlie as he moved towards his brother.

"No, you can't. You're likely to chop your blinking leg off. Come on, let's find the best place for a tree house and then we'll see if we can find the keys. They must be around somewhere."

★ ★ ★

Back in the house, Olivia had just finished unpacking the last three boxes in the pantry. "I've finished these ones, Mummy," she called out.

"Oh, well done. Thank you, dear. I've nearly finished sorting these out too," replied Laura, as she stepped down from placing a bowl on the top shelf.

"Can we go and see the ponies now?"

"Yes, I suppose we can, dear. I'll just put these empty boxes outside and check on the boys, then we'll go."

Laura opened the back door and placed the boxes down. "Ben?" she called out. No reply. "Ben!" she shouted again. Hearing nothing, she next tried calling Charlie's name and still neither of them replied.

"Why don't those boys ever listen?" she said to Olivia, now at her side.

Olivia shrugged her shoulders and replied, "They're probably making a camp at the bottom of the garden or building bits for Ben's tree house."

"Yes, they probably are," sighed her mother, moving back into the kitchen. "Oh well, I guess they'll be okay and we won't be long. I'll leave a note on the table to let them know where we are and not to leave the house."

She scribbled the note and pinned it down on the table with the biscuit jar. The boys were always scoffing biscuits, so they should find the note easily enough. "There, they can't miss that," Laura said to V. "Come on, we'll take a biscuit for the walk and go and see if we can find the ponies."

V followed her mum through the house, past the boxes that were still piled up in the hallway. Without any soft furnishings, the hall echoed with the sound of their footsteps on the wooden floorboards – one or two creaking with looseness.

Chapter 3

On reaching the front door, Laura realised she had forgotten to lock the front door before going to bed. In fact, it wasn't even shut properly.

"Oh my goodness, that was stupid of me," she said to V. "Good job we're out here in the wilderness; don't suppose anybody ever comes up here."

Compared to the town life they had been used to, this really was a wilderness, and there was a stillness in the air that would take a little getting used to. *But what a view*, Laura thought as she stood under the front porch.

They walked down the path that led to the broken picket-fence gate – hanging only by its top hinge – and on past the roughly mown grass and overgrown flower borders that obviously had not been tended for many years. Gazing over her new estate, Laura commented, "It was probably a very nice garden at one time."

"Yeah, I wonder what happened to the person who lived here before," replied V.

"Yes, it's strange that it should be left for so long. I'll ask in the village. I'm sure someone will know something. People don't normally just disappear. After all, they knew a lot about us before we got here, so they should know something about the people who were here before they went away."

They walked out onto the lane. A short distance away was a footpath that looked as though it led to the field with the ponies. Laura took hold of Olivia's hand and led the way down the narrow path, which was just wide enough for them to walk side-by-side.

The ponies were in the second field that they came to, which was separated from the first by a fence. Between the two was a large metal rectangular water trough propped up on bricks. There was also a shelter in sight, enclosed on three sides by timber cladding.

Just past the water trough, Laura and Olivia stood on the bottom rail of the wooden fence and called to the ponies. Olivia bent down and pulled a handful of grass from behind her. She then leaned back over the fence and tried to attract the animals' attention with her tempting morsel. One of the ponies looked up from their grazing and started to amble towards them.

"There's not much grass for them in there, Mummy," V said, noticing the very short grass in the field.

"We could do with them in our garden; they'd mow the lawn down," she laughed.

The pony, wearing a blue headcollar, made its way towards the two of them, followed not long after by the second. After some hesitation, one of the ponies took the offering of grass from V's hand. They stayed there for a few minutes and then Laura decided it was time to return home to check on the boys. The ponies had got bored anyway and wandered off across the field.

As they turned round to walk back up the path, a boy appeared and walked towards them, pushing a bike by his side. He looked a similar age to Charlie.

"Hello," Laura said as he got closer.

"Hello," said the boy with a wide smile. He dropped his bike into the bushes on the side of the path and walked across to the fence. He was wearing a pair of blue denim jeans and a worn T-shirt, and had a leather satchel slung over his shoulder.

They watched as he approached the fence and whistled loudly, before shouting some phrase that Laura couldn't comprehend. Whatever it was, the ponies obviously recognised it as they galloped towards the boy. He had now climbed over the fence and was standing directly in their path. Not having any knowledge of horses, Laura was quite concerned at the sight and instinctively grabbed V by the arm, pulling her towards her. Although slightly alarmed at the speed of the horse's arrival, Laura assumed the boy knew what he was doing.

He then undid his bag and grabbed a handful of what looked like solid brown pasta tubes. The ponies immediately came to skidding halt, which threw up a cloud of dust. He held out a flat hand of feed to each of them. Intrigued, V ran over to him and asked, "What's that you're giving them?"

"Oh, just pony nuts."

"Nuts?"

"Well, not nuts – they're just called that. They are a sort of crushed up corn and grass, I think," replied the boy. "They love them."

"I guess the ponies are yours, are they?" enquired Laura.

"Yes, this one's mine," he said, patting the smaller pony with the blue headcollar. "This is Archie."

"Wow, do you ride him?"

"Yes, when I can."

As he stroked Archie, they watched the others try to raid his satchel for more nuts. The boy slipped the satchel off his shoulder and emptied the contents on the ground for them both to feed on.

"Is the other one yours, too?" asked Laura, who had now joined them.

"No, she's my mum's."

"What's her name?" asked V.

"Annie."

Although it seemed obvious, Laura then asked, "Have you come down here on your own?"

"Yeah, I usually come down here twice a day to check on them. I should've come down earlier but I had to help Mum in the garden."

"We were just giving them some grass before. They looked hungry," said V.

"I hope you don't mind," added Laura.

"No, that's okay. They've got plenty really, although it doesn't look like much."

Olivia nodded, before asking, "What's your name?"

"George."

"Well, I'm Olivia and I have two brothers, Ben and Charlie. This is my mum and we've just moved into the house over there," she said, pointing to the top of the path.

"Oh, right. I've never known anyone to live there. It's been empty for as long as I can remember. Dad said a bloke lived there on his own once, but one day, when I was little, he just seemed to disappear and nobody knows where he went. I think he was a pilot on the old airfield, but I'm not sure. I live down the lane, in the house with the little table outside and the wooden archway into the garden. You must have passed it on the way down. Mum sells eggs from our chickens and vegetables from our garden. She did tell me there was a new family moving in soon."

"That'll be us. Well, there you are, V. We now know it was a man living on his own in the house before us. I think the lady at the shop said his name was Oliver."

"You're right. I think that's what it was, miss."

"Call me Laura," she smiled.

"Do you have any brothers or sisters?" Olivia asked.

"No, it's just me, Mum and Dad. Dad works on the farm and Mum helps out at the school in Windslea Green."

"You'll have to come and meet the boys," said Laura. "Have you got much to do here now?"

"No, I just need to check the water and that the

ponies are okay. I'll bring extra feed down in the evening and check on them again."

"Well, why don't we wait while you do that and then you can come with us to the house to meet the boys?"

"Okay, I'd like that."

Chapter 4

"I've got the key," shouted Ben, as he ran towards the shed.

"What?" said an invisible voice, which sounded a lot like Charlie.

"The key, I've got the key for the shed!"

Charlie now appeared from behind the shed.

"I found it above the door in the woodshed," continued Ben. "Look, there are two. One must be for here and one for the other shed."

Ben fiddled one of the keys into the rusty lock and, after a few attempts, by which time Charlie had joined him in wishing the lock would open, the lock released. He wiggled the padlock out of the hasp, grabbed hold of the door handle and tugged at it. At first, it didn't move. Then, with a few more pulls, the rusty hinges slowly gave way and the door creaked open. Charlie joined in to help open it, pulling enthusiastically on the edge of the door. Once the door was opened, it revealed a dimly lit room full of objects that were covered in a thick layer of dust and cobwebs.

As they moved slowly inside, they could see there were a couple of tables and a chair with objects piled on top and tucked underneath. Looking around, they saw shelves and chests of drawers stacked with even more interesting-looking objects. In a corner stood some garden implements, a fork and spade among others, which had long gone rusty with disuse. Charlie went one way round the tables and Ben the other, lifting up things and poking at others. There were lots of tins of all shapes and sizes, old oil lamps, a small green flag, a bicycle, spare wheels, rope – all of it covered in cobwebs. Ben looked to one wall where a number of photos hung. *That's strange for a shed*, he thought as he approached and wiped some of the dust off the front of them.

"Look at these, Charlie," he said.

Charlie's head popped up from behind a table to glance at the pictures. Several of them featured, what looked like, the same man, posing in different costumes in a play. One as cowboy, another as a knight and another next to some people dressed like Victorians, all of which hung under an old aeroplane propeller. In each one, the man in the photograph was holding a camera at his waist.

"Wow, look at that," exclaimed Charlie, pointing at the propeller. "I want that in our bedroom."

"Okay, but we'll have to speak to Mum first," replied Ben, who continued examining the photos before noticing a large mirror in an elaborately carved wooden frame at the end of the shed.

Charlie, meanwhile, turned his attention back to the clutter that surrounded him. He started to notice more unusual things; a spear, for example, which he immediately picked up and started prodding things with. Swinging it round, he knocked a painted vase off the table, which broke on the floor near Ben's feet.

"Watch it, Charlie!" shouted Ben as it crashed around him.

Charlie propped the spear back up against the wall and carried on searching through the junk. He came across a large old trunk, topped by a brass plate that had some writing embossed onto it. He wiped away the dust and read: 'Flt Lt O. T. Bramley' and beneath the name 'Private'.

It must be interesting if it says private! he thought. There was a padlock on it but it wasn't locked, so Charlie removed it from the hasp and lifted the lid. Charlie sighed. It was just full of old clothes and he wasn't into dressing up like his sister was.

He rested the lid against the wall behind and rummaged through the trunk of clothes, which were all a bit too big for him. To his left was an old wooden tea chest containing a large pile of hats. The words 'East India Company' were branded on the side. He grabbed the one that was nearest to the top of the pile, a cowboy hat, and tried it on. He pointed his finger and pretended to shoot at things in the shed for a moment.

"Pow! Pow! K-pow!" he shouted.

Out of the corner of his eye, Ben thought he saw something move. He turned and looked to the far end of the shed. There was a picture of an old aeroplane hanging and he was certain that it had moved. He walked over to take a closer look. Oddly, it was the only thing in the room that wasn't covered in a layer of dust.

"Shut up, Charlie!" he shouted.

Charlie looked around, "What's the matter?"

"I dunno. I… I just thought. Oh, never mind."

Ben studied the photograph a bit longer. It was of a beautiful old bi-plane from the early days of aviation. He'd seen pictures similar to it in books before, but this one looked bigger and had windows in its side. Looking closer, he could see the figure of a man standing next to it – a man very similar to the one that appeared in the other photos. He could see the man was of slim build and average height, with close-cropped hair. In his hand, he held an old-style, leather helmet. His head was tilted slightly to one side and a broad smile spread across his narrow face. Ben turned away from the picture to investigate what looked like a suit of armour stacked up in the corner.

Charlie chucked the cowboy hat down and picked up a tall black top hat; a huge amount of dust flew off as he bashed it against his knee before placing it on his head. At the same time, Ben's eye once more caught something twitching in his periphery. Snapping his head around, he caught sight of the picture coming to rest. He flicked his head from side to side, up and down looking for a clue. His heart jumped a beat.

"Did you do that, Charlie?" he shouted.

"Do what?"

"Do something to make that picture move?"

"What? Nope I 'ain't done nothing! How could I move the picture?" said Charlie. It was true; Charlie was halfway across the shed and in no position to affect the picture. Charlie continued, "Hey, what do think of my fancy hat?"

Ben shook his head and inspected the picture even more closely, dragging an old chair with him. Moving a couple of boxes aside, he placed the chair against the shed wall, stepped onto it and took a look at the sides of the picture frame. Poking it with his finger first one way, then the other, he could see no reason for it moving.

Wearing his rather big hat, Charlie strutted across the shed towards Ben. "What is it, Ben?" he enquired.

"I'm sure I saw this move," he replied. "Look how clean it is compared to everything else." Ben looked at the man staring out of the picture at him. "I don't know what it is, but there's something fishy about this."

He turned his back on it and stepped down off the chair. "Come on, Charlie, I think we ought to go back to the house now. Mum said not to be too long."

"But we should have a look in the other shed, too – see what that's like," said Charlie as he lobbed his hat back on the pile.

"Okay, but not too long."

Having been a bit more than spooked, Ben was keen to go somewhere else. Charlie led the way to the smaller shed that was slightly further down the garden. It didn't take them long to get inside, but it wasn't quite as exciting once they were. It turned out to be a workshop, mainly for woodworking, with a long wooden bench that was fitted with a vice on one end and surrounded by woodworking tools. Chisels, mallets, planes, saws of all shapes and sizes were hung on the wall with their shadows painted behind. Ben noticed that it looked as if some of the tools were missing. He scanned the workshop, but none were lying around in the sawdust and wood shavings.

"Wow, this is great, Charlie, everything we need to build our tree house. We can bring Dad's old stuff down here, too. Mum will be pleased to get it out of the house," said Ben.

Their father had been killed in a car accident a year ago while on his way to work and for a number of reasons their mother had wanted to move away and make a fresh start. It was what had led them to Pegasus Ride.

Ben now started pulling open various drawers and sniffing about in the little wooden boxes on the shelves, investigating the assorted nails, screws and other fixings. To the side of the bench was a neat stack of dark red timber planks and pinned to the wall above was a large dusty sheet of paper with, what looked like, plans for a wooden chest. Judging by the colour of the majority of the wood shavings, this was the wood that had last been worked on.

Charlie was not so enthralled with the workshop and after a few moments made for the door. He had other plans. He left the workshop shed and stared towards the gateway that led to the airfield.

After a few minutes, Ben left the shed to join

Charlie. However, Charlie wasn't outside the shed, he was further down the garden. It took Ben no time to realise what Charlie had in mind.

"No, Charlie!" he shouted. "You know what Mum said."

"Yeah, but she can't see us from the house, so how will she know? We could just go and have quick look. Come on, Ben, it's not far to those buildings."

Charlie stepped through the gateway beckoning Ben with a wave of his arm. "Come on, it'll be all right."

Ben was still thinking about the picture in the junk shed; he was so sure it had moved. "For goodness sake, Charlie, don't you ever listen?" he sighed as he followed his brother through the broken gate.

Charlie ran on towards the first building, which was about fifty yards from the gate. It looked rather like a massive shed as it was made of planks of wood. There was another identical shed alongside it, and a third beyond that. As Charlie rounded the corner, he saw a door on the side. With a twist and a tug on the handle, the door opened and he crept inside. Ben rounded the corner just in time to see Charlie disappearing inside.

"Jeepers, Charlie," Ben muttered to himself, hurrying to the door. He peered inside and saw Charlie inspecting an old car.

The building, which was actually an old aircraft hangar, was like a much bigger version of the garden shed they had just come from. A few dusty windows let in some light – just enough to see what was inside. There were a few workbenches and some very old posters pinned to the walls. There was also an antique car, which Charlie was nosing about in, and an old lorry parked near a big pair of doors. As Ben moved further inside, he could see large green drums with 'Castrol Oil' printed on the side, as well as an assortment of oil cans and funnels.

By now Charlie was bouncing up and down on the driver's seat and pretending to steer the old car. "Hey, Ben, this is great," he shouted. At first Ben ignored him, preferring to wonder why all this stuff was still here, who it belonged to and, if nobody wanted it, how it could be useful in building his tree house. After all, Mum had been told there were plans for the old airfield to be built on and all of the buildings demolished.

"Ben," shouted Charlie, shaking him out of his daydream.

"What?" he replied.

"Have a look in here."

Ben stepped into the car, through a door that opened the wrong way, and sat next to Charlie, who was still busy pretending to drive. He sniffed the pungent, old leather smell in the vehicle, which had been isolated from fresh air for years.

"I've never been in a car this old, Ben," he said as he tried to move the gear lever.

"Neither have I, but I have seen them on the telly." Ben wiped away some of the dust on the dials in front of him. "This must have been here for ages, like the stuff in the shed at home. It's like we've gone back in time."

"Must be a hundred years old," said Charlie.

"Well, I don't think it's that old, although it does smell strange!"

"Wouldn't it be great if we'd gone back in time, Ben, and then I could be a pirate."

"What? In a car? I don't think many pirates had cars, Charlie!" Ben laughed.

"No, but if we had a time machine, that's where I'd go first, to a pirate ship and get all the treasure."

"With any luck, you'd be left on a desert island," said Ben. "Anyway, we don't have a time machine, just a load of old dusty stuff that nobody seems to want. Mum is going to go mad when she sees the state of our clothes and finds out we've been here."

Getting out of the car, Ben said, "Come on, we'd better be getting back."

Charlie climbed out the driver's side of the car for a last look around the hangar and then walked to the door ahead of Ben. As he left the hangar, he couldn't resist walking towards the front of the other building. As he couldn't see a door in the side, he thought there might be a way in at the front.

Ben noticed Charlie heading away and shouted, "Oi, Charlie! Where are you going now?"

"Oh, come on, Ben. Let's have a quick look in this one."

"Jeepers, Charlie, why can't you do as you're told for once in your life."

"Come on, it won't take long."

Ben muttered to himself again as he followed Charlie round to the front of what was another old hangar.

"Look, there's nobody about, Ben," said Charlie as he made his way to what looked like a small door in a much bigger one. He tried the door handle but it came off in his hand.

"Now look what you've done," said Ben.

"It wasn't me. I hardly touched it."

"What do you mean it wasn't you, it's still in your hand!" Ben exclaimed. "Come on, trouble, we'll give this a go."

Ben pushed his fingers in between the gap in the doors and pulled on one of them. To his surprise, the door opened quite easily. After wiggling the broken handle back in, Charlie hurried to Ben's side.

"Wow!" exclaimed Charlie as his eyes caught sight of an old aeroplane inside the hangar.

The two boys pulled the door ajar, just enough for them to get in, and entered the hangar. It was a very old-looking aeroplane with two big wings. It had a single engine at the front with a big propeller on it, the top of which reached well above Ben's head. He went to take a closer look and could see that something was written on its side, near the engine. He wiped away the dust that was covering it and read the artistically painted word 'Jenny'.

Meanwhile, Charlie made his way around the wings to the fuselage of the aeroplane. He stepped onto the lower wing to access a door in the side and tried opening it, without success. He wiggled the handle up and down and pulled as hard as he could, but still it would not open. The noise he was making attracted Ben's attention.

"Oi, stop that, Charlie, I don't want you breaking anything else," shouted Ben.

Charlie left the door and wiped away some of the dust on the windows. "Ben, you wanna come and have a look at these seats in here. They're like Granddad's garden chairs, made out of cane."

"Don't be silly, Charlie. Why would they have cane chairs in an aeroplane?" replied Ben.

"Dunno, but look for yourself."

As Ben walked around to have a look, Charlie found the way up to the pilot's seat.

"Don't go up there, Charlie."

Charlie ignored Ben's plea and continued to climb up the footholds that led to the pilot's cockpit. "I want to see where the pilot sits."

Ben knew that it wasn't a good idea, but wasn't in a place to stop him. He just shook his head in disapproval and continued towards the windows in the side of the plane. Peering in through the dirty windows, he could see that there were, indeed, wicker or cane chairs. He looked up to see Charlie about to reach the cockpit.

"No, Charlie, come down here," he insisted.

"Aw, go on."

"NO!" Ben said, firmly.

As Charlie clambered down, he slipped, slid forward and his foot punched a hole through the wing. The old aeroplane was made with a wood frame covered in fabric, which could be easily damaged if you were careless.

"Blinking heck, Charlie, now look what you've done."

"Wasn't my fault! You told me to get down."

"What!" shouted Ben. "I told you not to go up there in the first place!" He reached up to help Charlie down. "Come on, let's get out of here before anyone sees us."

Charlie jumped off the wing and they made their way to the door, pushing it shut when they got outside. They started their way back to the garden.

"I think you might be lucky, Charlie. I don't think anyone around here cares about what's in the hangars. And I don't think anyone has been in any of them for years anyway. Come on, let's go back to the house and see what Mum and V are up to."

Chapter 5

After checking the ponies one last time, George collected his bike and walked with Laura and Olivia to their house. As they entered the front door, the boys came in through the back.

"Mum?" they called.

"Coming," was the reply from their mum, as she walked down the hallway to the kitchen. The boys trooped in, followed a few seconds later by V and George.

"Hello," said Ben.

"Hello," replied George.

"This is George," explained Laura. "One of the ponies we went to see belongs to him and he lives just down the lane."

George was only a little taller than Charlie and looked every bit the farm boy. Well-worn jeans with patches over the knees were topped off by a baseball cap, which was decorated with an image of a tractor. His trainers had seen a long service, too. Charlie viewed George with great interest and a grin appeared on his face. He might now have a new partner in mischief!

Laura introduced each boy in turn, and they acknowledged each other with a nod of the head.

"How old are you?" enquired Charlie.

"I'm eleven and a bit."

"I'm nearly eleven."

Charlie was very keen to make a new friend to play with, because he knew how quickly his brother now tired of him. A new playmate his own age would be just the sort of person Charlie could have some fun with. He already had ideas rushing through his head of taking George down the garden to show him the shed and take him to play in the hangars.

Laura stood in front of the glazed earthenware sink and ran some water from the hot tap to wash her hands. A minute later, the water was still cold.

"Oh goodness, I'd forgotten. No blasted hot water. Ben, I'm going to need your help to get the stove going so we have some hot water. Can you get some wood and coal in from outside?" she asked.

Laura planned on getting the electric heater fixed in as soon as possible, but for now she needed to get the fire going. Ben didn't exactly jump at the request, but muttered, "Okay, Mum."

Drying her hands, Laura enquired, "So, what did you two get up to the garden?"

Ben turned and stared into the biscuit tin. "Nothing much," he replied, guiltily.

"What's 'nothing much'?" Laura probed. 'Nothing much' usually meant something. Ben continued to peer keenly into the tin, as if he were picking out a particular biscuit.

Seeing Ben struggling, Charlie chipped in, "Nothing, Mum. We just found somewhere to make a tree house and… well… found the keys to the sheds."

Ben took a sideways glance at Charlie and scowled.

"Keys? You found some keys?"

Ben was now making a beeline for outside, trying to ignore his mother's question.

"Ben!"

He squeezed his eyes shut and stopped at the kitchen door. "What?" he asked innocently.

"Keys, Ben. Charlie just said you found some keys to the shed."

Ben was thinking hard how to play it down. "Oh yeah," he said, rather nonchalantly. "Yeah, we did. I found them in the woodshed."

"Well, what's in there, anything useful?"

Running one hand through his hair and stuffing the other in a pocket, he said dismissively, "Oh, a few garden tools but mainly lots of old junk. You know, the sort of old stuff Dad used to keep."

"Well, if that's the case, we'll have a clear out and get someone to take it away," said Laura.

"It's not all junk," interjected Charlie, "some of it looks quite useful." Charlie thought that there must be a lot more interesting stuff in the shed and would do his best to keep his mum away from it for the time being.

"There might be some garden tools we could use, Mum," said Ben. "I suppose Charlie and I could try and sort it out first and then chuck out the rubbish."

The boys had already discussed the idea of making

it their den, as well as building a tree house as a look out. Ben had suggested they could rig up a piece of string between the two camps with a tin can on each end, and thereby make a primitive telephone. He'd seen some kids do it on the telly.

"Well, just be careful if you do. I don't want you having something fall on you if it's piled up with stuff. And don't play with any tools you find. Are you listening, Charlie?" said Laura, her voice rising a few more decibels.

"Yes, Mum. We'll be careful," Charlie assured her.

She nodded, before turning to Ben. "Go on now and do something to get this fire going."

Ben disappeared outside. He was still thinking about the moving picture. Had it really moved or was it his imagination? It puzzled him, but it wasn't going to stop him going back to the shed. The garden and the old airfield were going to be a fantastic place to play and the stuff in the shed could be used for games. There was the workshop shed, too, and a new friend to share the fun with.

★ ★ ★

The boys showed George around the house and ended up in their bedroom. Charlie jumped onto his bed; from the extra height, he had a better view of the airfield.

"Look, George, you can see the airfield from here."

He was about to continue talking when he saw Ben subtly shaking his head. With V around, Ben thought it better that they not mention their exploration of the airfield just yet.

The subject changed and each enquired about the other's lives. Ben explained where they had come from and why they had moved to Pegasus Ride. George described a completely different lifestyle. He had grown up in the village and went to the small village school run by Miss Templeman. There were just twenty-two children in the whole school. It was an old Victorian school building with '1886' proudly picked out in red brick over the entrance door. The local authorities had tried to close it twice over recent years due to the low attendance, but the parents and locals had forced it to remain open.

George often spent weekends and holidays helping his dad on the farm or his mum at home. The farm had a small herd of Friesian cows, some sheep and about a hundred acres of arable land. The work made him a very fit and strong little boy, as well as earning him a good deal of pocket money. There was always something to do and George had not grown up sitting in front of a TV or computer screen. However, as most of the children who went to the school came from a wide area surrounding the village, he had very few friends close by to play with.

Much to the boys' surprise, he told them that his dad had taught him how to drive a tractor. Which, of course, for a boy of nine – which he was at the time – had been a great thrill. Admittedly, he was only allowed to drive the small Massey Ferguson 35, but it was big enough for him. Sometimes he even drove it with a two-wheel trailer hitched on behind, used for moving the hay bales around. In the winter, his dad attached a metal crate to the rear of the tractor to take straw, hay and nuts to the ponies. Next winter, he was hoping to do it on his own.

George went on to explain that he'd been given the pony for his eighth birthday and enjoyed riding out, especially to the heathland common on the other side of the village. There, he could get Archie up into a gallop or, at least, a canter over one of the many bridle paths that crossed the bracken-covered ground. His mother had taught him to ride when he was very young – so young, in fact, he couldn't exactly remember when.

V was desperate to ask whether she could have a ride on the pony, especially when she heard how young George had been when he began. It wasn't long before she couldn't resist the temptation any more. Leaning her head to one side in a particularly cute fashion, she said, "George, do you think I would be able to have a ride one day?"

"Yeah, sure, have you ridden a pony before?" he asked in reply.

"Not really, but I did sit on one at a pet farm once."

"That doesn't matter," he said. "Archie is very good and gentle. I'll speak to Mum about it."

V started to jump up and down with glee. "Really?" she squeaked. "Do you mean it, George?"

"Yeah, course. Mum'll put you on a leading rein in the paddock first, to get you used to it."

V ran off, buzzing with excitement, to tell her mum the news.

"Great, she's gone," said Charlie. "Now we can tell you about the airfield."

"What about it?"

"Well, we weren't supposed to go over there, but... well, we did. Didn't we, Ben?"

"Yes, we did. And you broke the aeroplane."

"I didn't break it. I just... err... put a hole in it."

Ben's face was about to explode, so George quickly asked, "What aeroplane?"

Charlie continued enthusiastically, before Ben could detonate. "Well, we went over to those buildings..." he pointed out of the window, "and found an old car and an old aeroplane. It's made of wood and some sort of cloth."

"Yeah, and you stood on the wing and put a hole in it," Ben said, sharply.

"It's not that bad, and it doesn't look as if it's being used anyway. It's covered in dirt and dust."

"Maybe it belonged to the guy who lived here," suggested George. "Dad said he was a pilot and flew from the airfield. After all, he's been gone a long time."

"Could be," said a now calmer Ben.

The boys agreed that they would all go and see it together. Ben explained that their mum had told them not to go over there, so they would have to keep it quiet and just say they were going down the garden.

With his tummy beginning to rumble, Charlie asked George if he would like to stay for lunch.

"Yeah, thanks, but I shouldn't be too much longer or my mum will be wondering where I've got to."

"Come on then, let's go downstairs," said Charlie as he hurried out of the bedroom, the others following behind. When they got downstairs, Charlie located his mum and asked if their guest could stay.

"He is quite welcome to, but won't your mum be expecting you home?" Laura directed her reply to George.

"Yeah, she will."

"Can't you phone George's mum?" enquired Charlie. He had hoped that George would be able to stay for the afternoon, too.

"No, unfortunately the phone is not going to be connected until tomorrow," said Laura. "And anyway, I probably ought to go and meet her first."

Charlie's shoulders sagged and his lips pouted. His face was one of great disappointment. This failed to affect Laura much, however, who had other plans for the afternoon. She needed to go into the nearby town of Cheshampton where there was a supermarket and wanted the children to go with her. The local village shop was okay for some things, but not everything.

She compromised, "Maybe you would like to come and spend the day here tomorrow?"

"Yes, I'd like that," George replied, eagerly.

"I'll drop in to meet your mum later and we'll arrange it then."

★ ★ ★

Charlie wasn't impressed with the idea of the shopping trip at all, especially in comparison to the excitement he was likely to find in the garden or over at the airfield. But at least it seemed that George would be back in the morning, which meant that he could show him the treasures in the shed and sneak back to the hangars. He didn't think Ben would go with him again, not just yet anyway.

And he really, really wanted to get in that aeroplane. Being covered in dust and with no one caring for it, he already had plans to make it his own playground. It was like the house, forlorn and forgotten and desperately neglected. He just needed a way of getting into it, of opening the jammed door to the cabin. If he could not actually fly it, then he wanted to at least imagine he was flying it!

His mind drifted. *Perhaps I can clean it, give it a good wash and oil up the hinges. It is in a sort of workshop after all, but where was its key?* He couldn't remember seeing one in the cockpit. Whatever he did to get in, he would have to be very careful.

Unbeknown to Charlie, there was indeed a secret surrounding the aeroplane. It was a secret that had remained undiscovered and undisturbed for years, and was something that only the owner, who had disappeared, and two others in the village knew about. It was way beyond Charlie's understanding, or any of his family for that matter, but they were destined to discover the truth. Charlie's meddling would see to that.

Chapter 6

After an enjoyable lunch, George said goodbye and they all waved as he rode off down the lane on his bike. Then, after clearing up the remains of the meal, Laura loaded the children into the car and drove off to Cheshampton for the afternoon.

On the way, she stopped off at George's house to introduce herself to his mum and to arrange the visit for the following day. Helen, George's mother, was of a similar age to Laura and worked part-time at the local school as a cleaner and cook. Her husband worked long hours on a nearby farm as a labourer and tractor driver. George was their only child.

Within a few minutes of meeting, it was obvious that the two women were going to get on well with each other. Both were easy-going, with a great tolerance of their mischievous kids. Although, with apron donned, it looked to Laura as if Helen was more familiar with the kitchen. Baking had never been her strong point. Preparing dinners and laying on breakfast were one thing, baking cakes quite another. While the children chatted outside, Helen invited Laura into the house. Once inside the kitchen, Laura was stunned by the row upon row of jars containing pickled everything. Shelves on each wall were filled with jars of beetroot, cabbage, cucumber, onions and chutneys – all of which was quite alien to Laura.

Seeing the expression of wonder on Laura's face, Helen offered her a jar of her vibrant yellow piccalilli. "It's probably a bit strong for the children, but it goes really well with strong cheese – if you like that sort of thing," she said.

"I do, thank you." Laura paused. "Do you make all these yourself?"

"Well, Gerry and George help me sometimes, but otherwise yes."

Laura was amazed at the collection. "Wow, I wouldn't know where to start!"

"There's more in here, too," laughed Helen as she opened the pantry door. She was a real, down-to-earth country girl and worked in the family's garden just as hard as her husband, Gerry – known by his friends as Spud. The truth was that the produce from the garden helped to supplement the low income that Gerry received from the farm. "It's just something I've always done," she added. "I sell some to Mrs Hobbard in the village stores. You'll meet her when you go in there."

"Oh, I already have. When we first arrived I had to ask for directions."

"She's lovely, and so is Mr Hobbard," said Helen.

Laura was fascinated by the thought of growing and preserving your own food. However, it would be a big ask for her children to do the work that George obviously did here. Maybe they could be persuaded if there was the right incentive. After all, they now had a big garden and it sounded like they might have the tools to do the job in the shed. There was also the dilapidated greenhouse that they might be able to restore. Perhaps, she should go and investigate the contents herself after all.

After a brief conversation, Helen and Laura agreed on George coming over after breakfast the following day. Laura thanked Helen again for the piccalilli and called the kids to get in the car.

Before she had even closed the door, Charlie enquired, "So is it okay? Can he come tomorrow, Mum? Can he?"

"Yes," she replied with exasperation. "Yes, he can, after breakfast."

"Great!"

It wasn't a long drive to the town, but it was a journey that Laura wasn't familiar with and so they had to stop several times to check directions. At one point, the journey was halted by cows crossing the road.

"You don't get that in town!" exclaimed Laura. "Life really is going to be different round here, kids."

It was about thirty minutes to Cheshampton, but took less time on their return. Once home, Laura kept the children occupied with more unpacking and organising.

Chapter 7

After breakfast the next morning, Charlie busied himself in the front room by planning what he would do when George arrived. Every now and then, he looked expectantly out of the window for his new friend's arrival. Olivia, meanwhile, continued to help her mother unpacking boxes and finding places for books, ornaments and other odd bits and pieces, and Ben had been tasked with trying to fix the locking catch on the bathroom door.

"Here's George!" shouted Charlie, and he ran to the front door to let him in. George propped his bike against the front wall and smiled as he walked into the house.

After they had all said hello, Charlie asked if they could go and play in the garden. Thinking that they would all get on better if Charlie was out of the way, Laura agreed on the condition that they stayed in the garden.

"Of course, Mum," Charlie said, not really meaning any of it.

"Come on, George," he shouted, as he ran out into the garden. George, only half looking where he was going, tripped as he went through the back door and pedalled his legs quickly to stop himself falling over. Somehow, he managed to remain upright and looked up to see Charlie standing in front of him. He hadn't seen his near trip fortunately, but was instead looking up in the direction of the roof.

"What you looking at, Charlie?" he enquired.

"Oh, nothing. It's just… never mind. Come on, George."

★ ★ ★

Laura closed her eyes, shook her head and whispered, "Goodness knows what they will get up to." She then told herself that they were boys, after all, which meant two things: that they attract trouble like flies to a cowpat, but that they were also hardy beings. Even so, she reminded herself where the first aid box was and hoped that would be all she would need. It was a long way to the nearest hospital! Turning her mind to the other jobs that needed doing, she picked up another box to open and unpack with Olivia.

★ ★ ★

George caught up with Charlie at the big shed where he was fiddling with the catch to open the door.

"What's in here, Charlie?" he asked.

"Come in and see for yourself, George," he said, as he slowly opened the door.

George followed Charlie into the Aladdin's cave, twisting and turning to look at all of the objects around him. "Wow, what a lot of stuff!" he exclaimed. "Is all of this yours?"

"It is now," Charlie replied. "I suppose it's Mum's stuff really, but she won't want it."

George's eyes were nearly popping out at the sight of it all; he didn't know what to pick up first. Time slipped by as they began to sift through their private treasure trove. Both thought it was a dream come true. The excitement of it oozed out of them. They laughed about how it was going to keep them occupied for a long time; in fact, it would probably take all summer.

Charlie found some tins of paint, held one up and said, "We need to make a sign saying 'NO GIRLS ALLOWED'."

"Good idea," George replied. "I'll try to find a piece of wood and some nails." Turning around, he tripped over an old oil lamp and fell onto some boxes that were filled with old tins of food. "Look at this," he said, as he promptly forgot his quest for the wood. He picked up one of the cans and wiped away the dust, which revealed a picture. "It looks very old, Charlie."

"Everything in here seems very old, George."

"This looks like the sort of tin I saw in a museum once with my dad," said George as he closely inspected the tin in his hand. "There was a whole town there that was made to look like as though it was at least a hundred years old. There were all sorts of shops and a tram and people dressed up like it was in the olden days – even older than my dad!" George picked up a different tin and rubbed his cuff over it to reveal the words 'Bully Beef'.

"George, come and have a look at this lot."

Charlie had returned to the trunk that held the great assortment of costumes; he now picked up the cowboy hat and threw it towards George. "Cor!" George exclaimed, as he caught the hat and placed it on his head. Both boys had their backs to the picture hanging at the far end of the shed, so did not see it become excited. It rocked to a halt.

"This is wicked," said George.

They spent the entire morning rummaging through the old boxes in the shed, a place where time seemed to have stood still for so long. They were completely engrossed in their discoveries. For them, it was almost as good as being left alone in a sweet shop! They lost themselves in their imaginations; one minute a pirate, the next a cowboy, then a sultan in the desert or an explorer fighting a tiger in the jungle. They had struck gold as far as they were concerned. With an overgrown garden for a stage and shed of goodies, they would be able act out any daydream that they had ever had. This was going to be the best summer holiday of their young lives.

After tiring of dressing up, Charlie busied himself by making the sign. They found a hammer and nails in the workshop shed and secured the sign to the door. Then, they returned inside. Charlie went to discover more of the hat collection, noticing more hanging on a tall hat stand. He selected a turban this time and placed it over his fair hair. It covered his head and dropped down over his eyes too! Laughing, he turned to face George. "Look at me!" he said. Walking forward, he held his arms out and pretended to be an Egyptian mummy.

Again, unseen by both of them, the picture on the end wall moved gently to and fro on its mounting. It was like a dog wagging its tail in excitement, wanting to go out for a walk or a run. Neither boy seemed to notice, though it wouldn't be long before the dog would get its exercise.

After tripping over something, Charlie threw the turban back in the box and grabbed a pilot's leather flying helmet that was hanging on the hat stand. Charlie examined it for a moment, then dipped his head forward and, holding on to each side of the well-worn leather cap, pulled it down over his ears.

George, meanwhile, still with a cowboy hat on, was examining an old rifle he had found propped up in a corner behind some boxes. He pretended to shoot at the various pictures that hung on the walls, when suddenly one of them moved. The surprise made him jump with amazement and stumble backwards.

Nearby, Charlie also stumbled and fell over at the sound of a strange voice in his head. "Where to today, Captain?" it whispered.

"Did you hear that?" Charlie shouted.

"Did you see that?" shouted George, who was still looking towards the end wall.

"The voice!" Charlie exclaimed.

"The picture!" George replied.

They both looked at one another. Then, the picture rocked again and Charlie's ears heard a repeat of the message. Charlie grabbed the helmet by the ear pieces and removed it from his head. He turned it over and over to inspect if it was connected to anything, which it wasn't.

They both got up and moved cautiously towards the picture, staring intensely at the image. There was a man holding the pilot's helmet that Charlie had in his hand and he was standing next to an old aeroplane. As they got closer, they could see the man was smiling and holding onto the aeroplane as if it were a close friend.

"That looks like the aeroplane in the hangar," said Charlie.

"What?" said George.

"The aeroplane. It looks like the one Ben and I saw in the old hangar on the airfield." Charlie's face took on an expression of confusion, with a hint of worry. "I heard a voice when I put the helmet on."

"A voice?" questioned George.

"Yeah."

"Let me try."

He took the helmet from Charlie, before slowly pulling it over his head. At first, he heard nothing, then: "Where to today, captain?" With a snatch of his hand, George quickly removed the helmet. His mouth wide open, he quickly looked left and right to see if someone was nearby. Nobody was there except Charlie, who now saw the picture rock from side to side once again. There was real panic in their eyes now and they tried to digest what was going on.

"Did you hear it, George?" Charlie enquired, frantically.

"Yes, I did."

Nervously, they looked at each other, not really knowing what to say or do. They both had racing hearts and were very twitchy, looking this way and that for an answer. They began to inch their way towards the door, George still holding the helmet in his hand.

"Ben said he saw the picture move yesterday and thought it was me. I bet he's playing a trick on us. I bet he's rigged something up."

"Yeah, he'll be laughing his head off at us," replied George.

They crept out of the shed as if to surprise someone.

"Ben!" shouted Charlie as he peered round the corner of the shed, but no one was there. Ben was still in the house.

"This is creepy," said George. "Didn't you say you found an old car and aeroplane yesterday, too?"

"Yeah, they were on the old airfield," replied Charlie as he pointed in the direction of the airfield, before explaining where they were to be found.

"Why don't we go and look at those instead?" asked George.

"Good idea."

George followed Charlie through the gate onto the airfield. As they rounded the corner of the hangar,

Charlie stopped abruptly, stepped back and put his arm out to stop George. He was surprised to see that the main doors of the hangar were wide open.

"The door was shut tight last time we were here," whispered Charlie. "There must be someone about."

"Come on, Charlie, let's go back."

"Nah, it'll be alright. We'll just have a quick peek."

They slowly walked towards the open doors, furtively looking around for another person, but nobody appeared to be about. They peered around the door and still nobody could be seen.

"Wow!" exclaimed Charlie.

"What is it?" George asked, urgently.

"That, that..." pointing to the aeroplane "was old and dirty when we saw it yesterday," Charlie stuttered as he looked at the now pristine aircraft. He braved a step forward, shouting, "Hello?" No reply. "Hello?" He paused, expecting someone to say something, but there was total silence.

"Come on, George, let's have a look inside."

George was more cautious and hung back, but Charlie beckoned him on.

They slowly walked up to the front of the aeroplane, continuing to look around for any sign of life. Charlie marvelled at how different the plane looked. Sure enough it was still old, but it was now gleaming as if it had just come out of the factory. There was also no damage on the wing, which he had caused just yesterday. It was bizarre.

Charlie stood and scratched his head, and then noticed the door on the side of the aeroplane was open. The day before, he and Ben had tried to open it without any success. *Somebody must have cleaned and repaired it*, he thought. *What if they are still here? They might still be here.*

"Come on, George. Let's have a look inside."

"You sure it's okay, Charlie?"

"Dunno, but it can't hurt. We're only looking."

George looked at his watch. "We can't stay too long, Charlie. It's lunchtime already. You don't want your mum to come and look for us; after all, we were supposed to stay in the garden."

"Stop worrying, George. We won't be long."

George really wanted to have a look anyway, so they crept further into the hangar and walked around the wing of the aeroplane. As they rounded the end of it, Charlie noticed the aircraft seemed to rock slightly from side to side as they approached the open door. He looked back to see if George was touching the plane, but he wasn't.

Although he felt a bit anxious, he lifted his hand that was still holding the flying helmet and goggles and pulled them on. He was beginning to feel a bit worried about what was happening. There was definitely no one there except the two of them, yet the plane had seemed to move on its own.

"Come on in. Where are we going?" said the flying helmet suddenly, a certain amount of expectation in the voice. Charlie jumped and looked round at George, while the aeroplane once again rocked on its wheels.

With the voice ringing in his head, Charlie

nervously pulled George towards him and they edged closer towards the open door. Leaning into the open doorway, he could now clearly see the wicker seats with their plush cushions on a carpeted floor. They both looked over their shoulders to see if anyone else was there, but it was all clear.

George was getting ever more nervous. "Charlie, I'm not sure about this anymore."

"Come on, George. Let's get in."

"I don't like it, Charlie. There's something spooky about this place. I think we should go home."

Charlie ignored George's worries. "It can't hurt us. Let's just have one look and then we'll go." He then peered into the cabin and studied its interior, noticing a scrap of old paper underneath one of the seats. He leant across and pulled it out from behind the leg of the chair where it had become wedged.

"What's that?" asked George.

Charlie slowly began to read the note out loud:

Dear Harry,

Please could you get me a brass pocket compass from Emilie's and then send it back?
> *Thanks.*
> *Oliver*

Charlie turned the paper over, but it was blank. "Why would you get something and then take it back?"

"I dunno," shrugged George. "It doesn't make sense."

Charlie screwed it up and stuffed it in his pocket. They didn't know who Harry or Oliver was anyway. He then grabbed hold of the side of the cabin and clambered into the plane, helping George up into the cosy passenger compartment. They sat down opposite one another, as the door suddenly closed on its own. Semi-frozen, they both looked sideways, almost without moving their heads. Looking through the glass, neither could observe anyone and slightly, only slightly, they began to relax and once again make eye contact with each other.

George was the first to utter a word, which was more like a whisper, "How... What... Did you see anything, Charlie?"

"No, I think it just shut on its own."

"What?"

"On its own, just as we sat down."

They weren't so much worried about the door, but who might be behind it. After a couple of moments, they plucked up enough courage to peek out of the windows again.

"Can you see anyone?" asked Charlie.

After a short pause, "No," was George's answer.

They both relaxed back into their chairs with a sigh. They could hear nothing. The door closing must have been their fault.

"It's 'cos you sat down a bit hard, George. You made the door swing to."

They relaxed a bit more and began to smile, puffing out their cheeks.

"Come on, Charlie, we better go."

But then, the strange voice spoke again. "Come on then, I'm ready to go." It made him jump and sit bolt upright.

"What is it, Charlie?"

"It's the helmet again. It's talking to me. This is all very scary, George. I only wanted to see what it was like in an aeroplane. I've never been in one and it must be great fun to fly and whirl and spin around the clouds."

"Is that all? Very well, let's go," spoke the voice.

Charlie jerked his head from side to side to look once more for the speaker. There was a sudden clattering noise from the front of the aeroplane and a shaking vibration started through the whole machine as the engine burst into life.

"Someone has started the engine!" shrieked George.

They both looked through the little window into the pilot's cockpit, but saw no one. They both grabbed at the door handle, with George just beating Charlie to it. He tried to open the door in order to jump out, but it held firm.

"What on earth is going on?" exclaimed George.

"It started as soon as I said it would be great fun to go flying! It's as if it was doing it itself, George!"

"Are you ready? We'll be taking off soon," spoke the voice.

"It is, George, it is! The aeroplane is going to fly by itself."

"Rubbish, it can't do that."

"Well, look for yourself! It must be some kind of

magic. It asked me if I wanted to go and I suppose, in a way, I said yes."

"Charlie, what have you done?"

"It's not my fault, it's doing it by itself!"

The aeroplane now eased forward out of the hangar and its tail swung round as it cleared the doorway. Charlie tried the door one more time, but they were still prisoners. His heart nervously pounded in his chest, racing like a steam train at full throttle as the aeroplane began to bump across the grass. George looked out at the tatty windsock as the aeroplane lined up in the direction of the wind.

Chapter 8

The Greens' new home used to belong to Oliver Bramley, before his mysterious disappearance years earlier. He was a quiet character and had tended to keep himself to himself, and not get involved with village life. Some said he had been born at the wrong time because he would often talk passionately about the past. Although he knew most of the locals, very few of them knew much about Oliver in return – except Harry Hobbard. Indeed, Harry had known him best and knew that he frequently went away on trips. Rather obscure journeys they were too. And on one occasion, he had not come back.

Oliver had lived in the house alone for more than twenty years. He had moved in, with his beloved aeroplane, after the Royal Air Force had moved off the airfield. Before that, he had been a pilot officer in the RAF for many years and had served at bases all over the world.

His life in the RAF had begun in 1936 when he was sent to the Eastern Mediterranean, perhaps more commonly known now as the Middle East, with 70 Squadron. At that time he was based at Habbaniya, a new airfield being built near Baghdad, Iraq. His job was to fly senior officers to other towns and airbases, such as Cairo in Egypt, in a small transport biplane. The aeroplane had a small passenger compartment, or cabin, for his passengers, accessed from a door above the lower wing, while the pilot sat above in an open cockpit.

Habbaniya was a growing RAF base next to a large lake by the Euphrates River. When Oliver had arrived, much money was being spent on making the airfield a comfortable place for British officers to live and work, and workers were busy everywhere erecting new billets and laying new roads. There was even a large billiard hall, which looked rather like an aeroplane hangar, being constructed near the centre of the complex. Oliver would spend many of his leave hours there, thanks in no small part to the drinks bar that was attached to its side. The boat club was also a popular destination for the off-duty pilot, especially in the sweltering heat of the day.

Oliver flew a plane he had called 'Jenny', but he was disappointed not to be flying one of the more exciting fighter planes that were helping the army trying to bring peace to the region. A peace that was being disturbed by tribes at war in the area of Kurdistan. Sometimes he would fly over the pyramids to Cairo; other times, to a base in Palestine. He not only relied on Jenny, but had formed a special bond with the machine and made sure that the engineers took the utmost care with her. Whenever he wasn't flying, playing billiards or sailing, he could be found cleaning and polishing Jenny, and generally tinkering around with the aeroplane. The longer he spent in her company, the closer the bond he formed. It is a strange bond that a pilot can form with his aeroplane; some say, almost a love affair.

In American airbases during the Second World War, pilots would get artists to paint the name, and often an illustration of a lady bearing the name, on the nose of their aeroplane. The British RAF, however, did not usually allow pilots to do so, but Oliver's special relationship with his superiors did allow him to get just the name of his plane painted on the engine cowling.

His job meant that Oliver got to see a lot of places and meet many interesting people – far more, perhaps, than the average fighter pilot. He even met Lawrence of Arabia once while hanging around an army camp for a few days, waiting for his passengers to finish their business. None were quite as special, though, as an old man he had once saved from a group of desert bandits on a track in the middle of nowhere.

He had been flying alone on one of his trips to pick up officers, when, looking down at the road he was following, he saw what looked like a group of men attacking another person. He was flying at about a hundred feet off the ground, so could clearly see what was happening. Low flying was an activity he thoroughly enjoyed, although it was frowned upon by senior command of the RAF.

On seeing the man, he turned the plane around sharply and dived at the ground towards the group, swooping low over them. They must have thought he was flying an aeroplane with guns, because they quickly jumped on their horses and fled the scene. He had then zoomed into the air, rolling the plane nearly onto its side, and swung back towards where the person was lying. He landed just past him. Stopping the engine, he leapt out of the plane and rushed towards the victim, who was lying motionless on the ground.

He knelt down next to a very old man and gently lifted his head into his arms. A frail figure with a face that was thin, drawn and wrinkled like a prune, and partly covered in a thick, grey beard. His hands, which were protruding from his tunic, showed evidence of much arthritic pain and swollen joints. Raising him further, he could see the old man was still alive, but unconscious and with some cuts to his head.

Oliver had lifted him up and carried him towards the aeroplane, where he laid him down against the tail in the shade. He carried a first aid kit in the plane and now grabbed it out of the back and tore into it. He had no training in what to do with its contents, but ventured that anything was better than nothing. He grasped his water bottle and proceeded to wash the old man's wounds.

Looking at the withered frame, he wondered why the bandits had been trying to rob him in the first place. He had nothing on him except a small wooden cross on an old piece of leather, which was now lying in the road, and, what looked like a very old book that the man was still clutching. Oliver began to bandage his head wounds. He was now getting his senses back and smiled painfully at Oliver. He released his grip on the book, which slipped to the ground.

Having done the best he could, Oliver lifted the old man up and said, "Come on, I'll take you with me. There'll be a doctor in Alexandria." He wasn't sure that the old man understood, but he responded with a look of gratitude.

After settling him into the aeroplane, Oliver turned round and walked back to pick up the book. It was bound in tatty brown leather, with scrapes and other scars that were an indication of its age. On the spine were seven ribs, three of which were more worn than the others, virtually poking through the leather. The front of the book bore an inscription in an ancient writing that Oliver did not fully recognise. Some of the letters, embossed in gold, looked like Greek handwriting, others were more like Egyptian hieroglyphics.

A glimpse inside revealed pages made of parchment and more of the text he didn't recognise. Again, it was a mixture of vaguely recognisable letters and hieroglyphics. He mused about it for a moment, before returning to the plane and handing it over to the old man. He clutched it tightly against his chest with one arm and held the other up as if to try and point to something. Then Oliver remembered the cross that was lying some distance away behind the aeroplane. He held up his hand in acknowledgement and walked off to get it.

As he picked it up, he said aloud to himself, "I hope the old boy will be okay," followed by some vulgarities about the attackers picking on a defenceless old man. Then, as he turned to return to the plane, he was puzzled and surprised by what he saw. The rear cabin seemed to be glowing with a bright light.

"What on earth?" he exclaimed and rushed back towards it.

As he got closer, the light dimmed and disappeared. He rounded the back of the plane and stood facing the doorway to the cabin, glancing at the old man. All seemed normal and there was no evidence of the strange glow. He decided it must have been a trick of the desert sunlight reflecting off the glass of the cabin. It did that sort of thing sometimes, but he'd never seen anything quite like that before.

As Oliver handed the old man the cross, he reached out and clasped Oliver's hand, still holding the cross, firmly with both hands.

"Thank you so much. I believe I have now found my mission," he said, slowly, in broken and heavily accented English. "You are the worthy one." He had smiled and lowered his head before releasing his grip on Oliver's hand.

Slightly mystified, Oliver thought that the old chap was already looking a lot better. In fact, if he hadn't known better, apart from wearing Oliver's bandages, he looked pretty good. *Never mind,* he thought to himself. *The docs can check him out in Alexandria.*

As he went to close the door, the old man stopped him and asked, "What is your name?"

"Oliver, sir. Oliver Bramley."

The old man smiled again and nodded. With that, Oliver closed and locked the door, and in no time they were on their way. Shortly after getting airborne, Oliver looked down through the small glass window to the cabin and observed the old man sitting and holding the cross on the book as if nursing a child. *Perhaps he is some kind of holy man,* he thought. *This is probably the first time he has been in an aeroplane, but he seems content.*

After that, Oliver never looked down to see how he was and concentrated on navigating to his destination, Alex – as they tended to call it. But by not looking down, he did not witness a second glow of light in the cabin, brighter than the first and lasting no longer than a few moments.

On arrival at Alex, Oliver landed with his usual finesse and kissed the ground gently with the wheels. He taxied up to the group of huts and tents that were known as the aerodrome control, and shut down the engine. He was greeted by several ground crew who held onto the wings and put the wooden chocks in front and behind the wheels. He knew them all quite well as he was a frequent visitor to the base.

"Hello, sir," one of them said with a sharp salute.

"Hi, Jimmy," he replied as he leapt down from the wing.

As an officer, he had to be addressed as 'sir' and saluted, but Oliver wasn't fussed by such officialdom and preferred to be on first-name terms.

"Got a passenger today," he announced.

"Who's that?"

"Don't know."

"What do you mean you don't know?"

"Just someone I picked up on the way."

"I didn't think that you were allowed to do that, sir," said Jimmy.

"I know, but this poor chap needed my help. He was being attacked by a group of thugs. It's not hurting anyone. Come on, he needs to see a doctor. No one will know. Well, not the brass anyway."

"Okay, sir, we'll sort it out."

With that, Oliver turned around to walk towards the aeroplane, but a burst of white light rushed out from the cabin window. It was so bright that he and Jimmy had had to cover their eyes with one hand. At the same time, Oliver felt a warm calming glow of emotion flow through him and a swirl of dust flew up around the aeroplane. It was like a mini-tornado, but around the aeroplane.

As Oliver protected his eyes from the light and dust, he heard a voice in his flying helmet, which he was still wearing, say, "Thank you for your kindness. I will be with you always, but for now goodbye."

The light stopped beaming and the dust settled almost as quickly as it had begun. For a moment Oliver stood confused, staring into the aeroplane window and wondering what on earth had just happened. He looked around for the owner of the voice.

"What on earth was that, sir?" exclaimed one engineer, dusting himself down from the sand blown on him.

"What, or who, did you say you have got in the

plane, sir?" quizzed Jimmy, still wiping his eyes.

"Er… hold on," puffed Oliver, as he began walking over to Jenny. "I need to check."

He opened the door and stood aghast at the sight that greeted him. An empty plane. He leant in and looked around, but nothing. It just didn't make sense.

Still rubbing his eyes free of sand, Jimmy came over and asked, "What was all that about?"

"I'm not really sure," replied Oliver. "One minute there's no wind and the next there's a blooming whirlwind right on top of us. And I guess it was the sun reflecting in the windows, but I couldn't see for the light shining in my eyes."

"Where's this passenger you picked up, sir?" asked Jimmy.

"Well, I don't rightly know. He was in here," replied Oliver, looking into the aeroplane again.

"You sure you picked somebody up, sir. Not been out in the sun too much, have we?"

"No, I bloody haven't," barked Oliver.

"Sorry, sir."

"Not your fault, Jimmy. I just… oh, forget it. Just forget it, okay."

"Yes, sir; whatever you say, sir."

Jimmy saluted and walked off. Out of sight of Oliver, he raised a finger and pointed in a twisting action to the side of his head. His two fellow fitters chuckled and left Oliver staring at the aeroplane.

He never did see the old man again.

Chapter 9

The aeroplane taxied out of the hangar and was soon on the end of the runway, ready to go.

"Ready?" said the strange female voice.

The boys decided that they might as well say yes, as it didn't seem they had another option anyway.

"Okay," they said, hesitantly, as they cast a worried look at each other and strapped themselves in. The engine began to roar, and the aeroplane accelerated and bounced down the grass runway. The tail then lifted slightly and, within a few moments, they were airborne and climbing up into the sky.

"Wow, look at that," Charlie exclaimed as he looked down on his house getting smaller and smaller. The countryside began to spread out all around them and, not too far away, they could see the village of Rosemie Common, the junction with the garage nearby, the post office and pub. Up and up they went towards the brilliant white clouds that were spread out around the sky. They looked like massive balls of cotton wool drifting along in the breeze.

As Jenny approached the first cloud, she turned slightly sideways and started to turn around it in a great big arc like a rainbow on its side. The boys gripped the edge of their seats tightly and screamed with a mixture of fear and delight. They weren't sure what was happening, but were beginning to enjoy the ride. Jenny rolled her wings level and then pulled up to loop over the top of the cloud. Again, the boys shrieked.

"Are you okay, Charlie?" said the voice in the helmet.

"Err, umm, I think so. Who am I talking to?" enquired Charlie.

"I'm Jenny, of course. That's what Master Bramley calls me."

There was a pause while Charlie thought about it. "But where are you?"

"I'm all around you. I am you and you are me." This was a bit much for Charlie's brain!

"What is it, Charlie?" asked George.

"I, I, err, I think the plane is talking to me."

George wasn't sure what to believe anymore and could do little more than stare blankly at Charlie. "What?"

"The voice. It's coming from the aeroplane."

"Yes, Charlie, it's me, Jenny. And I'm more than just an aeroplane," spoke the voice.

Charlie wasn't sure whether to be more alarmed or excited. "What do you mean?"

"Well, it depends what you want to do and where you want to go. We can go wherever you like. If you wear the helmet, you are the captain," said Jenny.

"Are you serious?"

"Of course."

He thought for moment, then, "Okay, take us to

the seaside – somewhere where it is hot, sunny and sandy," requested Charlie.

"No problem."

Jenny weaved through some clouds, then went straight towards a massive, grey, menacing cloud that reached high up into the sky.

"Wow," shouted the boys in unison.

One moment they were surrounded by a beautiful blue, then the aeroplane plunged itself into the monster cloud. It began to get darker and darker until, suddenly, a brilliant white light shone in the cabin inside and out.

Instinctively, they closed their eyes against the bright glare.

"Wow," they screamed again and blindly leant forward to hold each other.

From behind their eyelids, they could see flashes of lightning – three, four maybe more – but no thunder. They waited for the bangs, but none came.

Then, the lightning stopped and they were back in the blue again. Sensing the blinding light had gone, they blinked their eyes open.

"Charlie, was that your fault? What did you ask it to do?" queried George, with some concern.

"No. Well, Jenny says she can take us anywhere so I've asked to go to the seaside – that's all," replied Charlie.

George looked out of the window as Jenny swooped down under the clouds again in the direction of a distant coastline. He said nothing, sat back in his seat and looked out of the window again.

He wasn't quite as adventurous as Charlie and many worries raced through his mind.

It did not take long before they were flying above miles of sandy beach and a blue-green shimmering sea. Peering out of the side window, Charlie and George were stunned by the view.

"Wow! Can we land?" asked Charlie.

"Yes, we can land on the beach," replied Jenny.

Rolling over into a gentle dive she flew down towards the beach, skimming over the waves with her wheels and barely missing the surf. The engine became almost silent as Jenny drifted down onto the firm sand just above the rippling waterline. After a couple of bounces, the aeroplane settled down on to beach and slowly came to a stop.

As the boys undid their seatbelts, the door popped open and they both leapt eagerly out of the plane. Running aimlessly about and shouting to each other, the boys each found a piece of driftwood and began a duel. It wasn't long before they were fencing in the water, jumping through the salty surf and trying to score the winning blow.

Charlie's sword suddenly snapped in two and George prodded him in the ribs, then raised his sword in victory. He repeatedly shouted out loud, "I'm the winner," dancing around Charlie in delight.

Charlie sulked off and began to use his broken sword to scratch lines in the sand.

"Pity we haven't got a bucket and spade," he said. "I'm great at making sandcastles."

"I wonder if we could borrow..." started

George, looking around as he spoke. He had been going to suggest that they borrow someone else's, but realised the beach was completely deserted. *Strange*, he thought to himself. It was such a lovely day and a lovely beach, and it was school holidays, too. It was also very warm – actually quite a bit hotter than at home. It didn't make any sense at all.

The top of the beach was covered in grassy sand dunes and trees. He mused about it for a few moments, then said, "Look, Charlie, there are palm trees here."

"What?" Charlie replied, looking up from his scribbling in the sand.

"Palm trees. I've never seen a palm tree for real before."

Slightly puzzled, Charlie got up and followed George, who was now making his way to the top of the beach.

"My dad has taken me to the beach before, but I have never seen it look like this," George said, as his eyes scanned up and down the line of the beach. He was quite puzzled. They had both been too excited when they arrived to notice, but now they thought about it and George said, "And the sea is really warm and it is normally cold."

"I thought it was nice," replied Charlie.

"Oh, yes, it's nice, but it's not right."

Sure enough at the top of the beach, sand dunes were spread amongst the trees and there was still no sign of anybody else being there. About one hundred metres to their right was a small rocky outcrop where the beach disappeared around a corner.

"Let's go and look up there," said George. He was now beginning to take the lead, as he had some concern over their whereabouts.

"Okay," said Charlie, starting to run. "Last one there is a rotten egg!"

Although slightly smaller Charlie was quick on his feet and, with his little arms swinging wildly back and forth, he got to the rocks first. He took no time in announcing his victory to George.

"Now I'm the winner; now I'm the winner," he boasted with glee, standing proudly upon the rocks. He pointed his small stick to the sky with one hand and held his other up with his fingers forming an L. "Loser," he exclaimed.

"Okay, okay," said George. "Let's go and see if we can find anybody."

The two of them clambered over the rocks and round the corner to the next beach. This beach was more of a bay that swept around to another clump of rocks in the distance. It was a calm, peaceful and beautiful beach, but again no one to be seen.

George was just about to speak when a loud roar was heard just ahead of them. They both nearly jumped out of their skins! Still on the rocks, they ducked down like synchronised swimmers beneath the water to hide behind a boulder. With their eyes nearly popping out of their heads, they looked at each other with horror.

"What was that?" shrieked Charlie.

"I don't know! How should I know?" replied a trembling George.

There was another frightful, fearsome roar and a clattering through the trees, alongside an almighty commotion of screeching and squawking from the birds flying out of the woodland. The noise continued but did not seem to be getting any closer to them, so after a few moments the boys decided to brave it and peer over the top of their hiding place. For the second time in as many minutes, the sight that greeted them nearly made their eyes pop out and they ducked back down behind the rock.

Charlie's mouth moved up and down but nothing came out.

"Ch-Ch-Charlie," George said with a trembling, stammering voice. "It… it's a lion."

Now visibly shaking, the boys took another careful look. Yes, there was no doubt about it; a lion was eating a monkey on the beach.

"I know what it is, but… er… what is a lion doing here?" asked Charlie.

"I haven't got a clue. What are we going to do? Where are we?" replied a panicky George.

The boys were now really worried about what was going on. Neither were strangers to doing things they were not supposed to do or being in places they shouldn't be. However, this was something that was really worrying them. What had they got themselves into? Where were they? Wild monkeys and lions didn't run along beaches in England.

They decided they had had more than enough adventuring for one day, so climbed down the rocks and raced back towards the aeroplane. They hoped they would not get any more surprises before they got back to Jenny. She was still sitting where they had left her, basking in the sun just above the water line.

With their hearts racing, they jumped aboard through the open door into the passenger compartment and let out a joint sigh of relief.

"Phew, thank goodness this is still here," said a relieved George, collapsing backwards into one of the wicker seats. Once again, the door closed without help from either boy and this was followed by a now friendly voice, "Where would you like to go, Captain?"

"Home!" shouted Charlie. "Home."

"Ok, hold tight then."

The pair fumbled for their seatbelts and strapped themselves in. The engine burst into life and Jenny trundled forward a little, pointing straight along the beach. The engine revved up and with a roar, they were soon rushing along the beach. Jenny then gently lifted them into the air. George and Charlie looked out of the window with much relief as they flew higher and higher, and further away from the beach. In the distance, they could just make out the lion on the sand below. They were still in a state of shock from what they had seen.

"Was it what you wanted, Charlie? Did you enjoy it?" enquired Jenny.

"Well, we're not sure," replied Charlie. "It all

seemed a bit strange, and quite different from what I expected the local beach to be like."

The voice laughed. "I am not surprised; you didn't say you wanted to go to the local beach. You said you wanted to go somewhere hot, sunny and sandy. So I took you to a beach in Africa."

"Africa!" Charlie screeched.

"Why yes, I thought you would like it."

"Well… er… yeah… but Africa."

"Africa!" George repeated.

"Yes, Jenny said she… she… took us to Africa."

Jenny spoke again, "I said I could take you anywhere at any time."

"Well, that sort of explains a lot," said Charlie, and told George what Jenny had said.

"Well, I just want to go home now. We are going to be missed and then we'll have to answer questions on where we have been," said George. He looked at his watch. "Bother! My watch has stopped – now I've no idea what the time is and we are really going to be for it."

Jenny zoomed up through the clouds again and soared around the tops, of what looked like, beautiful giant white puffs of cotton wool. The boys were still in such a state of shock that they didn't notice the big cloud and the flash of light this time. Just moments later, Jenny descended down through the white puff balls to reveal Rosemie Common below.

"Look, Charlie," shouted George, "Look, we're home."

They both glued their faces to a window and their

shoulders dropped as they let out a sigh of relief. Jenny swooped down towards the old airfield, circled round once and came in to land. With a gentle bump, they were once again back on the ground. Jenny rumbled to halt in front of the hangar and swung around to face the airfield. The engine fell silent. The cabin door popped open and the boys leapt out.

"Come on," said George. "We'll shove her back into the hangar."

The boys pushed the aeroplane back into the hangar and pulled the doors shut. George instinctively then looked at his watch, hoping, rather than expecting, that it would tell him how long they had been away – but it showed the same time as when they had first got into the aeroplane. Twelve-thirty, which was the time they were expected to be back for lunch! He shook his wrist furiously a few times and moaned at the watch for not working, then noticed it had started again.

They ran as fast as they could back to the garden, pausing briefly so that Charlie could throw the flying helmet back into the shed and slam the door shut. Racing down the garden path and fearing the worst, they burst into the kitchen and started to apologise with out-of-breath voices.

"Sorry, Mum," said Charlie.

"Sorry we are late, Mrs Green," blurted George. "I didn't notice the time, and my watch stopped and then started again."

"Yes, Mum… sorry."

"What's the matter? You're not late, it's only just lunchtime," laughed Laura.

George looked at Charlie and then the clock on the table with puzzlement. His watch agreed with the clock.

"You two look like you've been up to no good. What's happened?" asked Laura, shaking her head.

"Nothing!" they said simultaneously.

"Come on, what have you been up to?" she said with a slight crack of a smile.

"Nothing, really, just, well, playing and stuff."

Laura didn't look convinced, but said no more and went back to preparing their lunch. The two boys collapsed onto the chairs in the kitchen, put their elbows on the table and cupped their foreheads in their hands. Both let out a sigh of relief. Then they looked at each other, but said nothing, just exchanging a stare of wonder. They were just pleased to be back safely for dinner – they were certainly feeling hungry!

Chapter 10

Ben tripped over a box and fell into the kitchen, crashing into the back of Charlie's chair.

"Careful, Ben," cried Laura, as she stepped out of the way holding up a plate of food.

"Get off, Ben," shouted Charlie.

"What have you been doing?" Ben enquired, ignoring Charlie's protest.

"Just mucking about in the shed."

"Yeah, Mum said you were down there but I couldn't see you," queried Ben.

The two boys looked at each other. "Well, er, um—" Charlie hesitated.

George piped up, "We were hiding in our camp. We saw you coming but…"

"Yeah, we were watching you from our secret camp," said Charlie.

"What secret camp? Where?" enquired Ben, dubiously.

"Can't tell you that or it wouldn't be a secret would it?" stated Charlie, with a smile.

"Can I see it?" asked Olivia, pulling her chair up to the table.

"No," Charlie swiftly replied.

"It's not fair you have all the fun. I've been helping Mum all morning."

"Well," said Charlie, "Maybe… it's not really much of a camp yet, but we were getting some stuff from the shed to make it."

"Some secret camp," sniped Ben.

The discussion about the camp continued over lunch, involving discussions around the extent of it, who could see it and when, and what it was going to be made of. The boys mentioned nothing about their adventure in the plane, but Charlie really wanted to tell Ben all about it. He was itching to tell him and maybe even Olivia. However, he didn't think it was something his mum needed to know. Not just yet, anyway. Of course, Ben wouldn't believe him. Just another one of Charlie's pranks he'd think. But this time it wasn't, Charlie and George both knew what they had seen, what they had done and where they had been. By the end of lunchtime, Charlie was practically exploding with desire to tell Ben.

With the last mouthful still working its way to Charlie's stomach, he pushed his chair back and leapt to his feet.

"Ben, do you want to come with us to the shed?" he enquired.

"Well, Mum wanted me to—" he was interrupted by his mother.

"Don't worry, dear," she said. "You go with them. We can do that later; there's plenty of time."

"Okay then, I suppose so," he said nonchalantly, as if he wasn't really bothered.

"Can I come too?" chipped in Olivia.

"The shed is not for girls," announced Ben, firmly.

"Oh, go on. Let her join in, Ben," said Laura.

Ben sighed in disapproval. "Okay then, but we bagsied it first. It's going to be our den. Well, 'til we build a tree house. And we don't want it messed up."

"Thanks, Ben. I'll be good, honest," Olivia cheerfully replied.

"I can't believe there's much to mess up, Ben, from the way you and Charlie described it," retorted Laura. "Or perhaps I should come and have a look myself just to check it over."

"No, Mum! No. It's, it's… all right really," Charlie blurted out as he gave Ben a hard stare.

"Why is it yours, anyway?" Olivia challenged.

"It's not really, but if you find something you like…" continued Charlie, trying to prevent any further interest from his mother.

Ben was a bit mystified at Charlie's reaction as it had been his idea to make it a "boys-only" retreat in the first place and he was already inviting girls in!

George was first to the door, pulling it open so hard that it banged loudly against the side of the adjoining cupboard.

"Careful," said Laura.

Bumping into each other, the other children followed him out into the garden. Various stares and whispers were exchanged as they made their way from the house.

"Phew, that was close," said Charlie, once they were well down the garden path.

"What do you mean?" enquired Ben.

"Mum saying that she wanted to come down to

the shed. You won't believe what happened to George and me this morning – you really won't. You won't, Ben."

"All right, all right, what won't I believe?" said Ben.

"Yeah, what won't he believe?" squeaked V.

"Come on, I'll tell you in the shed."

Excited, they all started to run down the garden towards the shed. Charlie hastily yanked the door open and they all bundled past him. With everyone inside, Charlie took a quick look down the garden to check they hadn't been followed, then grabbed hold of the door and firmly slammed it shut.

V was amazed to view the contents of the shed, craning her neck around and around, and up and down. She was totally astounded by what she saw.

"Charlie, this is like that shop at home. The one on the corner of the high street. The one that Mum called the Junk Shop."

V carefully lifted a cloth and squealed with delight at the sight of a beautiful hand-painted doll's house. The cloth had kept the worst of the dust out so it had retained its original ornate detailing despite being in a shed. The smile on her face stretched her lips from ear to ear, her eyes sparkling with excitement. Although initially speechless, it wasn't long before, "Wow," squeezed out. The boys turned to see what deserved the expression of joy from V.

She found a catch on the side that, once released, allowed her to open it and see the exquisite miniature furniture adorning the inside. Another happy sound found its way from V's mouth and her whole body oozed with excitement at what she had found.

Before she had even asked, Ben said, "Yes, V, you can have it. We don't want that sort of thing in here. This is just for boys, remember."

"Anyway, what's this all about then, Charlie?" demanded Ben. "What happened?"

Charlie cleared some stuff from a stool and George did the same with a chair, so that they could sit down to tell their story.

"Well, you know that plane we saw on the airfield?"

"Yeah," Ben replied.

"What plane?" interrupted V, looking up from the doll's house.

"Ssh," hissed Ben, "what about it?"

"You tell them, George. They won't believe me," said Charlie.

"We've been for a ride in it."

"How? With who?" queried Ben.

Charlie and George looked at each other. "With no one," they both replied.

"What do you mean with no one? You just said you went for a ride in it. I s'pose it flew itself, did it?" scoffed Ben.

"Yes," blurted Charlie, "it did."

Ben turned around, losing interest at the obvious lie, and started to busy himself with a search for something interesting. He moved towards a dark brown, plainly decorated bureau and pulled down the front of the desk to form a writing table.

Inside, small compartments were stuffed with

bits of paper, alongside some pencils and pens. In the middle were two books. Ben picked them up and read the titles to himself. The first was *'The History of the Long Island Native Indians'* and the second was *'Captain William Kidd – Pyrate or Pryvateer'* by Captain James Kelly. Each had a number of paper bookmarks inserted in them. More interested in the pirate book, which was obviously very old, Ben put the other down. Opening up some of the bookmarked pages, he noticed that the bookmarks had notes written on them. He didn't bother to read them all, but one he pulled out said:

'Find William Kidd or Bartholomew Sharpe – Kidd on the ship Adventure Prize and Sharpe on the Trinity. 1698 Santa Carolina – Mozambique or Libertatia – Madagascar.

Must get board before they sail from Caribbean.'

Chapter 11

Ben was extremely baffled. The book looked very, very old, but the message was written on paper that didn't look very old at all. How could someone be writing a note on modern paper about trying to board a ship over 300 years ago? His confused mind was brought back into the room by V's persistence to get Charlie to tell her his story.

"Tell me," said an excited V. "Tell me."

"Yeah, tell her about your dream, Charlie," scoffed Ben. "Tell her how you went for a ride in a plane without a pilot!"

The boys were really struggling to start telling their adventure. It was hard for them to believe and they had actually been there! But Charlie tried again. "Look, we went to see the aeroplane. I just wanted to show George what we'd seen the day before. The aeroplane looked new, clean and shiny today."

"Yeah, right," sneered Ben. "And that blinking great hole you made in the wing has been fixed as well, I suppose."

"Yes, Ben, it was. It was fixed. It was as if there had never been a hole!" Charlie stuttered.

"It must have been a different aeroplane, you idiot."

"No, it wasn't, it wasn't, Ben. It was the same one."

Ben ignored him, put the book back down and moved on from the bureau. He started to look into a large wardrobe made of black hand-carved wood that was standing against the back wall. He wondered why all the clothing, which resembled a fancy dress collection, was in a shed. In a drawer below, he discovered shoes of all sorts – some he recognised from his history lessons at school.

On top of the wardrobe was another collection of hats. He reached up and grabbed one that looked like that of a sailor. A sailor of tall sailing ships, like one of Nelson's men, maybe? It was a large, black three-pointed affair, which he inspected and then put down on top of the clutter on the table. He had remembered seeing a jacket to match in the wardrobe and fumbled through it to find the coat. Here it was! Pulling it off the hanger, he slid it over his shoulders. It was slightly too big on his young frame, but passable. Of course, it had been quite common for boys of his age to go to sea in earlier centuries. The lucky or privileged ones would serve as midshipmen and assistants to the officers; others would be cabin boys or general dogsbodies, working very hard during their time on board. Ben started to drift away imagining life on board a sailing ship – he quite fancied himself as a buccaneer!

"Carry on, Charlie," said an interested V.

"Well, that's not all," interrupted George. "We

went to the plane and Charlie had this flying helmet, the one he found in the shed, and it talked to him."

"What do you mean, talked to him?" asked V.

"When you put the helmet on… you hear a voice, as if it's talking to you."

"Yeah, Charlie, course it did," muttered Ben, adjusting his new head gear.

George continued, "Anyway, we got in the plane and it took off, and then it flew to a beach and then it landed." He was getting faster and faster in his explanation.

"You got in it and it took off," laughed Ben. "And I thought it was V that was best at making things up, with her fairy dolls in fairyland."

"We're not in fairyland," blurted Charlie as he stood up. "We're not making it up. We did go flying, and we did land on a beach and we also… saw a lion!"

"And you expect us to believe that," said Ben. He moved towards the large mirror to inspect his midshipman appearance, dusting himself down as he did so.

Charlie was beginning to think he'd made a mistake in telling Ben.

"A lion!" squealed V.

"Yep," said George.

Ben was quite impressed with his look and decided to see if he could find some trousers to match, continuing to ignore the boys' nonsense.

"Ben, really, please come and see the plane. You remember we couldn't get into it yesterday, could we?"

"No."

"Well, today the door was open."

"That doesn't prove anything."

"No, but the voice asked me where I wanted to go and I just said to fly in the clouds or something. Then the plane started up, drove out of the hangar and off we went."

"'Course you did, Charlie," sighed Ben in a partial whisper, his head now buried in a second trunk of old clothes.

"Can I see the aeroplane, Charlie?" asked V.

Charlie looked towards Ben for his approval, but Ben wasn't interested – or, at least, pretended not to be. He then gathered up the helmet and goggles, and looked up at the old photo on the wall. The moment he placed the helmet on his head, the picture began to swing gently to and fro.

"Look!" he shouted. "Look, Ben, the picture moves."

V glanced over and squealed with surprise. She made across the room to grab hold of her oldest brother. Now, with Olivia by his side, Ben too swung round to look at the picture, then back in George's direction to see how he might be doing it. "Very good, boys, how do you do it? Come on, Charlie, you must be doing something. You can't honestly expect me to believe your porky pies and that you have nothing to do with it?"

However, both George and Charlie were standing motionless, staring at the picture that was still rocking gently on the wall.

When he was finally able to, Charlie again protested their innocence and continued with his story. At times, he became quite animated, waving his arms this way and that. He also reminded Ben about the time he too had heard the voice in the helmet and insisted that he now try it on. Ben was beginning to pay a little more attention, but still had a disbelieving look on his face.

He snatched the helmet from Charlie, gripped it with both hands and slowly pulled it over his head – but not before checking the inside, as he expected some trick was about to be played on him. But no, it was okay; there was nothing disgusting lurking inside, ready to drop onto Ben's head. He pulled it slowly down over his ears. For a few seconds, nothing. Then the voice spoke.

"Where to today, Captain?"

It was just as Charlie had said.

"Jeepers, Charlie!" Ben shouted, yanking the helmet off.

Ben's attention was suddenly transformed into one of mild panic mixed with eager excitement. His heart rapidly increased its pace and adrenalin raced around his body, infusing a tingling feeling all over. It was a natural human flight or fight reaction. He was certainly a bit more focused on Charlie's story now. Having initially thrown the helmet on the floor, he picked it up and carefully examined it again.

"See, I told you so, Ben," Charlie said.

"I know, but how?"

"I don't know. I just know it does."

By now, the picture had stopped oscillating on its nail and, without realising it, they had all moved together for comfort. Perhaps for safety in numbers. V gripped hold of Ben. "What's happening?" she enquired.

"We don't really know, V, but somehow I don't think we're quite as alone as we think we are. Come on then, Charlie, tell us again what happened."

"Ben," he huffed, "weren't you listening at all?"

"Sort of."

Charlie explained again to a more attentive Ben, and expanded a bit more on the story.

After properly hearing about Charlie and George's adventure, Ben began to think about all of the clutter in the shed – in particular, the clothing that filled various chests and the wardrobe.

"What if all of this stuff has something to do with what you said happened to you, Charlie?" said Ben, not that he, at this stage, really believed the part about the aeroplane flying. However, they could have some fun pretending. Indeed, Ben was beginning to warm to the idea of an adventure. Building a tree house of his own could wait a while.

"If you could go anywhere, Ben, where would you like to go?" enquired V.

Still dressed in the navy blue suit, he raised his arm in salute and said, "Oh, I should like to sail the seven seas catching pirates and making them walk the plank." He then lowered his arm and gestured as if he had a sword and was poking a pirate along a plank. "Yo, ho ho," he teased Charlie.

"And Charlie could be the first off the end!"

"But that's what I said," protested Charlie.

"Well, if the plane's that clever, we can both go," Ben sneered, squeezing his nose and mouth to make a weasel face.

"Why pirates?" asked V.

"Well, we were reading about pirates last term at school – and I'd also like to find and capture some pirate treasure, because then we'll be rich. There was a famous one called Blackbeard that we were told about. He captured lots of ships and collected their treasure."

"Where did he live?" asked Olivia.

"On his ship most of the time, but he did return to a place called… now, what was it?" Ben pondered for a moment. "Oh, yes, Godolphin Bay. I think it was somewhere in America."

"Come on then, Ben," challenged Charlie. "Let's go and see if you can get yourself a pirate, or maybe he'll get you!"

"Yeah, let's!" agreed George.

"You'll be all right won't you, Ben?" said a slightly worried V.

"'Course I will. Do you really think we're actually going to go somewhere?" he replied with a slight shake of his head.

After a while rummaging around in the shed, they each found at least an old top to put on over their normal clothing – one which they thought suited the period in history where pirates roamed the seas.

"Come on," grunted Charlie, "let's go."

They started to make for the airfield. Charlie led the way, with Ben still carrying the helmet and goggles in his hand. The four passed through the broken garden gate. Ben glanced back down the garden to see if their mum was watching. He couldn't see anything, so followed on behind the others. Unbeknown to him someone was watching, but it wasn't his mother.

As they approached the hangar Ben looked around for signs of other people, the owners perhaps, but again it seemed deserted. He entered the hangar and there, just as Charlie had described, was a beautiful, gleaming aeroplane. As far as he could tell, it was the very same one they had seen yesterday that had been covered in dust and grime.

"There you are, Ben, I told you so," said Charlie with a smug grin.

Ben was staring at the plane with eyes that were on stalks and a jaw that fell earthwards. "You weren't lying."

"Look and there is no hole in the wing," Charlie continued.

"Come on, Ben, put the hat on and tell it where you want to go," said George.

"Yeah, come on then, Ben. Where do you want to go? Jenny says she can take us anywhere, remember," said Charlie, as they moved closer to the aeroplane.

"Yes, come on, Ben. Where shall we go?" said an excited Olivia, not really understanding what was going on.

They approached the rear of the aeroplane and the

door that led to the passenger compartment. It was wide open, just as Charlie had described, offering a clear view of antique wicker chairs and floral curtains around the windows.

"Come on then, Ben. Let's see if Jenny can take us there," said Charlie as he grabbed the helmet off Ben and put it on his own head.

Urging each other on, they bundled into the rear of the plane and seated themselves in the wicker seats of the passenger compartment.

"We have to be careful, Charlie. Pirates can be very cruel and mean," said Ben, getting slightly apprehensive now, as his bluff was about to be called.

"Will Captain Hook be with them?" asked V.

"I don't think so," snapped Ben.

Charlie buckled the strap on the helmet and waited for the voice – the voice of adventure, the voice that was going to take them into their dreams.

"Where shall we go to today then, Captain?" it spoke.

"Hello, we want to see some pirates on sailing ships – real old ones, like someone called Blackbeard."

"Okay, let's get going."

The door closed on the cabin, the engine chugged into life and the aeroplane taxied out onto the airfield.

"Cripes, Charlie, you weren't kidding about this either," puffed Ben.

With hearts racing, they excitedly looked out through the cabin windows as they bumped gently across the airfield. Slowly the craft accelerated, the tail lifted up and then, as the bumps disappeared, they became airborne. V let out a squeal of excitement and grabbed hold of her seat, though she still didn't fully realise what was happening.

As they rose higher into the sky, Jenny asked, "Do you know the name of Blackbeard's ship, Charlie, or where he will be? What year would be best?"

"No, I'll ask Ben if he knows."

"Who's Ben?"

"He's my older brother – he knows lots of things."

Charlie asked Ben the questions.

"Well, his hiding place was somewhere called Godolphin Bay in America. I think it was around 1700 or something like that that he sailed around robbing ships there."

"Oh yes, I think we've been there before. Master Oliver had some business there once," said Jenny.

"Who?" asked Charlie.

"Oh, it doesn't matter. It won't take long," replied Jenny as she climbed up through the clouds. Above the clouds, the sun shone brightly. Jenny next headed for a giant cloud, one that was more grey than white in colour, and flew straight into it. Then, a blinding flash surrounded the aeroplane, which made all the children squeeze their eyes tightly for a moment and turn away from looking outside.

"That happened this morning," remarked George, squinting.

"Yeah, the same really bright flash," said Charlie, looking through one eye.

Wheeling around another big white cloud, the plane gently started to go down through a thin veil of cloud. Then, way below, they saw a scene that was completely different from Rosemie Common. It comprised of a long, curving coastline, where rocky cliffs rose out of the ocean to form a headland in the distance.

Jenny drifted down with graceful turns, gradually losing height. As she descended, the faces in the passenger compartment were glued to the windows in an attempt to absorb the wondrous view below.

Then Charlie shrieked, "Look, Ben! Look over there," as he pointed at a ship in the direction of the bay beyond the headland. They all crowded over to one side of the plane, desperate for sight of the vessel. And there it was, a sailing ship with three tall masts – although the sails were not unfurled – just around the rocky cliff of the headland. Even from their distance, the sun glinted off the windows in the stern of the ship like jewels in a crown. It appeared to be moored just offshore from a little creek.

"Crikey," exclaimed Ben.

"Wow," from V.

George just gawped, open-mouthed at the sight before him. It appeared that Jenny had indeed taken them to a place that pirates might frequent. She continued her descent towards the sand and landed gently on the beach. Rolled to a stop, the engine silenced and, pop, the door sprang open.

"You should find what you're looking for beyond the cliff face," spoke Jenny.

A rush of warm air, which was well above the temperature of home, engulfed the cabin. George jumped out of the plane first, closely followed by the others. Charlie whipped off his helmet and goggles and threw them back into one of the chairs. He then repeated the message he was given by Jenny to the others, while Ben closed the compartment door behind them.

V looked around starry eyed at the strange scenery. She held a hand to her forehead. "It's really hot, Ben."

"Yes, squidge, it is. It's not England, that's for sure."

"Where are we then?"

"I don't know, ask your other brother."

About fifty metres along the beach, the landscape turned a corner. Charlie was quick to lead the way towards it.

"Hey," called Ben, "not so fast. You don't know what's around the corner."

"Yes we do," he replied. "A ship!"

Ben put his arm around V. "Oh goodness, what are we doing," he muttered.

George paced ahead alongside Charlie with an innocent anticipation.

"Is it alright, Ben?" enquired V.

"I really don't know. Mum's going to kill me if we get into trouble. It will all be my fault."

"Don't worry, Ben. I'll tell her it was Charlie's idea."

"Come on, Ben!" Charlie shouted as he got to the rocky overhang on the corner.

"Wait there," replied Ben, who was worried that

they didn't know what to expect beyond the rocks. Did they really see a sailing ship? Ben was beginning to sweat a bit, partly because of the thick coat he was still wearing and partly through nerves. He pulled off his three-pointed hat and waved it in front of his face to create a breeze. Ahead, the other two sat on a rock and waited for him and V to catch up.

Chapter 12

Laura picked up a cardboard box from the corner of the lounge and placed it on the table. Inside was a collection of rectangular parcels stacked against each other. Pulling one out, she carefully unwrapped the picture of the three children in their school uniform. It had been taken just over a year earlier and she gazed at it for a moment. *They change so quickly*, she thought. Standing on her own, staring at the family portrait, her thoughts drifted back to before the accident that took Simon, her husband, from them. *Why can't he be here to see them now?*

A tear appeared in the corner of her eye. She bit her lip and took a deep breath. Her eyes began to leak more. Grasping her lips with one of her hands and, putting the picture down, she told herself to stop. Simon would not want her to be unhappy and this was supposed to be a new start.

Just then there was a loud knock at the front door, which echoed through the unfurnished hallway. *Who could that be?* she mused. Finding a tissue in her pocket, she wiped her face before approaching the door – just as the knock was repeated. A tad more composed but still brushing herself down with her hand, she opened the door.

"Hello, my dear," said a friendly voice in country accent. It was the face of Harry Hobbard.

"Oh, hello Mr…" replied Laura, still trying to compose herself and to remember his name.

"Hobbard, Harry Hobbard, miss."

"Yes, yes, of course it is. Hello."

"I was just passing the end of the lane and thought I would pop down to see how you are settling in. You know, see if you need anything." He paused for a moment, "Oh, are you okay, my dear?" he enquired, seeing her slightly troubled appearance.

"Oh, yes, yes, I'm fine. Just a bit of dust getting up my nose, keeps making me sneeze!" she fibbed, brushing her fingers through her hair. "It's going to take me a while to get the place properly clean and tidy – although it was supposed to have been cleaned before we arrived."

"Yes, I imagine it will take some time, my dear. It has not been lived in for quite a few years now," he said. "They did send a large white van, I think, to clear out the place, but maybe the blokes didn't do such a good job of the actual cleaning, eh."

"No, you're not wrong there, Mr Hobbard!"

"Oh, please call me Harry, miss, everyone does. And forgive me, but I can't remember what you said your name was. 'Course when your post starts to come through, I'll learn it soon enough!"

"It's Laura, Laura Green, Harry."

"Yes, that's right, Laura," he nodded as he spoke.

Harry often repeated parts of a sentence said to him because his hearing was not quite as good as it used to be. Although his wife kept going on about it, he wouldn't go and get an appointment to get a hearing aid. So, if he didn't hear something the first time, he found cupping his hand around his ear usually did the trick.

Laura was now beginning to feel a bit more relaxed and thought it very kind of Harry to come and check on her, especially when they had only met briefly the day before. In the two days since she had arrived, the people she had met had already made a good impression on her. It had taken years at their old home to get to know a few locals. Nobody there seemed to have the time of day for anyone else. It appeared that it was going to be quite different here.

"Well, thank you for calling, but I'm okay for things at the moment. I was just going to take a break and have a cuppa, would you like to join me? If you have time, that is."

Looking out onto the lane, she could see the post office van he'd arrived in and guessed that he was on his rounds. Even so, there were a couple of things she wanted to ask him as a long-term local.

"Oh yes, my dear, I've finished the post round and am on my way back. A cuppa would do just fine. Lovely, thank you. Mrs Hobbard asked me to check you were getting on all right and that. You know, you being new to these parts and all."

"That is very kind," replied Laura. "Do come in – we'll go through to the kitchen. It's at the back."

"Oh yes, I've been in before – when master Oliver

lived here. I used to bring him his groceries as well as the post, you know. Lovely man, he was."

As he stepped through the front door, Harry removed his brown flat cap and held it firmly in his left hand. He always wore the cap, even in the height of summer, but never indoors. A tie, too – no matter what the temperature. He now also wore a check shirt with the sleeves rolled up to above the elbow, and braces that held up a pair of brown corduroy trousers that looked at least one, if not two, sizes too big and were worn at the knees. This attire was bottomed with a pair of well-scuffed brown leather boots.

Laura was somewhat bemused, as the postmen in the town were always smartly dressed in a uniform. She closed the front door and led the way through to the kitchen with Harry close behind.

Dipping his head slightly to one side, he said, "It's still the same, except for your stuff of course, miss!"

Pulling out a chair at the table, Laura said, "Please have a seat."

Harry seated himself with a view of the garden, though his eyes surveyed the whole kitchen.

"Guess you'll be wanting to modernise this place a bit, miss, won't you?" he said as Laura busied herself making them tea.

"Yes, it's going to keep me busy for quite a while. Actually, you might be able to help me there. I was wondering if you knew anyone local that does decorating who could get some of this done – rather than get a firm from the town?"

"I know just the person for you, miss, Frankie Miller. He works at the garage in the village, but often has time for other work, too."

"Do you think he'd be interested in a bit of decorating for some extra cash?" Laura asked.

"I'm sure he'd be pleased to, as I don't think he earns a lot from Mr Seward. Mr Seward owns the garage and can be a bit misery. Some days he's fine, the next he's like a bear with a sore head." Looking out of the window for a moment, Harry added, "He could sort out your garden, too. He's very green-fingered."

"Sounds like a really useful person to know," replied Laura.

"Oh, he is. Frankie is very handy. A very handy man to know."

Laura then placed a freshly brewed cup of tea in front of Harry and he stirred in two well-heaped spoonfuls of sugar. They chatted over the kitchen table about things to do with the village and village life, and Laura enquired about the previous owner of Pegasus Ride. She learnt that he had moved to the village after the airfield had closed down and set up as a pilot, taking people up for pleasure flights. Then, out of the blue, he had mysteriously disappeared about six years ago. He had had no close family and, although well liked around the village, he tended to keep himself to himself most of the time. It was therefore quite a while before anyone realised he was missing. In fact, it was Harry himself who had raised the alarm when he noticed the post building up behind the front door.

It had not been unusual for Oliver to not be around for a few weeks at a time, though he normally told Harry or Beryl of his absence so that they could keep hold of his post. On this occasion, though, they'd heard nothing. Suspecting the worst, they notified the police, who broke into the house and found nothing. They had also searched the garden and checked the airfield, where his aeroplane was kept in one of the old hangars. The aeroplane had been there but there was no evidence of Oliver.

Because the house had been found locked up and with everything left there as if its owner was expected to return, nothing further was done for some time. In due course, however, the police had opened a missing person's file and Oliver's picture had been circulated around the country. Detectives had come to the village and asked around for information, but nothing ever came to light.

It had then turned out that Oliver was not particularly good at filing his tax returns and the Inland Revenue was seeking back payment of several years. They had put an investigator on the case, who worked even harder than the police, to find Oliver. It was as if he had just disappeared off the face of the earth. Neither he nor the police could trace him.

And so the property lay empty for years until the Inland Revenue got a court order to force the sale of the house to recover the money due. For the house to be sold, all his possessions in the house had to be cleared. There had been an attempt to find any living relatives, but, again, no one could be traced. So in the end, his house and all his belongings had been sold at auction and the state was the benefactor. E.H. Cotton and Sons, a house clearance company, had cleaned the house in advance of the sale. They hadn't bothered with the back garden, though, as it was already very overgrown, which is why the shed had been left untouched. However, Harry hadn't been sure whether anyone at the auction house was aware of Oliver's aeroplane tucked away in the old hangar. For all he knew, it could still be there.

Back in the kitchen, Harry suggested that the best thing Laura could do with the back garden was to get some animals to chew the grass and weeds down! He thought that any one of several local farmers would oblige, and it would be much easier than trying to mow it.

The tea and biscuits had gone down well, although Laura had been slightly bemused at the way Harry drank his tea. As it happened, Laura had served the brew in a cup and saucer – not something she normally did, but they had just been freshly unpacked.

Harry had taken the cup in one hand, the saucer in the other, and then poured the tea into the saucer before drinking from it. It was a habit that annoyed his wife no end when they were out in public. The practice was always met with a tutt and a frown. Laura had just raised an eyebrow and smiled to herself, wondering if it were a tradition in these parts.

With their refreshment nearly over, Harry asked after the children. "How are the children settling in? They doing all right, are they?" he enquired.

Staring out of the window over the wilderness that was her new back garden, she said, "Oh, early days, but they seem to like the garden. It's sort of an adventure playground for them – and at least they're out of my hair for a while! Hopefully they can't come to much harm out there."

"No, I don't suppose so."

"They've hacked out a path through the grass to the shed and are down there now trying to sort it out. I think."

Harry nearly spat out his tea and spluttered, "Shed, you say? The shed?"

"Yes, I suppose it gives them somewhere to go while I'm still trying to sort out the house. And you never know, they might find something useful."

Harry wiped his mouth and chin with the back of his hand, "Of course, the shed." He cleared his throat. "I'd forgotten about the shed."

"Forgotten?" quizzed Laura. "Forgotten what?"

"Oh, nothing, nothing really."

Of course, it had been years since he'd last checked it when looking for evidence of Oliver's whereabouts. Harry and Beryl – and they alone, as far as they were aware – were the only ones that knew of Oliver's secret. Oliver usually informed them of his trips, but not always.

If Oliver was not in when he delivered the post, he would usually go out back and check if Jenny was there or not. If she were, he would check in the cabin for any messages. It was not unknown for Oliver to request some object or for an item of clothing to be sent. If that were the case, then Harry would go on a mission to buy whatever was required. He quite liked being part of Oliver's little schemes, searching out odd, very old items.

Oliver's shopping lists had meant that Harry was a frequent visitor to Emilie Brackets' Emporium, an old curiosity shop. Most thought Emilie was an old curiosity herself! Her shop was a collection of rooms and corridors in a large, old, Tudor timber-framed house. It was full of the weird and wonderful from all ages of history. Always adorned in a large flowery frock, Emilie was a spinster of senior years with some of her marbles missing. She wore thin, wiry spectacles on a fine chain around her neck and a woollen shawl around her shoulders. With the full-length frock on, she seemed to glide through the shop like a skater sliding silently across the ice, always humming as she went. To a new visitor, the shop would appear unattended on entering and then, when it was least expected, she would appear behind them. "Can I help you, dear?" she would announce, in the low hissing sound of a deflating airbed.

The house clearance and sale had, in the end, all happened so quickly. He had meant to come and clear out the shed himself, because Oliver had asked Harry, in total confidence and with definitive passion, to do so and to burn everything if anything happened to him.

Harry had never let on to anyone that he had a key to the house and sheds, and he now felt that he'd let his old friend down. What would be found or discovered? He thought most people would just think it was full of old junk and party costumes. Even so, an agreement was an agreement and Harry was now a bit worried.

The flying helmet was the main thing he should have retrieved. He had removed it from the aeroplane and locked it in the shed with all the other clothes. The helmet was the key to the secret life of Jenny and Oliver. *Was it too late?* he thought. Though, how could he do anything now? It all belonged to the new owners.

He tried to conceal his worry and finally responded to Laura, "Really, it, er... it doesn't matter... I'd lent Master Oliver some garden tools a long time ago and, er, I'd meant to call in and ask about it when they were clearing it out."

"Oh, is that all? It sounded like something important or dangerous. They're not dangerous, are they? The tools, I mean. Perhaps I should go down and check on the children."

"No, no, just hoes and the like – nothing that could possibly harm them. I was helping Master Oliver plant up the garden and left them here," he fibbed. "I can pick them up another time."

★ ★ ★

When Harry left, he promised Laura he would speak to Frankie about the decorating. He also laughingly explained the reason for his workman-like attire: he tended to his allotment-style garden inbetween his post office duties. In the morning he dressed as other postmen, but in the afternoon his time would be spent digging, weeding and planting in the garden. This would be followed by the late delivery of post.

Sometimes, if there were only a few letters, he would leave them for the morning delivery – not that he was supposed to, but there was no one to check. This allowed him all afternoon in the garden or to help out with the shop, which meant going into town to get supplies. For those trips, he used his very old, faithful, half-timbered Morris Minor estate car. The vehicle was his pride and joy, and it was washed and polished every Sunday until Harry's face could be seen in the bottle-green bodywork. The external timber frame surrounding the rear was a novelty compared to a modern-day car, but didn't seem out of place in a village where modern developments had largely passed it by.

On saying a final goodbye to Laura, Harry closed the door firmly and raised his arm through the open window to wave goodbye. The post office van soon disappeared down the lane in a cloud of dust.

Laura returned to the front room and the task of unpacking the pictures. Feeling more phlegmatic now, she began to arrange the family photographs in the lounge and the hallway. Ben could use his expertise with a hammer to fix them to the walls. It would only be a temporary measure, as the walls needed repainting, but it would brighten up the place and make them feel more at home.

Chapter 13

Pleased that they had waited for him, Ben, with V in tow, caught up with Charlie and George sitting on the rocks.

"Now what are we going to do, Ben?" Charlie enquired eagerly.

Ben didn't reply, instead walking on a few more paces so he could see the ship moored a little way in the distance. He stopped and stared, transfixed for a moment. He was still trying to make sense of what was happening.

"Well?" enquired Charlie again.

"Okay," said Ben, getting a grip on the situation. "Let's get a bit closer to see if it really is Blackbeard. We should keep to the top of the beach and you should all stay close to me."

The top of the shoreline was covered in small trees and scrub. It was good for hiding. They stayed close together with Ben in the lead, keeping close to the scrubland at the top of the beach. There wasn't much wind about, but now and again a slight breeze stirred the flag flying from the back of the ship – it was the Jolly Roger.

"I wish I had a telescope," said Ben. "Then I could try and read the name of the ship."

"Why's that?" asked George.

"Well, they're obviously pirates and if it's Blackbeard, the name of his ship was the *Queen Anne's Revenge*."

They were now about halfway towards the ship and were noticeably walking more slowly. Ben was crouching down and creeping from tree to tree with the others lurking behind him. Then, suddenly, Ben held his arm out behind him and waved the others to take shelter in his shadow. He had just seen a small boat, a skiff, come out of the river inlet. It appeared to be heading for the ship. They could see a tall, dark-haired man with a ragged beard standing at the back of the boat waving his arms and they thought they could hear him shouting at the six men rowing the vessel. A pistol shot rang out, fired in the air by the tall stranger in the skiff. The boat seemed to quicken its pace a little and all the children spontaneously jumped and grabbed each other.

Crouching down in the undergrowth, they watched the skiff tie up alongside the ship. The men in the skiff took hold of the ropes that had been lowered and struggled to load some heavy boxes into a net on the end. The activity made the small craft rock wildly to and fro, and one of the men fell in the water with an almighty splash. Once again, the tall dark-haired stranger was gesticulating wildly, this time with a cutlass in one hand, at the men trying to get the crates into the net.

As the boatmen appeared to be preoccupied, Ben decided to move closer. He was desperate to find out the ship's identity. Keeping a careful eye on the ship, they edged closer to the bank of the small river but could still not read the identity of the mysterious ship. Where the beachhead met the river inlet, there was a small clearing in the scrub with a tree stump bench. It offered a vantage point where one could spy on the sea without easily being seen. The children watched intently as more boxes were loaded onto the ship. The tall madman, meanwhile, had climbed up the side and was now on board. A short time later he reappeared at the gunwale of the ship, clutching, what looked to be, a small sack under one arm.

Firstly, he had some discussion with a man next to him and then shouted down to the crew in the skiff. At the same time, he alarmingly pointed in the direction of the young observers. Seeing him point in their direction, Ben backed up and pushed the others behind their cover.

"Has he seen us?" said a worried V.

"I don't think so," sighed Ben, staring as hard as he could from eyes that felt ready to pop out of their sockets. He wished he had a telescope.

"But I think they will be coming this way soon, though."

"What should we do now, Ben?" asked George.

"Why don't we find out where they're going?" suggested Charlie.

Ben sighed, "You would say that, wouldn't you, Charlie."

While they were having their discussion, the tall

madman descended back into the skiff, which then started to make its way towards them.

"Come on," said Ben, "we should move from here."

There was a footpath leading from the spying bench that cornered a bend and went further up the river inlet – which was actually more of a creek than a river. Ben decided to follow this path, as they couldn't go back the way they had come now without being seen. He grabbed V's hand and hurried them from their hideout, "Come on, we need to run." They had to get around the next bend before the skiff entered the creek or they would be seen.

As they got round the bend and now out of view of any boat entering the creek, Ben stopped and bundled the group into the undergrowth once more.

"Hey, Ben, what are you doing?" protested Charlie, as he fell into the bushes.

"You obviously didn't see it," Ben whispered through gritted teeth.

Just in sight, ahead of them, was a wooden shack with a landing stage on the bank. In fact, there were several buildings that were all made of roughly cut timber planks. Outside one of the sheds stood a number of large wooden barrels, and a section of fence to which a horse was tied. A thin veil of smoke rose above the building from a chimney pipe and drifted slowly skywards.

It was a lot warmer here than at home and after their short run, the kids were all breathing heavily and sweating. Ahead of them was some form of habitation and behind was a madman in a boat, waving a cutlass about and catching up with them fast. Should they continue or risk being seen by a raving nutcase? Ben had often called his little brother a loony or a nut-job, but the tall stranger in the skiff really did look mad, and he had a gun and a sword. Ben ushered them further into the undergrowth, picking Charlie up by the collar.

"Come on, we need to get out of sight. There's some sort of settlement further up the path. It's probably where the boat is going and I don't want us to be seen."

Still with a tiny view of the creek, they waited for the men to pass.

"Ben," whispered Charlie.

"Sssh, you idiot," replied Ben. He put a finger to his lips and looked intently at each one of them.

A moment later, they could hear the splash of oars on the water and the skiff floated past, with the tall dark-haired stranger still barking orders at the rowers. His hair was tied in a collection of small plaits, including his beard.

"Put yer back into it, yer lazy narks. I don't wanna be missin' the nex' tide or dat Captin bloody Morgan'll be on us," he shouted as they drifted past the children.

Ben's face held a frozen expression of disbelief, with his jaw slightly dropped and his mouth open. As the back of the boat came into view, Ben finally caught sight of the name of the ship: *Queen Anne's Revenge*.

Ben unfroze, turned around to the others and stuttered the words, "My God, it is. It's Blackbeard."

"What! It's Mr Blackbeard?" asked V.

"There's no Mr about it, V. He's just known as Blackbeard. If I remember correctly, his actual name is Edward Teach."

"So, is he a real pirate, Ben?" enquired a now excited Charlie.

"Real all right, and he can be really nasty from what I was told at school."

"He was shouting a lot," chipped in George.

Charlie pushed past Ben and inched forward from their hiding place, so that he had a better view. Leaning forward, he watched as the skiff pulled in alongside the jetty outside the shed with the smoking pipe. One of the men in the boat jumped out and another threw a rope, which was used to tie the boat to the jetty. Another rope was thrown from the stern to a man in a wide-brimmed hat, who had just come out of the shed. He used it to pull in the rear of the craft and tie that off too.

By now, all the kids were peering around the tree that had provided them with shelter, with Ben's face at the top, V kneeling on the ground and the other two squashed between them. They keenly watched as Blackbeard stepped across and out of the skiff, still tightly clutching his small bag. He greeted the shed occupant with a completely different disposition. He seemed positively jovial and slung his arm around the shoulder of the man in the wide-brimmed hat. He then began talking in a calm manner as the two of them disappeared into the shed. It took a few more moments before the other six crew members had clambered out of the skiff and followed their leader out of view.

As the last one disappeared into the shed, Ben, Charlie, George and Olivia fell out from behind the tree into a pile on the ground. With a lot of moaning and groaning, and shushing and tutting, they gathered themselves back onto their feet.

"Come on then," said Charlie. "Let's go and have a closer look."

"Not so blooming quick," warned Ben quietly, grabbing hold of Charlie's sleeve.

"I think it's time we went home, Charlie. We've seen enough for one day."

"I haven't," he quickly replied.

"Look here, Charlie, you didn't see them, but I read some notes in the book about pirates in the old shed at home. They must have had something to do with the man who lived at the house before us. We need to go back and find out more, as there may be a clue about why the man disappeared. Now that we know the possibilities of the aeroplane, maybe he went on a journey and something went wrong?"

Ignoring Ben, Charlie pleaded, "But we could just go and have a quick look, please."

"Oh, you're a pain, Charlie."

Charlie grinned so that his special smile, with a slightly curled top lip, spread over his cheeky little face.

"Okay, we'll just go close enough to try and see what's going on and then we better scarper home."

He'd hardly finished his sentence and Charlie was off.

"Oi, not down the path you twerp!" Ben bellowed.

Ben took hold of V's hand and led them through the undergrowth of tall grass, bushes and trees – keeping away from the path, as they would easily be seen approaching the shed that way. They edged around to the front of the buildings and got to where the horse was tied up on the fence post. As they rustled the bushes a few metres from the animal, it lifted its head and turned towards them, thrashing its tail a few times in an attempt to flick some flies off its back.

Ben ducked down into the grass, pulling the others down with him. "Okay, this is close enough; we're going to get caught if we're not careful."

They were now in a position to hear people talking, but not close enough to make out what they were saying. Charlie felt frustrated; he really wanted to move closer, as he could see an open window. There was no glass in the frame, just rough wooden shutters on the outside. Charlie reckoned he could squat under the open window and listen in to the conversation. He wanted to actually hear someone call the dark-haired madman Mr Blackbeard. Then, he really would have a story to tell.

Ben surveyed the scene in front of him. There were four different buildings: one looked like a log cabin where someone would live, which also had a pipe sticking through the roof, though no smoke was coming from it. He could now see that the shed in front of them was actually some sort of supply store. It had a sign above the door, written in black tar, which announced it was "Taylor's Stores". Both buildings stood on a wooden platform, which raised them off the ground, and had a covered veranda across their front.

Isaac Taylor had constructed the timber buildings on the banks of the creek, about ten miles south of Charles Towne, South Carolina, to supply pirates like Blackbeard. Charles Towne, a busy port, did not generally welcome pirates, but they brought Isaac good trade. He did not care where their money or valuables came from, as they always paid well for the supplies he could provide. The outer reaches of the creek inlet was only accessible to smaller ships like *Queen Anne's Revenge* as it was protected by a vast expanse of sand banks and small channels. The large naval ships that tried to hunt down pirates could not get anywhere near, for fear of running aground. The likes of Blackbeard would try to get in and out on one tide to avoid being seen by their pursuer. Having exchanged some of their plundered treasure for supplies, they would then carefully navigate back to the open ocean.

The other barn-like structures had a pair of large doors, one of which was open. Through these, Ben could see a four-wheeled wooden cart parked just inside, alongside which were more wooden barrels. While Ben was distracted, he hadn't noticed Charlie and George creep up to the open window. V tugged at Ben's sleeve and pointed silently at Charlie.

"Charlie!" Ben hissed in dismay. "What are you doing?"

Charlie ignored his big brother. There were several empty wooden crates on the veranda just outside the door and Charlie and George were hiding beside them. Ben knew this was likely to end in trouble, but wasn't sure what to do. He moved himself and V back undercover, while keeping an eye on Charlie.

Charlie had put his little hands on the window ledge. He could hear a gravelly voice complaining about the price of something and tried to see what was going on. Suddenly, the door was thrown open by a giant of a man, covered in tattoos. Charlie and George had nowhere to go and nowhere to hide. They froze on the spot.

It was Irasmuth Kelly, a fearless gunner on board Blackbeard's ship. He had a face that could melt steel and a body that had a patchwork of scars from numerous battles. Behind him followed a much leaner, but just as fearsome, man. His name was Ned Pook; he only had one ear and one eye, and most of his teeth were missing. They had been sent to go and get some crates from the nearest of the two barns.

"Why, what 'ave we 'ere, Ned?"

The boys cowered beside the boxes.

"Looks like we got ourselves a couple a dormice, Rasmuth," Ned replied.

"What you doin' 'ere, lads?" enquired Irasmuth.

As well as being scared, the boys were slightly

bemused by the accents of the two imposing figures in front of them. On seeing the pirates, Ben recoiled further into the tall grass, making sure he and V couldn't be seen. Although both were fearless in battle and appeared fearsome in character, Irasmuth and Ned were actually relatively normal men – relative to some pirates, that is.

Seeing that the little ones were a bit overcome by their presence, Irasmuth bent down in front of Charlie and said, "What's up sonny, cat got ur tongue?"

In his squatting position, Charlie pressed his back against the wall and tried to move away from the awful smell of Irasmuth's breath. It was the equivalent of sticking your head into a bucket of dead fish guts.

"I… I just… wanted to meet Mr. Blackbeard, sir," stuttered Charlie.

Irasmuth turned his head sideways to look at Ned. "Aah, 'e wants to see Mr Blackbeard, Ned."

Ned raised his eyebrows (he still had two of those) and scratched his one ear. "Well, let us introduce 'em then."

"Come on den," said Irasmuth, as he took Charlie by the arm. Ned grabbed hold of George and led them back into the store.

From his hiding place, Ben was moaning, "I knew something like this would happen, V. Going off on his own like that. He never stops to think."

"What are we going to do?" said V as she started to cry.

"I don't know yet. Let's just wait for a moment and see what happens. I'll have to think of something."

★ ★ ★

Inside the store, the boys were presented to Blackbeard.

"These boys were outside, wanin' to sees yer, Teach," said Irasmuth.

Blackbeard stood in front of them. He was an imposing man of more than six feet tall. Two leather belts sat diagonally across his chest, into which he had six flintlock pistols secured. On one side hung a cutlass; on the other was a dagger. A scruffy, three-cornered hat sat on top of his head, from which long black hair sprouted. The hair was roughly twisted into plaits and held in place, it was rumoured, by dipping the ends in molten candle wax. His long beard looked more organised. It was neatly plaited in six strands, with each end bound with thin, brown, hemp rope that dangled a couple of inches below the beard. In one hand, he tightly held a leather bag that was tied at the top with a thin strap of woven leather.

On seeing the boys, he thumped the bag down on a wooden counter top. The resounding chinking sound immediately gave away its contents. He eyed the boys up and down for what seemed like an age, though in reality it was only a few seconds.

"So yous wanted to sees me, eh?" he said as he leaned over them both.

A pause enveloped the scene. Then, Blackbeard raised an eyebrow, encouraging a response.

"Yes, sir," they both replied.

"I heard about you from my brother Ben," added Charlie.

"Ahh… famous, am I?"

"Oh yes, sir. He read about you in a book."

"Book, yer say. Now there's a thing."

"Yes, definitely a book, sir."

"Did yer hear dat, boys? Me in a book. What abut Rasmuth and Ned?"

George nudged Charlie in the ribs with his elbow, who then chipped in, "Oh no, don't think so, sir. You're the famous one. We… err just wanted to see you for ourselves."

Isaac looked at the boys. "I don't remember seeing you around the village before?" he questioned.

Hawkestowne was a village that was around four miles away and Isaac made regular visits there on his way to Charles Towne, where he bought most of his goods to sell to the pirates. Charles Towne was a big port where all manner of goods were brought in on trading ships. He also sold his wares to the people of Hawkestowne and knew the majority of people who lived there. Most people in the area, apart from the Edisto Indians, had arrived as settlers on board ships that had docked in Charles Towne.

"I guess you're new arrivals, are you?"

Charlie looked at George and George looked at Charlie.

"Yes, you could say that we are!" remarked Charlie.

They chatted for a few minutes, asking questions about what it was like to be a pirate and it seemed that Blackbeard wasn't that terrifying after all. Neither were Rasmuth or Ned, or the other four that had been loading boxes onto the skiff from the back of the store and had now come in to stare at the boys inquisitively.

Charlie decided to go the whole way and ask if he could see Blackbeard's ship.

"Wat do yer think, boys?" he said to the other men. Some of them grinned a knowing smile and nodded. Two new cabin boys to do their chores! "Tides going out, captin," remarked Ned.

"Yes, we best be off." Blackbeard turned to the motley crew behind him and said, "You take 'em boys out so's I can settle the payment with this 'ere blaggard. Ned and Rasmuth, yoos get that barrel of powder. Careful, mind."

Ned and Irasmuth disappeared out of the front of the store. As they were led out the back by one of the other crew, George whispered something in Charlie's ear, but he wasn't listening. George looked back and wished they had not got into this situation. It didn't feel right to him.

The band of seemingly nice cutthroats helped Charlie and George into the skiff. This was hidden from Ben's view, so he couldn't see what was going on. After settling the fee for the goods, Blackbeard supervised the loading of the powder barrel, which Irasmuth and Ned had collected, into the skiff and then demanded they 'get to it' and row.

136

Ben's attention had been drawn to the two men coming out of the front door and he had watched as they had brought a barrel out of one of the barns. They had then carried it around to the back of the stores, with it suspended on two ropes on a pole. Ben could see nothing else, until, some moments later and to his dismay, the skiff was rowed into view with Charlie and George in it.

Charlie turned to where he knew Ben would be and raised his arm slightly and waved. He smiled with his top lip curled over, knowing full well he was up to no good. Ben buried his face in his hands in desperation. As it happened, none of the other members in the boat saw Charlie waving, so they continued down the creek unaware of Ben and Olivia hiding in the bushes.

Chapter 14

Harry pulled up outside of the Post Office and hurried inside to discuss his worries with Beryl.

"Oh, Harry, why didn't you get rid of the helmet years ago?"

"Well, you know I always believed Oliver would be back one day and then I just forgot."

Harry was pacing about like an expectant father waiting for a child to be born. He kept folding and refolding his flat cap in his hand. He twisted it first one way and then the other. "What if the children find out? What if they find Jenny? You know, Beryl, get in it and everything?"

"You'll just have to get back up there, Harry, and, and do what you need to."

"But what reason can I give? The children are already exploring all over the place. You know what inquisitive things children are. Oh lordy lord, Beryl."

Poor Harry was beside himself with worry. Should he go back? Maybe if he spoke to Frankie he could use the excuse of taking a message up there? In the end, he couldn't decide and spent the rest of the afternoon wrestling with the situation in his mind.

★ ★ ★

Laura returned to the front room and delved into the open box on the living-room table. Pictures of their past packed up in a cardboard box. She unwrapped another frame and scanned the room for a place to hang it. As it was, the room had a picture rail around all the walls, which was a tradition in Victorian houses, and it still had a number of little brass picture hooks hanging from it. She selected one to go above the fireplace next; it was one of the children that had been taken at school last term. They looked like they were on their best behaviour – well, if you didn't count that give-away smile of Charlie's.

Laura soon unpacked the rest of the photos and found room for all but one on the little picture hooks. The last was one of Simon and Laura on their wedding day. *I'll have to get Ben to help me fix it on the wall*, she thought to herself, so for the meantime propped it up on the mantelpiece. With that box done, she tossed it aside and picked up another, which was full of ornamental knick-knacks, and placed it on the table.

Before tackling the next box, she paused and wandered what the children were up to. Something had worried her about the way Harry Hobbard had reacted when she said they were exploring the contents of the shed.

She went to the kitchen and looked out into the garden. She couldn't see them from the kitchen window, but the garden was so overgrown and little could be seen beyond the wild privet hedge that reached out across the garden like a demented

Chinese dragon. Laura opened the back door and shouted their names. No response. She tried again, but with the same silent response.

Little blighters, she thought. *Why do they never hear me when I call them?* But then, even if they were just upstairs it would take at least three or four bellowing shouts from their mother to get their attention!

"As if I haven't got enough to do," sighed Laura.

Still in her fluffy pink slippers, she stepped outside onto the grey paving slabs that led down the garden. It was the first time Laura had ventured into the back garden and, as she surveyed the rampant wilderness, she agreed with Harry that the best start would be to get some animals in!

The path was hemmed in by jungle grass and weeds that were half as tall as she was. Laura then passed the head of the Chinese-dragon hedge and tucked behind the overgrown laurel trees, spotted the first shed that the boys had been talking about. She stopped and shouted their names again. Nothing. She tried "BEN!" at a greater volume, but still no reply.

She walked on with her arms folded tightly and an annoyed look on her face, which caused the two wrinkles on her forehead to crease. Expecting to find them all in the shed, she opened the door ready to shout at them for not listening – but no one was there. She glanced briefly at all of the junk, but didn't take much notice of the contents. She just sighed and left the shed in a huff. She then continued down the path and stopped to check the second shed. Again, however, the children weren't there.

Where the heck are they? she thought as she walked from the shed to the gate that led to the airfield. She suddenly noticed that there were two footpaths that went in opposite directions across the end of the garden, as well as the gateway onto the airfield. Laura quickly came to the conclusion that the children weren't in the garden. They could be anywhere.

She tried to shout for them one last time and came to the conclusion that George must have taken them somewhere. She decided that as Ben was with them, they probably wouldn't come to much harm, so began to make her way back to the house. Even so, they would be in for a talking-to when they did come back for tea.

Chapter 15

V tightly clutched Babbit, who she had brought with her, and twiddled her fingers around the purple ribbon that tied around his neck. Removing her thumb from her mouth, she nervously asked Ben what they were going to do.

Ben wasn't sure how to get out of this one, though; they'd been in a few scrapes before, but this was in a new league altogether.

"We'll wait a couple of minutes and then we should go in there and see what we can find out," he said, looking in the direction of Taylor's store.

With the skiff well on its way down the creek, Ben took V's hand and they left the cover of the elephant grass. They cautiously stepped onto the wooden platform outside the door and peered into the glassless window, trying not to be seen. Isaac had his back to them and was stacking some jars from a crate onto a shelf.

"Go on, Ben," squeaked V. "Go and ask him."

Ben took a deep breath, gripped V's hand a touch more tightly and crept slowly towards the door – although the creeping bit didn't really help as the door creaked on its hinges as Ben opened it. Isaac turned around immediately.

"'ello, young sir," he said, politely. "Don't be shy now, come on in."

Ben and V were statues in the doorway, but managed to relax enough to slowly approach the counter.

"What can I do for you young 'uns?"

V hid behind Ben with her head down, her thumb back in the sucking position and Babbit held tightly under her neck.

"Well, sir," started Ben, "I'm looking for my brother. He came here a little while ago."

"Was he with another young lad?" asked Isaac.

"Yes, sir, that's right."

"The one that wanted to meet Blackbeard?"

"Yes, sir, that's him."

"Well, he's gone off with him. Not so sure that was a good idea, but it's not for me to say. He asked to go and see his ship and that's where they've gone."

Olivia sidled out from Ben's shadow and asked, "Why's that not a good idea, sir?"

Isaac explained that by the time they got to the *Queen Anne's Revenge*, Blackbeard would probably want to set sail as the tide had changed and was going out fast. If he did not leave at this point, he risked being grounded on the sandbank and would be a sitting duck for any of the eighty or ninety-gun Royal Navy warships that were looking for him. With their big guns, they could pound his ship, while staying out of range of Blackbeard's smaller guns.

The *Queen Anne's Revenge* was a fast and manoeuvrable corvette, but it relied on getting close to its prey to use its battery of small cannon. It was no match for a Man-O-War ship of the line that the British Navy had looking for him. As it was, Blackbeard was currently short of gunpowder in the skiff. Still, the chance of Charlie and George being returned that afternoon were very slim.

Unbeknown to them, however, Blackbeard had other plans for the boys. He could make good use of a couple of young cabin boys. They would be good for fetching, carrying, helping in the galley, and generally doing light and menial tasks around the ship.

Isaac asked Ben how they knew Blackbeard would be there. Ben fibbed and said they had been told by people in the village that he sometimes went there, and Charlie and George had run on ahead.

He thanked Isaac for the information and started to lead V out of the store, but paused before opening the door. Turning around, he enquired as to when Blackbeard was likely to be back if he did not return today.

"I don't expect he'll be back for a couple of weeks."

Ben grimaced a smile and left with V.

Once outside, he said to her, "Come on, let's go and see if we can watch from the spying bench."

The two started to walk down the footpath to the end of the creek, but on the way heard what sounded like explosions in the distance. Ben directed a startled look at V, grabbed her hand tightly and immediately started running down the pathway. Their return to the spying bench was much speedier than their departure, with their sprint to get there witnessed by numerous native birdlife fleeing the noise. The birds' high-pitched screeches, in some cases, exceeded the level of the distant explosions.

It seemed that Blackbeard had stayed too long at anchor. *HMS Cornwall*, a ninety-gun warship, had found them and was busy sending ranging cannon shots towards the *Queen Anne*. So far, none had actually hit the ship and were landing short of their target with an almighty splash, sending a plume of water high into the air.

As Ben and V got to the end of the path, they could see Blackbeard gesticulating wildly and shouting up at the ship as the skiff came alongside the *Queen Anne*. Men were scurrying up the rigging and releasing sails, which made the ship come to life from its dormant state. A breeze had also picked up and quickly filled the canvas sails as they were dropped and hauled out. Cannon shot suddenly ripped through one of the main sails and headed for where Ben and V were watching. It splashed down on the edge of the surf and buried itself deep in the beach, throwing up a fountain of sand. Blackbeard was first on board, his arms still waving instructions and shouting commands at his crew.

Several men threw a rope and netting over the gunwales of the *Queen Anne* to the skiff below, which was rocking to and fro as the men panicked to leave it for the mother ship. Leaning over the side himself, Blackbeard reminded them in no uncertain terms, using words that Charlie and George were not used to hearing, that the contents of the last visit to Isaac's store must be got on board first. He then untied a large brown key from his belt and handed it to Irasmuth. "And get those boys locked in my cabin," he yelled.

From his viewing point, Ben could see Charlie and George being ushered up the wooden steps on the outside of the ship, both hanging on the side ropes for dear life. Charlie had stopped smiling. He now wished he had listened to Ben.

On deck, they were pushed and shoved by sailors rushing about their duties. Commotion was everywhere as they were dragged to the rear of the ship and Blackbeard's private cabin. Below deck, they could hear men chanting some sort of song as the capstan clattered round raising the anchor. Another cannon shot whizzed through the rigging, taking one poor soul with it with a great scream of pain.

Irasmuth opened the oak panelled door and threw the boys in, then slammed it shut and turned the key in the lock. He wrapped a leather cord around the key and tied it onto his wrist, before going in search of Blackbeard. Inside the locked room, Charlie immediately tried to get out, but no amount of twisting the handle released the door. "Now what are we going to do, George? Ben will be going mad!" For once, Charlie was beginning to worry. He remembered Ben's look of annoyance when they had passed him on the river. It appeared that they really were in trouble now.

"Come on, Charlie, let's see if there is another way out," said George.

The boys spotted another door, but that was also locked. They turned their attention to the rest of the cabin. There were several sturdy wooden round-topped chests, with equally impressive locks. In the centre, towards the back, was a large mahogany table with four grand chairs around it. A large book dominated the table, with two quill pens and an inkwell on the side, and a flintlock pistol resting next to them. Sticking vertically up from the top of the table was a dagger with an elegantly carved ivory handle. Behind the table, a row of small windows reached across the rear of the cabin. Oil lamps hung from the walls and ceiling, and to one side were several solid wooden chests. A bed on the opposite side was built into panelling.

Moving towards the table, Charlie's attention was drawn to the pistol, which he picked up and began to examine. He pointed it at random items around the cabin and pretended to shoot them. It was loaded, but, unaware of this, Charlie pulled the trigger back. On this type of pistol, you had to pull the firing hammer back before it would fire the shot. George took hold of the dagger and wriggled it to release it from the table, then turned to the large book. After admiring the carving of a lion's head and the jewels encrusted in the leather cover, he opened it.

It was a record (also known as a ship's log) of events during the *Queen Anne's Revenge*'s journeys, together with her conquests. George thumbed through some of the pages, reading of the plunder the battles had brought Blackbeard.

"Look, Charlie," he exclaimed as he started to read one of the pages.

"Look at all this stuff he's got. It can't all be in those chests."

As they carefully turned the pages, they studied the entries with increasing amazement. It detailed ships conquered and treasures stolen. Gold, silver, jewels and coins with names they had never heard of filled the pages.

Loud shouts could be heard outside the cabin and a rumbling noise came from under their feet. Joseph Foley was winding the rudder around to bring the ship about for their escape through the shallows. The ship started to lean over to one side, making each boy take a steadying step. George also supported himself on the edge of the table. Charlie went to look out of one of the windows at the back.

"We're turning round, George," he exclaimed. "There's the beach, I wonder if Ben's watching this?"

Ben was. He and V were at the spying bench. Ben was holding his head in his hands and shaking it in disbelief in at the mess Charlie was now in.

"Why does he always have to do it, V? Why can't he just keep out of trouble?"

"What are we going to do, Ben?" asked V, innocently.

"I don't know, V. I just don't know."

"Can we get a boat and go out to them?"

"No, V, we can't get a boat and go out to him."

"Should we go home then?"

"No, V, we can't just go home."

"What we gonna do then, Ben?"

"Oh for… just… just let me think, V."

V clutched hold of Babbit and sucked her thumb sullenly. Ben took a couple of paces away and clenched his fist in anger.

★ ★ ★

On board, George continued to look at the book, which also contained details of deaths and injuries to the crew.

"Listen to this, Charlie," he said, reading out the information on Henry Petter. "Leg partly blasted off from cannon shot and wood splinters shattering his arm." A further comment read: "Leg amputated and stump covered in tar. Splinters removed and bandaged. Died two days later." Another, Charles Crowhurst, died from disease, but it didn't say what disease. There were many diseases, like scurvy, that affected sailors. Lack of clean, fresh water and rotten food played a part in the poor health of crews who were at sea for long periods of time.

Charlie rejoined George, placed the pistol back on the table and read on a bit further, before saying, "Urgh. Cannon broke free and squashed him flat against the main mast." It seemed each death was recorded in its full gory detail.

A crashing noise somewhere else on the ship vibrated through the floorboards of Blackbeard's cabin. It was accompanied by a great deal of shouting and cursing from unseen men. The ship also seemed to lurch forward, as the sails suddenly caught hold of the wind.

As he looked down and away from the book, Charlie saw two metal handles hanging down from the front of a drawer beneath the table.

"Look, George," he exclaimed, grabbing hold of one of the handles, "there might be key in here."

George grabbed the other, hoping to help Charlie pull the drawer open. It stayed firmly shut. George tried poking his dagger in the gap between the drawer and the table, above where a lock was mounted in the middle. He wriggled it around in the hope that it might release the lock. It was in vain. No amount of tugging on the drawer would release it.

"It usually works when they do it on the telly," said George.

Charlie sighed and turned his attention to one of the large chests to the side of the cabin and wriggled the padlock that secured the lid. He stared at it with a frustrated frown wishing it to open.

"Why is everything locked up in here?" he moaned.

"Oh, come on, Charlie, it's a pirate ship! They don't trust anyone."

"What about the pirate code?"

"I don't think Mr Blackbeard would believe in that one," said George.

Then they heard another distant bang, followed by a whistling, whooshing noise outside. Loud footsteps were running about on the deck above and they were brought back to the reality of situation. George stuffed the dagger through his belt and went over to try the door again. As he did so, it suddenly released and opened.

"Hello." The massive frame of Irasmuth Kelly stood before them. "The boss wants you two to 'elp out on deck. Fings need doin', so yer gotta come wiv me."

Charlie's head sank. George pulled his T-shirt down to cover the dagger. Outside the cabin was a scene of mayhem. Cannon shots were shooting through the air from the Royal Navy ship; although many were still missing the *Queen Anne*, some had struck various parts of it and several injured pirates lay on the deck.

Irasmuth led them up onto the deck above the cabin at the rear of the ship, where Blackbeard was shouting instructions to the crew and swearing at the British captain – although there was no way he could have heard him.

"Ah, me boys," he started, "I'll be needin' yous to help me men who's got 'emself hurt." He turned away and shouted, "Are they be turning yet?" to a man with a telescope high up the main mast.

"Aye captin, there just startin' now."

The cannon firing stopped as the *Cornwall* started to turn around to follow the *Queen Anne*. On board the *Cornwall*, Captain Forsyth was watching the escape manoeuvre that Blackbeard was pursuing. He knew the *Queen Anne* was a faster and more manoeuvrable ship than his own and was frustrated that his gunners had not been able to disable her while the ship was at anchor. Forsyth instructed that all available sail be let out to catch the wind, in the hope of increasing speed.

"That's better," declared a smiling Blackbeard as the shots stopped whizzing through his ship. "Mind yer line, Joe," he shouted at the helmsman, referring to the narrow channel they had to navigate past the rocky headland. However, Joseph Foley knew the waters as well as Blackbeard and expertly judged the position of the unmarked channel.

"Right you young 'uns, Rasmuth 'ere will show you where you can get some linen to 'elp cover these 'ere lads' wounds." He looked up from the boys and told Irasmuth that there was some linen under his bed that they could use. "But mind you don't go poking around in nuffink else, okay?"

"Of course, Mr. Blackbeard," said Charlie. George nodded.

"I'm trusting you, mind," said Blackbeard, pointing sternly at them.

"Yes, Mr Blackbeard," they replied together.

"That's my boys. I'm sure we're goin' to get along just fine."

Irasmuth led them back down to the captain's quarters, explaining on the way what they had to do. He would leave the door unlocked now that they were under way and the ship was picking up speed. There would be nowhere for them to go as soon as they were at sea. Just as Blackbeard had said, there was a pile of fine white linen cloth under his bed. They were to take enough to each man so that their wounds could be dressed.

"We're really stuck now, Charlie," said George, as he pulled out the cloth and waited for Irasmuth to leave the cabin. Charlie went to the rear of the cabin and saw, out of the window, the little creek disappearing into the distance as the ship passed by the rocky outcrop.

"There's Ben and V," he exclaimed.

George carried the cloth he had in his hand, dropped it on the table and joined Charlie at the window. They could see Ben and V running along the top of the beach in the direction of Jenny.

"Where's that cloth?" a voice shouted from outside the cabin.

"Look, George," said Charlie, "that little boat we were in is tied onto the back here."

George opened one of the windows and looked down at the skiff that had brought them to the *Queen Anne*.

"Maybe we can use it to escape?"

"How do we get down to it?" replied George.

"You take that stuff out and tell 'em I'll follow with some more."

George grabbed the pile of linen from the table and disappeared out of the door. He found Irasmuth cutting clothing off a man's arm. The arm had been lacerated by splintered wood from wrist to shoulder and blood was pouring from the wounds. George winced at the sight, but he'd seen plenty of blood from animals on the farm, so wasn't as shocked as Charlie would have been. At home his dad often brought rabbits home, and skinned and gutted them in the outside porch of their house. Occasionally he'd bring home a deer that had been hit on the road, which would then be strung up and skinned. George separated the cloths and passed one to Irasmuth, who used his knife to slice it up into a form of bandage.

Henry Moffat was the poor man propped against the side of the ship, in an attempt to support him in his semi-conscious state. His head drooped over his left shoulder, with the right side of his face also home to several large splinters of wood sticking out at various angles and dripping blood like a series of leaking tentacles. He yelled out in pain as Irasmuth pulled the last, large piece of the *Queen Anne's Revenge* from his arm.

"Sorry 'enry," he grunted.

More blood oozed from the remaining hole in the battered arm. For a big rufty-tufty sea-faring brute of a pirate, Irasmuth was surprisingly gentle in bandaging Henry's arm. "You hold it, son, while I wrap in this."

George needed both his hands to hold up the heavy muscular arm in front of him. Henry was a gunner – one of Blackbeard's best and a man they needed to save if possible. Blood streamed over George's hands while Irasmuth wrapped the cloth round Henry's arm from his shoulder to his wrist, pulling out a few smaller splinters as he did so. At that point, another sailor joined them and poured some brandy down Henry's throat. He coughed on it at first and then had another swig.

Irasmuth next turned his attention to Henry's

face and the bits of the ship that were sticking out of it. "Okay, boy, leave me wiv some of that and take the rest over to Reg over there." He nodded in the direction of the mast in the centre of the ship, where another poor soul was being sat down covered in blood. He looked like he had a bone sticking out of his leg beneath his knee and was yelling out in pain. He'd fallen from the rigging above.

"Then you should go back and get some more cloth. Where's your mate?"

George felt like puking at the sight of the broken leg. He dropped the cloth next to the two men looking after the screaming sailor and started to run back to the cabin. "I... I'll... I'll... go and see," he stammered.

In Blackbeard's cabin, he found Charlie leaning dangerously far out of a window at the back.

"What are doing, Charlie?" shouted George.

At that point Charlie very nearly fell out of the window, but just managed to grab the rope he'd being trying to reach. He held on to the window ledge by his feet. George rushed over, grabbed his ankles and pulled him back through the window.

"Look, George, we can slide down this rope to the boat."

"Then what?"

"Row ashore, of course."

"Can you row, Charlie?" asked George.

"No, but we can try."

"Yeah, go on then and I'll follow you."

"What do think they'll do if they spot us, George?"

"I think they're too busy looking towards that warship," replied George.

Holding tightly on to the rope, Charlie wriggled himself out of the window. As he left the security of the window ledge, the rope carried him away from the stern of the ship and then crashed back into it, and again. This second collision knocked out the pistol he had previously stuffed in his clothing and it fell downwards. It ricocheted off the top side of the skiff and dropped into the bottom of the boat, firing off a shot through the thin wooden hull.

Charlie immediately looked up above him to see if anyone had noticed. He stared for what seemed an age, but the shouting and screaming and general commotion above seemed to have disguised the shot.

"Get on with it, Charlie!" shouted George, who was now leaning out of the window himself and holding onto the rope that suspended Charlie.

"But I think I've just shot a hole in the boat," he said worriedly.

"Look," pointed George, "it's not far to the shore anyway."

At that time, the *Queen Anne* was passing Jenny on the sand. Luckily for them, only those who travelled in Jenny could see her, so even if any pirates on board happened to be looking in the direction of the shore, they would see nothing. Back home in the hangar she was there for all to see, but on a journey it was different.

On shore, Ben and V were now running towards Jenny while staring at the *Queen Anne*. In the distance they could see the other ship shadowing its movements, but it was well behind Blackbeard's ship. In less than a half mile, Joseph would have them clear of the sandbanks and they'd be clean away. Ben suddenly stopped in his tracks, as he caught sight of a little figure dropping into a small boat beneath the stern of the ship. It seemed an eternity, but in reality it was only a few seconds before George grabbed hold of the escape rope and swayed about as he slipped down to join Charlie.

There was still much shouting going on above their heads, and the pirates were too busy to notice the boys trying to escape. Charlie attempted to undo the rope that tethered them to the ship when George stepped forward. Charlie wasn't the only one with a trophy from Blackbeard's cabin! George pulled out the dagger that he had picked up from the table and sawed at the rope. It was obviously a very sharp knife. A few strokes of his new acquisition and they were free. Charlie picked up his gun and poked it more securely in his belt.

Luckily there were some oars in the boat and they set about trying to row to the shore. Having only watched others do it before, there was a fair amount of splashing about without actually going anywhere. Still, the ship was now moving away from them, even if they weren't making much progress! All the pirates were focused on was where they were going, and fixing up injured men and the damage to the ship.

"Look, V, I think it must be Charlie and George!"

yelled Ben as he watched the tiny craft slowly make its way towards them.

As the moments passed, Charlie and George got into more of a rhythm and the boat started to move more positively towards the shore. The bottom of the boat was beginning to fill with water, though, and both their feet were submerged.

"It must be them," Ben announced. The bow of the boat was now pointing directly at him and V, and he could just see the diminutive figures of Charlie and George.

Meanwhile, the *Cornwall* had turned slightly and was trying to fire some more cannon shots in the direction of Blackbeard. However, Blackbeard and his crew were picking up speed and within a few minutes they would be well out of range. Even these shots fell short.

On shore, Ben and V ran down into the breaking surf and helped pull Charlie and George onto the sand.

"You blinking little idiots," scorned Ben.

V threw her arms around Charlie and hugged him tightly. Ben didn't notice the two trophies wedged in the boys' respective belts; he just shouted at them to follow him back to Jenny. Half soaked in seawater, they all obediently jogged their way up the beach to where Jenny obligingly sat.

They clambered into the passenger compartment and this time Ben grabbed the flying helmet. Collapsing into the wicker chairs, he pleaded with Jenny to take them home.

"No problem, Captain," came the reply.

The engine rumbled into life, Jenny swung around into the wind and in no time they were airborne. They went up and up into the clouds and then: flash! Lightning appeared all around them and within seconds they were flying through the beautiful blue sky above Rosemie Common.

The journey back was a quiet one. None of them spoke inside the plane, instead choosing to stare at each other or the floor. Soon after Jenny landed back at the aerodrome, taxied up to the hangar and stopped. The door popped open and out the children tumbled.

"Come on, we'd better put her back," said Ben.

They pushed Jenny back into the hangar and closed the doors. It was only then that Ben noticed something sticking out of Charlie's trouser belt. "What's that you've got?" he asked.

Charlie immediately tried to cover up the pistol with his little hand. "Nothing." It was a standard reply from Charlie when there was, in fact, something.

"It doesn't look like nothing to me. It looks remarkably like something – something that's not yours." Ben moved in on Charlie and pulled at the pistol.

"So this is what you call nothing, is it?"

"Give it back! It's mine."

"It's not!"

"It is now."

Charlie grabbed Ben's arm and pulled it down to regain possession of the pistol. Ben didn't put up much of a fight and let Charlie have it back. He was already thinking of what their mother was going to say, without having a pistol in his possession. Charlie would have to explain that one.

They continued their way back to the garden and Ben enquired if George had acquired anything from their trip. George sheepishly pulled out the dagger, which almost sliced through his trouser belt as he did so.

"My goodness," exclaimed Ben, "you'll cut your own hand off with that if you're not careful."

"Yeah, I need to get a thing to put it in," he said.

"Hole in the ground would be the best place," smarted Ben.

"No, a cover of some sort, like a leather sheath."

Ben just shook his head and marched them through the garden gate. "I'll do the talking when we get back inside, okay."

"What are you going to say?" enquired V.

"I'm not sure yet, but you lot keep your mouths shut."

Chapter 16

"Hi Mum," said Ben rather nonchalantly as he breezed into the kitchen.

Laura was entering the kitchen at the same time from the front of the house.

"Oh, there you are," she said as they all trouped in. "I went down to find you lot, but couldn't see you anywhere. I told you not to leave the garden."

Then, she noticed that Charlie and George were dripping wet from the waist down. "And what on earth have you been up to? Look at you, you're all soaking wet."

They all bunched up together in a group as if to avoid being singled out for attention.

"Well," she demanded.

Searching his brain for an answer, Ben came up with a story about George taking them down to a stream where there was a rope swing, which they had all tried out, but Charlie and George had ended up falling in. Laura listened intently to the fabricated ruse as Ben got into full swing, making the whole thing seem plausible. After a few moments, the others began to join in with their own additions. Before long, the children were as convinced as Laura was!

"Okay, okay, but next time let me know where you are going." She noticed something sticking out of Charlie's trousers. "What's that you've got there, Charlie?"

"Where?" he said, innocently.

"There, that thing stuffed in your trousers," she said, pointing at the object sticking out of his belt.

Ben spun round to Charlie, thinking he'd blown it.

"Oh, this," Charlie said, looking down at the pistol as if he was surprised to see it there too.

"Yes, that."

He was stalling for time, but now had to come up with an answer. As he pulled the pistol from his belt, Laura gasped, "My goodness, it's a gun!"

"I don't think it works, Mum, it's very old," Charlie said as he held it up for inspection.

Laura grabbed the pistol from Charlie's hand. "Where did you get this from?" she enquired.

An awkward silence surrounded the young group.

"Well?" Laura persisted.

"I found it in the shed, Mum," Charlie proffered.

Laura took the pistol and inspected it closely. "Hmm," she muttered, "I don't like the idea of you having a gun, but this looks fairly harmless and, as you say, it is very old."

Having deduced it was an antique, and very unlikely to actually work, she handed it back to him. Little did she know that Blackbeard had used it recently and, through Charlie's carelessness, it had gone off! However, Charlie didn't know how to load it and he didn't have access to any sort of ammunition to load it with.

While this was going on, George had pulled his shirt down over the handle of the dagger that was stuck into his trouser belt. This was just as well, as Laura would have had a fit and confiscated it had she seen it.

"Well, you just be careful with the things down in that shed," Laura continued. "Sometimes you're just trouble on legs, Charlie Green. Now, you had all better get into some dry clothes while I start getting tea ready."

They all made a hasty exit to the hallway as Laura called after them, "Charlie, see if you have anything George can wear."

"Phew, that was lucky," panted Ben as they clattered into the bedroom.

"Shut the door, V."

"Now what?" said Charlie.

"For a start," Ben said, looking at George, "you'd better take that knife out and put it somewhere safe."

They sat down, stood up, sat down again and generally shuffled around the room excitedly discussing their adventure. They found a box in which to hide George's prized dagger and pushed it under Charlie's bed. For some time, they chatted about what they should do next and where they should try going. Should they tell Mum? No! This is just for kids, at least for now.

They argued for a while, mainly Ben and Charlie, but then Ben remembered the book he had found in the shed. It was the one about pirates, with the handwritten notes in it. With all the excitement of the day, he had forgotten about the notes in the book. *What if it had something to do with the disappearance of the man who owned the aeroplane?*

"Hey guys," said Ben, "do you remember the book I was reading in the shed?"

"No," they replied.

"I picked up a book from that writing desk?"

Blank looks all round.

"Oh, never mind. Anyway, I found a book about pirates that had some handwritten notes in it. We need to get it. It makes a bit more sense now. The notes in it, I mean, which said about finding a pirate ship."

The other three stood looking at Ben and then at each other with the same blank stare. It was as if someone had just asked them what they had had for tea last Tuesday fortnight.

"What are you on about, Ben?" queried Charlie.

Ben let out a huge sigh. "I picked up a book in the shed that may have something to do with the disappearance of the man who lived here before us. There were some notes in it about finding a particular pirate ship. It didn't make much sense to me this morning, but that was before we went on our flight. I need to go and get it. I only read some of the notes and there were more on other pages, and a second book about Native American Indians."

"I found a note," Charlie blurted out.

"What note? Where?" asked Ben.

Charlie put his hand into his wet trousers and

pulled out a scrunched up piece of paper. It was damp around the edges, but otherwise was surprisingly not too wet. He started to unfurl it and then handed it to Ben. Ben read out the note.

Dear Harry,

Please could you get me a brass pocket compass from Emilie's and send it back. Tortuga 1699.
Thanks.
Oliver

"I'm sure this is the same handwriting that was in the notes I saw," said Ben.

"Does it mean anything to you, George? You've lived here much longer than us."

He took the note and read it himself. "Well, I think the man that lived here a long time ago was called Oliver and Harry might be Mr Hobbard, the postman. His name is Harry."

"Yes," squealed Charlie. "Wasn't the name on the wooden chest in the shed "O. Brambles" or something?"

"And Emilie's might be an old shop in town. I've been in a couple of times with my dad. It's a strangely spooky place. It's full of old weird stuff, a bit like the stuff in your shed," George continued. "I think it's called Emilie's Emporium."

"What's an emporium?" asked V.

"I'm not quite sure, but I think it is a posh name for a junk shop," said Ben.

"Come on, we should all get into some dry clothes. I'm going to sneak down to the shed to get those books I saw and we'll look at them after tea."

V left the boys to it and went off to get changed. While they were getting into some dry clothes the boys hatched a plan to distract Mum after tea so that Ben could go back down to the shed and fetch the books.

* * *

After tea, they arranged for George to return the next day and he left with instructions that Laura would sort out his wet clothes. Having waved goodbye to George, V and Charlie followed their mother into the lounge and slumped in front of the TV. Ben had other ideas. He made his excuses and sneaked out the back door and off to the shed.

A few minutes later, Charlie heard him return. He saw Ben dodge the lounge door, clutching a couple of antique books, before going straight up to his room. Five minutes passed and then Charlie announced, "I think I'll go and see what Ben is up to."

"Don't annoy him, Charlie," said Laura. "I think he wanted to be on his own for a while."

"I won't, Mum, I promise."

"Well, see that you do."

V was quite tired and snuggled up with her mother on the sofa to watch the TV. Charlie made a hurried departure upstairs.

Chapter 17

Charlie's pace quickened as he approached the bedroom door. He burst in and found Ben with two books open on his desk, paper notes sticking out of each of them.

Excitedly, he asked, "What have you found Ben?"

"It's too soon to say, Charlie, but this is very interesting. I think it is going to take a while to sort out."

"Is it like a mystery then, Ben?" Charlie enquired.

"Well, it is really. Now we know what the aeroplane can do, we might find an answer to what happened to Mr Bramley."

"Who?"

"Mr Bramley. Oliver Bramley, the man who lived here before us."

"Oh, yes," said Charlie. "'Course."

Charlie fidgeted around the room as Ben, sitting at the desk, studied the books. Some time went by and Charlie bounced up and down on his bed. Then, Ben pulled another note from one of the books and read out:

"Research the connection between Major Thomas Jones and Capt. Kidd. Jones used some loot to buy land from the native Indian tribe on Long

Island. Kidd wanted to settle somewhere on Long Island. Jones at one time was a privateer."

"What's it mean, Ben?" said Charlie as he leaped off the bed towards him.

"I don't know, Charlie," he replied sharply.

"Look, you are going to have to leave me alone for a while to try and sort it out. I know I'm on to something, I just don't what yet."

As Charlie was getting a bit bored with it all anyway – he wanted an instant answer – he left Ben to it and joined his mum and V in front of the telly downstairs.

"What's Ben up to?" enquired Laura.

"Oh nothing much, just reading a book he found."

"That's good," she replied, not realising the implication of the text Ben was reading and what trouble it could get the kids into!

★ ★ ★

Ben spent the whole evening sifting through the books and reading through the notes. He decided to lay all the notes out and wrote at the top of each one the page number where he had found it. From the book about the native Indians, there was one that stated:

1688 Major Jones buys land from Massapeque Indian.

Others also paid very little for land from the

Natives Indians. Lion Gardiner dealt with Chief Wyandanch of the Montauketts.

There were other details of towns like Hempstead where Major Jones was buried, and more details of the dealings of Gardiner and the Indian chiefs.

From the book on pirates, there were lists of the movements of Captain William Kidd, Bartholomew Sharpe, William Dampier and Black Bart Roberts. It was clear that Kidd had had dealings with Lion Gardiner over some treasure he wanted to stash. Tucked into the back cover of the book, where part of the leather binding was coming apart, was a folded piece of paper that spelled out the story more clearly.

It seemed that Oliver had read about the way the Indian tribes had, effectively, been conned out of their birthright, the land they lived on, by unscrupulous colonists – those who sought to buy huge tracts of land for very little money. Later in the nineteenth century, the 'so-called' deals had been challenged in court but the Indian natives had got nowhere against the power of wealthy lawyers. Oliver had then decided to set out and try to get the Indians some compensation from the bounty and treasures of the pirates.

As such, Oliver was trying to trace some of the buried pirate treasure that was said to be missing after Kidd's last port of call before being arrested. He had made landfall in a place called Oyster Bay, but there was no guarantee that he had not stopped off somewhere en-route between there and Tortuga.

Captain Kidd had been a successful privateer for many years and it was assumed that he must have gained considerable wealth during that time. However, at the time of his arrest in America, he had little of his valuables with him. Oliver had written about some of Kidd's treasure that had been found and dug up on Gardiners Island, but there also appeared to be another site of buried loot, which Oliver had gone to find.

One of the notes Oliver had written read:

Kidd met Sharpe in Madagasgar 1698 after looting and taking the Quedagh Merchant.

Sail together to somewhere in Caribbean where they split up.

Kidd has renamed his ship the Adventure Prize.

Must get on board one of the ships in Tortuga to find out if clues in the reports from National Maritime Museum point to Oyster Bay.

Long Island being his last stop or where else did he go?

Ben opened another book and found a folded piece of old paper that read:

Where's the other half of the map?

Ben gently unfolded the yellow parchment. It didn't take him long to realise what he had in his hand. He thundered downstairs to find his mum asleep on the sofa and the other two watching yet another episode of *SpongeBob Square Pants*. Ben beckoned Charlie towards him, whispering, "I think I've worked it out."

V was snuggled under a blanket with Babbit, twiddling his ribbon around her finger and sucking her thumb. Her half-closed eyes didn't notice Charlie's exit.

As Charlie entered the hallway, Ben softly closed the door behind him.

"What is it, Ben?" Charlie asked, eagerly.

"I've worked out what Oliver, Mr Bramley, was up to and where he has gone."

"What's that?"

"Come with me," replied Ben and led Charlie back up to the bedroom.

Once there, Charlie was directed to sit down on the bed while Ben started to explain.

"Well, this Oliver Bramley, who lived here before us, was a bit of a traveller – and I think still is. It was, or is, his aeroplane that took us to see Blackbeard. "I've gone through these notes and books and I reckon he has gone on a bit of a mission and something has gone wrong."

"What do you mean 'gone wrong'?" enquired Charlie.

"Well, it seems to me he has gone in search of some pirate treasure."

"Wow."

"And there's more," said Ben, holding up the map.

Charlie jumped up, with his eyes popped out like organ stops, to inspect the map.

Ben continued, "The note you found was meant for Harry, but I guess he never got it. So Oliver never got the compass he asked for and the aeroplane never returned for him. He is stuck wherever he is."

"You mean he is still alive?" said Charlie.

"Well, I can't be sure, of course, but he could be. We need to try and rescue him."

Charlie jumped up excitedly and grabbed hold of Ben. "Wow, that's cool!"

"Yeah, but we will need to get a compass, and I really want to get hold of a telescope, too."

Ben rustled around on the table to find the note that Charlie had found in the aeroplane. "The place to go is Emilie Brackets' Emporium," he said, holding the note up. "I guess it must be in town. We need to get Mum to take us into town."

"How will we know where it is, Ben?"

"Good point, Charlie." Ben paused in thought for a moment.

"I know, we'll ask the postman. He'll know where it is."

The two boys spent the next moments planning a ruse to get their mum to take them into town the next day – but somehow they would need to stop at the post office in the village first. It was then that they heard their mother bringing Olivia upstairs.

After putting her daughter to bed, Laura looked in to see the boys, who were now getting into bed themselves. They explained that they wanted to go into town to get some paint for their new den, but needed to ask Mr Hobbard where they should go.

After a few minutes of discussion, Laura agreed to their idea as she also needed to go into town to buy some things.

★ ★ ★

The next morning, they stopped at George's house to let him know when they would be back, then made a stop at the post office, before making their way to Cheshampton. The boys had cunningly gone into see Mr. Hobbard by themselves, so their mum had not heard what they actually asked for.

"'Ello boys", replied the friendly voice of Harry Hobbard. "What can I do for you?"

"Well, we wondered if you knew where Emilie's Emporium in Cheshampton is."

"Oh yes," he started, but before he elaborated he paused and asked, "Why do you boys wanna go there then?"

It wasn't the first sort of shop a youngster would be drawn to and he obviously knew of Oliver's connection with the shop – a connection that went beyond the normal shopkeeper and customer relationship. Why would this be the one place the boys wanted to visit?

"Well…" started Ben, "nothing much really, just an old telescope. We found something in the shed with an old label attached to it with the shop's name on it and wondered, well, if it was the sort of place we could find one?"

Harry squeezed his lips together and took a deep

breath, which sounded like a puncture on a bicycle tyre. "Telescope, you say. What you be doin' with that then? Some star gazing?"

"No, no," said Ben, "it's for our tree house. I want to be able to see who's coming down the garden, in case we have invaders who want to take over it."

"Oh I see," said Harry, nodding. "You'll see 'em alright with a telescope."

He rubbed his chin and wrinkled his forehead, continuing to eye up each boy in turn. He was concerned they may have found something that would reveal the secret journeys that Oliver had taken. Little did he know that Ben had actually worked it all out and was on the trail to find Oliver.

Although they had the note that was meant for Harry, the boys thought if he knew what they had planned he would tell their mum and their fun would be over. For now, they wanted to keep it to themselves.

"I hear you found some interesting stuff in Mr Oliver's old shed?" asked Harry, looking down at the newspaper in his hand

"Yeah," blurted Ben excitedly, then stopped almost as quickly as he had begun. "Yeah," he repeated, but in a voice a couple of octaves lower. "It was mainly old boxes of rubbish, tin cans and stuff."

Harry looked up and raised an eyebrow, "Oh really, so nothing of much interest then."

"No," stated Ben in a more forceful voice, "I think Charlie was hoping to find some hidden treasure in it…" he paused, noting the relevance of the words he had just used.

"What, lad?"

"Nothing, nothing at all."

"And what about the shop?" says Ben.

"Shop?" echoed Harry. "Oh yes, the shop. There is a shop in town called Emilie's Emporium; it's in Church Street. I guess your mum is taking you into town?"

Ben and Charlie both nod in reply.

"Well, I suppose I could jot it down on a piece of paper for you."

Pulling at the skin under his chin, Harry slowly tore a piece of paper from a notepad and placed it on the counter top. He then scribbled a few instructions down.

Not wanting to stay any longer than necessary, Ben grabbed the note.

"Thanks, Mr Hobbard," they both shouted as they ran out the door.

As the door slammed behind them, the doorbell rattled wildly. Mr. Hobbard moved towards the window at the front of the shop and his eyes followed them into the car and away down the lane.

In the car, Ben whispered to Charlie. "I think he suspected something."

"What are you two whispering about?" Laura said from the front.

"Nothing!" they said in unison, looking blankly ahead.

"You've got the directions you wanted, I presume?" enquired Laura.

"Ah, ha," nodded Ben.

The rest of the journey into town was spent largely in silence and they eventually arrived in the high street, where Laura pulled into a car park.

Chapter 18

Once in town, Laura decided it would be better if Ben went to find the hardware store on his own while she took Charlie and Olivia to do some other shopping. Of course, she believed Ben was looking for paint, not a telescope!

With the note from Mr Hobbard in his hand, he set off down the high street in the direction of the bank. Just past the bank, he took a left turn into Church Street. Both sides of the road were a mix of old and very old buildings, some timber-framed, some stone and some brick. He passed a small bakery that looked like it was squeezed into someone's front room. It had a very tempting smell emanating from it. After passing a few more houses, he came to a quaint building, which had a sign above it that proudly announced in old English writing: "Ye Old Tucke Shoppe". Ben stopped and stared into the window and drooled over the array of sweets on offer.

That's tempting, he thought, but continued down the street. He then passed a very old thatched cottage covered in climbing roses. It had a sign on the picket fence that was buried in a privet hedge, which read "Saxon Cottage". His note said to take the left fork in the road after this cottage and it is the next building.

Around a slight left-hand bend, Ben found a large timber-framed building sitting that was positioned slightly back from the pavement. Beyond it, Ben could see an arched tiled entrance to a Norman Church, whose churchyard was lined with giant elm trees gently swaying in the light breeze.

The building was covered in heavy black timbers and panels of white render, which surrounded windows whose glass was criss-crossed with a diamond pattern grid. The ground floor was made up of redbrick panels between thick upright beams of blackened timber with larger window frames than in the upper storey. These windows were made up of small square panes of thick glass, with odd ones that had a wobbly circular pattern in the middle rather like the effect of dropping a stone in a pond.

As Ben stared at the old house, he felt an odd sort of shiver go through him. He turned around as he felt he was being watched, but no one was there. He then quickly scanned all the windows in case the person was watching from inside. As he did so, he thought he saw a figure vanish from the top left-hand window, but it had been so quick he decided he must have imagined it. A cold gust of wind brushed past him. He was starting to lose his enthusiasm for the place, but then reminded himself why he was there. He needed to get the telescope and compass if he could. He looked again.

At the front of the building was a small door, above which was a sign with the words "The Old Workhouse". Nearer the centre was a larger door; a heavy wooden door studded all over with large nail heads and an ornate wrought iron handle. To the left of the door, Ben could see what he thought was a handwritten sign and he cautiously moved closer. It said "Emilie Brackets' Emporium" and beneath the name was written: "Artefacts old and new, available only to a privileged few". He was in the right place.

Ben stepped onto the cobbles in front of the window and took a closer look. He marvelled at the amazing assortment of oddities that were displayed. Although he did not know it, the window display had been the same for as long as anyone could remember – though strangely no cobwebs or dust adorned the assorted artefacts on show. Peering through the thick glass, it looked rather dim inside and he wondered if it was actually open. However, a little sign in the lower right corner announced this odd place was open Monday to Saturday, and was closed for a half day on Wednesday.

He took the two steps up to the door and gingerly turned the heavy iron handle. With a gentle push, the door creaked open and Ben stepped into the shop. As he did so a smell of mustiness greeted his nostrils, mixed with the tang of old carpets. The shop oozed stillness and silence. It gave him the creeps. As he took a further step inside; the door closed by itself with a positive clank of the metal latch. Ben jumped, then froze. He wished he wasn't alone.

After a couple of moments, he bravely walked down the hallway in front of him. Doors led off on either side and he eventually came to a counter with a large ancient-looking silver cash register. A small handwritten card beside the till announced "Cash Only". He stood expectantly for a while, but no one appeared from the doorway behind the counter, so decided to investigate the room to his right.

The doorway was fairly low, as if made for a smaller than average person. The room was filled with tables and dressers covered in old stuff. From side to side and floor to ceiling, antiques and junk objects packed the available space.

He felt a tingle go down his neck and he was suddenly aware of a cold breeze pass by him. He immediately looked back to the entrance door to see if someone else had come in. No one was there – just the same silence. Ben rubbed his fingers through his hair and continued his examination of the curios that filled every nook and cranny. No telescope or compass, though.

Diagonally across the room was another doorway leading to yet another room, although it was slightly smaller than the first and crammed with old artefacts. On one shelf he spied a collection of microscopes, but there was no telescope.

A door on the opposite side of this room led to a short corridor with a further three rooms leading off that. Peeking into one of them, Ben found a narrow spiral staircase. It wasn't a smooth spiral, but angular and quite steep.

Back in the corridor, he studied the ornate wall carvings that decorated the oak panelling. He could not resist feeling the texture adorning the wall and gently moved his hand over the surface. Running his hand along to the next doorframe, he looked through it to scan the contents. Nope, just jewellery and fancy silver boxes in this room. Ben frowned and rubbed his forehead thoughtfully, bemused and slightly spooked by the quietness of the place. There was still no sight or sound of a shopkeeper.

Ben slowly turned around to visit yet another one of the rooms off the corridor and nearly jumped out of his skin!

"Sorry, my dear, did I make you jump?" hissed a voice, as the frame of an old lady glided down the passage towards him.

Ben shivered and tried to back away on his hands and knees. As the female figure got closer, Ben thought he could smell his own fear. Fear of what, though, he wasn't quite sure – an old woman?

"I... didn't hear you coming," he stuttered.

As Ben gathered himself up, he could feel his heart beating enough for two. The woman smiled and tilted her head slightly sideways. It was Emilie, the shop owner. A tall well-built lady with big grey hair. Sparkling wire-rimmed glasses hung on a cord around her slender neck and rested on her chest. As she approached Ben, she raised the glasses to inspect him.

"Are you alright, my dear?" she enquired through hardly open lips. The sound squeezed itself out like the last bit of toothpaste from the tube. People rarely heard Emilie coming, as she just seemed to glide over the floor with silent footsteps.

"Yeah… err, yes. Um, thank you. I'm okay. I was just a bit startled, that's all."

"Good," hissed Emilie.

"Are you looking for something in particular?" she asked with a thin smile.

As he looked up at her dominating posture, Ben was fixated for a moment on her choice of bright green eyeshadow and white face. Snapping himself back to the question, he answered, "Well, err, actually I was looking for a telescope and a compass."

"Ah, I thought so. Yes, I think I have what you are looking for down here."

She slid past Ben and went further down the corridor. Ben felt the cold breeze again. Before entering the room, Emilie turned around and beckoned Ben to follow. "This way, my dear."

Ben tentatively followed her into the room, still amazed at the way she managed to move so silently. She didn't so much as walk, but glide like a skater across ice. She gracefully swept her arm across her body, gesturing to Ben the contents of the room. "Would any of these suit you?" she said.

On the opposite side of the room was an old rustic table on which sat a large collection of old telescopes, with more on stands around the room and others on shelves behind.

Ben headed straight for the table and gazed at the collection in awe. "Wow, err, yeah, great. I'm sure I'll find… thanks," he stuttered.

"Yes, I'm sure you will," Emilie replied.

He started to finger through them and picked one

up at random. He felt the weight and smoothed his hands over the brass exterior, but thought it was a bit heavy. There was a little pocket-size one next to it that sat in a plain Mahogany box; it had a brass inscription plate bearing the name "Capt. H. Morgan".

Ben lifted it out of its resting place and rolled it around to take a closer look. It too had the name engraved around a brass collar on the end of the scope. Although he admired the detail and craftsmanship of it, it only expanded to about thirty centimetres, which he thought was just a bit small. Not that he really knew what he was looking for! Ben carefully replaced it in the case and carried on surveying the collection.

He reached up on to one of the shelves behind the table and picked up a leather-bound one that was decorated with brass studs and black tattoo marks. He held the small end up to his eye and pulled the telescope to its full length, which was around sixty centimetres. *This was more like it,* he thought. *Not too heavy, decent length and it had a carrying case, with a shoulder strap*. He pushed the ends together and grabbed the case.

"I think that would do you nicely," hissed Emilie, who had glided from his left to his right without him noticing.

Ben jumped again and flicked his head from side to side trying to make sense of Emilie's movements. "Yes," he gasped, "I think it will be just fine."

"Just right," she hissed back.

Ben slid the telescope into its case and clipped the end lid over.

"And a compass, I believe?" she asked.

"Yes," replied Ben.

"You should find what you're looking for over here," she said as slid back to her original place by the doorway.

Ben had not noticed the shelves of assorted compasses by the door. She hardly stopped as she exited the room, merely holding out an arm in the direction of the collection. With that, she disappeared out of the door and went down the corridor. As she did so, she called, "Just bring them to the till when you're ready."

The sooner the better, thought Ben. He stuck his head out into the corridor to see where she had gone, but Emilie had already disappeared.

Sifting through the compass collection, he picked up an old brass compass with a hinged lid, which was about the size of the palm of his hand. A subtle wavy engraving wrapped its way around the edge of the case. Underneath it, there were three small sockets drilled into the solid base. He looked for a box that it might sit in, perhaps with locating pins for the compass to sit on. It was only a guess, though, and there was no box to be seen. Ben decided it didn't matter anyway; the compass was the thing he was after and this one seemed about right. It was big enough to read and small enough to go in his pocket. He just wanted to get out of the shop now.

He fumbled his way back through the maze of rooms and eventually found himself at the counter with the till. No one there, of course. As he placed the items on the counter, Emilie appeared in silence beside him. He shot to the side in surprise, nearly falling over again. Emilie smiled.

"You'll be needing this, too," she said, holding up a small wooden box.

Ben frowned.

"For the compass," she said, opening up the lid of the empty box.

"Oh, thanks."

The telescope and compass each had a little brown label tied to it with the price on it. Ben reached in his pocket and pulled out his wallet.

"No need, my dear," Emilie hissed, as she raised a hand in Ben direction.

"I'll put it on Mr. Oliver's account."

"What?" exclaimed Ben.

"No need to pay yourself, I'll put it down to Mr. Oliver."

Ben was highly confused. For a moment, he just stared at her open-mouthed and with his mind racing.

"Really, my dear, I can assure you it's okay."

Ben had had enough; he'd already nearly pooed his pants more than once and just being in the shop gave him the collywobbles. He wasn't going to argue. He didn't understand at all, but then that wasn't the only thing he didn't understand. He replaced his wallet in his pocket, gathered up his new possessions and made a hasty retreat from the shop.

"Thank you," he called on his way down the corridor.

Emilie smiled. "See you again, my dear," she hissed loudly as Ben disappeared out the door.

Not if I can help it! His legs were moving faster than he could run. *That was the creepiest place I've ever been*, he thought, *and that includes the dungeons of the Tower of London!*

Clutching onto his new treasures, he scurried back up Church Street to find the others. When he met them, they all remarked he looked as if he'd seen a ghost, and Laura also remarked that he didn't seem to have any paint.

"Err, no, Mum. I think I went the wrong way," he explained.

"I can tell that, because there's the hardware store," she said, pointing across the road. "What have you got there?"

"Oh, this?"

"Yes," she replied, pointedly.

"Oh, I, err, found a junk shop and got a couple of things for our den."

"Hmm," sighed Laura.

They got some paint and then made their return home. On the way, Ben made up his excuses for the telescope and compass. Laura just sighed and remarked, "Well, it's coming out of your money when we get home."

Ben and Charlie smiled knowingly at each other.

Chapter 19

Ben's detective work was correct. Oliver Bramley had been reading a book called *A History of Native American Indian Tribes of Long Island* and felt sorrow at the treatment they had received at the hands of invading settlers. He read accounts of the local tribes such as the Montaukett and Lenape people, who had lost land rights to the British colonists. It appeared to him that many were fooled into giving up their land for a pittance of money in return. They had been conned by the colonists.

By the 1730s, the tribes were confined to a small parcel of land that could not sustain their hunting and farming practices. Later, in the nineteenth century, the native people challenged the legality of the land ownership issue in the courts, but had lost the case. Oliver felt their grievance. He felt he had to try and do something to redress the balance. After all, he had read in the book that a number of the settlers on Long Island had previously been privateers or pirates in the years before buying the land (or in some cases acquiring it through more forceful means). They were no more than common crooks and criminals, and had no doubt used bullying and threatening tactics to remove people from their rightful lands.

It was typical of Oliver to empathise with the natives' cause and to want to help them. No one else knew, but he had gone back in time to assist many people after having discovered their plight in a history book. This time, he would need to track down information on the pirates who had decided to settle on Long Island and see if he could acquire some of their ill-gotten treasure. He would then redistribute it.

To find out more, Oliver had gone to the National Maritime Museum where there is a large historical collection on all sea farers. The research took him several months to complete, which consisted of many visits to the museum and the British Library. In the end, he had several names to work with. The main characters were: Captain William Kidd, a privateer; Major Thomas Jones, who had moved from New York to settle on Long Island and Captain Bartholomew Sharpe, another privateer/pirate. Privateers were effectively licenced pirates.

Captain Kidd had originally commanded a British Navy warship named the *Blessed William*. Due to the British being at war with the French and Spanish, he was legally (as far as the British Government was concerned) allowed to plunder French and Spanish ships – and, indeed, any other nation's ships that the British were at war with at the time, provided a small contribution was given to the British Government on return.

A major and very profitable acquisition in the Indian Ocean was the French ship, the *Quedagh*

Merchant. After he had forcefully taken the ship and put some of his own crew in charge, he had renamed her *Adventure Prize*. It was at this time, in the late 1600s, that he had joined forces with Bartholomew Sharpe in joint ventures of buccaneering. They were both common pirates, taking any ship they could, with little intention of giving anything of value to the crown.

Bartholomew Sharpe sailed in the ship, the *Trinity*, on which he had an excellent map-maker named William Dampier. In these early days of world navigation, maps were notoriously inaccurate – even those of the British Navy. And if there is one thing that a ship's captain needs, whether pirate or not, is a supply of good maps.

In the book *A Full and True Discovery of all the Pyracies and Notorious Actions of William Kidd* by James Kelly, Oliver had found reference to William Dampier. It alleged that he had had involvement in creating maps for Kidd, including one reference to the possibility of maps showing the location of buried treasure. However, the book was written nearly 100 years after Dampier's death, so was possibly more speculation than a definitive history. Nonetheless, there could be some truth in it. Oliver had made a note of it.

It was known that Captain Kidd liked to hide his hordes in different places. One well-known stash was discovered and dug up on Gardiners Island (just to the north west of Long Island) by a man named Lion Gardiner. The treasure included diamonds, rubies, gold coins and silver bars, but Kidd got none of it. This happened before Kidd had met Dampier, so it was quite possible that there could be more to find with better map-making.

Kidd had planned to give up his piracy career and settle on Long Island, but he was wanted for poor treatment of his crew and his privateering. Not long after his arrival on Long Island, he was arrested, taken to London for trial, found guilty of various crimes and hanged – never really able to benefit from all the booty he had collected.

As well as being a brilliant map-maker, Dampier was also a committed diary writer. In the early 1900s, a collection of his work was discovered in the loft of a house in Bristol that was being demolished for redevelopment work. For a few years after their discovery, the papers had lain unappreciated in a local museum, before a naval historian had finally recognised their importance. He arranged to move them to London, where, for a short time, they were put on public display before being buried away in the archives.

Oliver had a friend that worked at the British Museum and he had used this connection to get access to William Dampier's personal effects, which were located in the depths of the long-term storage facility in the basement of the National Maritime Museum. The collection of books and diaries were brought to Oliver in the private library of the museum, which was normally reserved for senior academics and museum archivists.

The library was a cavernous room filled with rows of tall bookshelves and Victorian study tables. Each table had a centre partition about the same height as the table, with a brass lamp on top to illuminate the desk. Oliver had been guided to a solitary seat where a box sat on a table with the requested belongings inside. The brown-coated porter then left Oliver and exited by a second door at the rear of the room.

He lifted the books out and laid them on the table, before sitting down and switching on a light. He felt strangely alone in the silence, but something made him look around to confirm his situation. Nothing. The first book he looked at was quite large and contained illustrated maps of all sorts of ports and river inlets. Details of reefs and sandbanks, mooring points and tidal flows was all very interesting, but it was not what he was looking for.

It was while Oliver was reading one of Dampier's diaries that he made a fantastic discovery. As he thumbed through the pages, he admired how neatly written it was, although inkblots occasionally dotted the pages. On some pages were illustrations of what appeared to be coastal inlets or ports and other geographical features, which were drawn in black pen and ink.

It was as he brought the book closer to his eyes to study one of the illustrations that he spotted it. As he fully unfolded the book, the ancient leather spine cover opened up a small gap between the leather and the string binding, and he could just see what appeared to be a piece of parchment tucked between the two. There were only a couple of other people in the basement with him, but he instinctively looked over his shoulder to see if anyone was nearby. There was no one in view. His pulse quickened a little.

Nervously, he tried to get hold of the parchment between the tips of his fingers, but he couldn't get hold of it. He put his hand in his pocket and pulled out his trusty Swiss Army penknife. Oliver rarely went anywhere without it. He pulled out the tweezers from the end and used them to carefully extricate the parchment from the spine. It was folded concertina style. Again, he looked over his shoulder to check no one was watching. He placed the book to one side and cautiously pulled the parchment open.

As he opened up the folds, a map appeared in front of him that was drawn in the style of the other illustrations in the book. It took a few seconds before he registered what he had in front of him. Then, the cogs whirring in his head stopped. Jackpot! It was not a typical treasure map with a few lines and a big cross in the middle. Instead, a number of features were accurately illustrated on the top half, including a coastline, but it strangely faded out on the left as if it wasn't important. *Peculiar*, he thought. His eyes scanned down the parchment.

The lower half was devoid of map detail and certainly had no cross marking any treasure. There was just a verse that made no sense:

A day by cart on the seventh point to
Take the sob road for three degrees of
A pace for a place of three round
The crying tree shades the flowing.

A realisation was slowly dawning on Oliver; he only had part of the solution. This was just half of a map. His initial excitement subsided a bit. However, it was still a map – a good start. Where would the other part be though?

He grabbed the diary and squinted into the gap between the spine and the binding cover. Further inspection and poking about failed to reveal anything. Hurriedly, he checked the other diaries and books, but to no avail. There didn't appear to be any other old loose parchment. He frowned, wrinkling his forehead in frustration, and then held his head in his hands. *So close*, he thought, *so close*.

He picked up the map again and scrutinised it for more clues, running his finger down the right-hand side of the map. Although the other three edges were not perfectly straight, he could now see the map had been torn apart.

A door suddenly closed somewhere behind a row of bookshelves and Oliver heard footsteps coming towards him. He hastily refolded the map and, for the first time, spotted some writing on the reverse. Cursing himself for not looking before, he pulled it open to see some text in the same style as the riddle:

Falsle shall face the wroth of W. Kidd.

An excited smile raced across Oliver's face, like a child in a sweetshop. A shot of adrenalin pulsed through him as he heard a voice call out.

"How you getting on then, Oliver?"

Oliver looked up and over the top of the dividing partition. It was the voice of his friend, Frederick Peate, from the British Museum, who had got him access to the vault in the first place.

"Found anything interesting?" asked Frederick.

Oliver's hands were out of view and, although he knew he shouldn't, he swiftly refolded the map and stuffed it into his pocket. He was sure nobody else knew it was there anyway, so who was going to miss it?

"Oh, hi Fred," said Oliver, with an expression of slight disappointment. The trouble was he knew Fred was a stickler for doing things properly and would have strongly disapproved of Oliver taking the map for himself. He would have insisted that the museum be told of the find, but if Oliver let that happen, his plan would fail.

"Well, yes, sort of," continued Oliver. "I managed to find quite a few references that link Dampier to William Kidd."

As Fred approached, he quickly picked up his pen and pretended to write something in his notebook.

"Oh, that's good. I'm glad it's been of some use."

"Oh, yes, definitely," replied Oliver, nodding his head in agreement, though his face displayed a look of blank puzzlement. Many questions were now racing around his head: could it really be a Captain Kidd treasure map?

Where would the other half be? How would he find it? Was there still undiscovered treasure?

"Fancy a coffee then, Oliver?" asked Fred.

Oliver's thoughts were elsewhere; his hand was subconsciously doodling a series of symbols that would mean nothing to anyone else.

"Well?" enquired Fred.

No reply.

"Oliver, are you okay? Come on, old chap, let's go upstairs and get a coffee." Fred tapped him on the back, which seemed to break Oliver out of his trance.

"Yes, yes, of course, let's do that. There's a little more I want to do here and then I'll be finished."

After having a cup of coffee with Fred, he returned to the vaulted library and finished off a few notes. He then packed everything back into the box he had been given. Fred had explained that there was little surviving documentation of Kidd's, apart from a few logs that were also in the National Maritime Museum's library.

Before leaving the library, Oliver made the decision to go in search of Kidd himself. He would get Jenny to take him to meet Kidd and find the other half of the map. It was quite possible that the complete map had been deliberately torn in half to prevent either party running off with all the treasure. If that were the case, then Kidd would definitely have the other half. Oliver reasoned that there was a good chance his discovery of the half map meant the treasure may still lay unrecovered. It was his for the finding.

However, before he could set off on his journey, he also needed to locate the movements of Bartholomew Sharpe, as Dampier had originally sailed with him before joining Captain Kidd. Less was known of Sharpe, but Oliver was in the right place to find anything that was known of him.

Chapter 20

Oliver spent days in the library of the National Maritime Museum going through records of Captain William Kidd's sailing exploits. He pieced together the movements of Captain Bartholomew Sharpe and listed all of their voyages on a chart, rather like one would do on a family tree. A good friend of Oliver's, Dr Richard Ward, who was a genealogist at Somerset House, had suggested the idea and gave him a hand to get started. When their histories with various ships were complete, Oliver joined all of the information together. Bingo! There it was: the time, the place and the ships. Oliver had used official naval records to place them together at a particular point in history.

In 1698, William Kidd had sailed his ship, now called the *Adventure Prize*, to the location of the French ship, the *Rapourelle,* and captured it. He split his crew and sailed his prize, with all her wealth on board, to Libertia, Madagascar. There, he met Sharpe, who wanted to join forces and make a strong pirate force of four ships. For more than a year, they plundered French and Spanish merchant ships – most of which gave up without much of a fight when they saw the mini armada of Kidd and Sharpe's flotilla. Kidd and Sharpe weren't the cut-throat type of pirates, but were semi-official privateers with the British Government's good wishes. Therefore, what was thought to be unnecessary violence was generally avoided.

However, both knew it could not last forever. If peace were made with the countries presently at war with the British, the privateering would have to stop. Both were also aware that the British Government were expecting a cut of their ill-gotten gains on return to the UK and neither Kidd nor Sharpe were willing to give up their treasures. And so it was that in late 1699 Kidd and Sharpe, while moored up in Tortuga in the Caribbean, decided to end their privateering careers and settle down. Kidd had been sent an order to return to England, but he had other ideas. He had a plan to sail one of his ships to New York, which was then a fast developing town. There, he had an old pirate friend, Major Thomas Jones, who had said he would help Kidd find a place to live. Jones had given up piracy for a more settled life and was now a council leader or governor on the nearby Island of Nassau, which is now known as Long Island.

Although he arrived okay, it was not long before it all went wrong for the old buccaneer. The British had issued a warrant for Kidd for the murder of one of his sailors. Thinking he was safe and out of the way on Long Island, Kidd had given the news of the warrant little attention. However, his so-called friend Thomas Jones double-crossed him and soon the Redcoats of the British Army were knocking on his door. Kidd was arrested and sent to England for trial.

There was little sympathy for him in England and he was found guilty and hanged – not only that, his body was put into a metal cage and swung from a gibbet near Tilbury docks to warn others of the power of the British Government. They were more concerned about not getting their share of the bounty, than the poor sailor's death.

So there it was, Oliver had to get to Tortuga in 1699 and somehow get on board Kidd's ship to find out what happened to the map. He reasoned that William Dampier must have sailed with Kidd from Tortuga to New York with all his treasures and it would have been after that when they decided where to hide it. It was well known that one stash had been discovered on Gardiners Island, situated to the North East of Long Island, but also that it didn't account for all of Kidd's treasure. The hunt was on.

Oliver would volunteer to be a carpenter on board the ship. Sailing ships always needed good carpenters and Oliver was one. To help him prepare for the task ahead, he found a book called *The Carpenters Craft on a Ship O' the Line* by E. G. Hemmings in the library. Hemmings had sailed with another notorious captain, Henry Morgan, and everything Oliver needed to know would be in the book.

★ ★ ★

A few days later, he was ready for the trip. He left the books in the shed with the notes, including the half map and the scribble that said he'd been into Cheshampton to collect some clothes from the theatrical costumers and had seen Emilie Brackets to get some old coins. She had an amazing collection, which he had often needed to make use of – ranging from Groats to pieces of eight, and silver dollars to Roman coins. If she didn't have what he wanted, she somehow managed to acquire it! Nothing was ever too much trouble for her to get for Oliver. He was a special customer.

He also collected a good selection of old woodworking tools to complete the period tool kit he would be taking with him. He stacked the tools into a beautiful mahogany chest. On the outside the chest looked strong, but it was otherwise unimpressive. However, opening the hinged lid revealed two stacks of shallow removable trays, each with its own lid. Within each tray, Oliver had placed various tools of the carpenter's trade: chisels, spoke shaves, drill bits, a brace, hammers and more. At the bottom of the chest was a larger area for things such as saws and clamps.

During his studies and research, Oliver had made many notes on bits of paper that he left in the various books he had been reading. The last one he had written before his departure. It was the one that Ben would find and it read:

Change of plan.

Now know Kidd and Sharpe moor up in Tortuga 1699.

Kidd will be sailing for New York with all the loot on board.

Now it's Jenny's turn to help.

On the day he planned to depart, Oliver gathered the clothes together that he needed and wedged them into a canvas draw-string bag, and changed into the shoes Emilie had recommended. He struggled to move the heavy tool chest from the garden shed to the hangar, in which Jenny was stored on a two-wheel sack barrow. It twice fell off as he tried to manoeuvre it through the gateway between the garden and the airfield.

He began to wonder if he really needed all the tools he had decided to take or whether he should leave some behind. The decision was made for him when he got to Jenny. Grunting as much as he could, he couldn't quite lift the chest on his own into the passenger compartment of the aeroplane. After swearing at the inanimate object for being so heavy, he rummaged through the tools and removed those he thought he might find on the ship. With the rejected items placed on a nearby bench, he closed the lid and attempted another lift.

He continued his Anglo-Saxon cursing with the tool box to persuade it to get into the aeroplane. It was not going to work. He searched around the hangar for an alternative means of transporting his tools. He found a heavyweight canvas bag with leather handles lying on a shelf. He shook off the dust and pulled the top of the empty bag open. He would have to fit what he could in it. Oliver filled the bag with what he thought would be the most important, refilled the box with the tools he couldn't take and dragged it to the side near a bench.

He then carefully placed the canvas bag in the passenger compartment, pulled on the leather flying helmet and climbed into the pilot's cockpit.

"Come on, Jenny, I need you to take me to Tortuga in 1689."

The aeroplane soon burst into life and they were on their way – up, up into the heavens and far away. He arrived okay, but soon ran into trouble on landing. He cursed himself for not bringing a compass with him. There were no road signs in the seventeenth-century Caribbean! To properly find his way around, he would need to send Jenny back with a message for Harry to get one for him. He wrote a note and placed it on one of the seats before instructing Jenny what to do. He then put the helmet in the aeroplane and sent her on her way. After all the struggling with the tools, he'd made a big mistake by forgetting some important things!

He picked up the canvas bag with his tools in and slung his clothes bag over his shoulder, watching Jenny disappear into the distance. Having noted the approximate direction of the port on his way into land, he set off across a steep bank of tall grass towards a track that he thought would lead him to Tortuga. He found the cart track on the top of a rise and turned left towards the town in the distance. From his vantage point on top of the small hill, he could see the port laid out around a natural inlet.

The bay was surrounded on three sides by wooded hillside, with another track leading off in the opposite direction. It was hot and strange birds screeched in the undergrowth, which occasionally drew Oliver's attention as he approached the town.

On the outskirts there were small huts rather than houses, with domestic animals wandering around and some cattle grazing by the side of the road. A few townsfolk nodded in acknowledgement as he passed by, but most busied themselves with whatever they were doing. A blacksmith's shop was pumping out hammering noises as the smith thumped away at metal on an anvil. Next door, a cartwheel was being repaired. He continued on towards where he could see the tops of tall ships in the harbour.

His tool bag was becoming heavy as he wandered around the docks. He was surprised to see, what appeared to be, only French ships. Although the French and British would often take possession of each other's ships after a battle, something did not feel quite right and he felt a bit unsettled. Why were there no British ships? Ahead, he saw a company of soldiers marching towards him. As they got closer, he stepped aside – the sight made him swallow hard. These weren't British Redcoats. He blinked his eyes and took a second look. *They're French Marines. Why the hell are French Marines patrolling the area?* he thought.

Something was wrong, very wrong. He crossed the cobbled dockside to a narrow lane between two storage wharfs, wondering where he was. Jenny never normally made a mistake. A group of drunken French sailors bundled past, greeting him with a series of garbled, "Bonjours." He pretended to look for something in his rucksack and mumbled a reply.

His French was quite good, but not good enough that a sober Frenchman would not recognise him as English. He decided he would go to the tavern he had passed on his way to the dock.

With his canvas rucksack casually thrown over his shoulder, Oliver confidently entered the drinking den that was overflowing with jolly seamen. It could be dangerous to be an Englishman in a French town at this time, with the countries at war with each other. But why was Tortuga full of Frenchmen when it was, according to Oliver's research, supposed to be under British occupation? He had to find out.

Through the smoke-filled haze that hung in the air, he could just see a wooden bar on the far side of the room. Oliver pushed his way through the crowd, stepping over one horizontal sailor that had passed out on the floor, with tankard still in hand. On his way through the mob, he was molested, hugged and kissed by a number of very drunk sailors, who all smelt of hard-working men who had not washed for weeks. It was enough to make your eyes water! Oliver wanted to put his hand over his face, but had to endure the acrid body odours because he was pretending to be one of them. As it was, with beer and wine sloshed everywhere, the place also smelt like the inside of a beer barrel – so much so that he feared the fumes might overcome him.

Behind the bar, a portly bartender was handing out large wooden tankards of beer and wine. Many of the patrons were holding on to the bar for support as they downed yet another glug of ale. Some managed to pour the juice into their mouths, but some missed altogether.

On reaching the bar, before Oliver could say anything, a jug of beer was slapped down on the bar in front of him. When he offered payment, the innkeeper dismissed it with a wave of his hand and a smile on his face. With his tankard in hand, Oliver turned around and scanned the crowd.

Then, just as he went to take a drink, a large man with a bushy moustache and a huge scar across his face slung his arm around Oliver's shoulder. As they both nearly collapsed on the floor with his weight, he roared some incomprehensible French from his dribbling lips. Oliver staggered to keep them both upright while the Frenchman spun around as one of his legs gave way. They both careered into a nearby table. Beer and wine tankards went flying everywhere, to a great cheer from those around. Oliver's new companion rolled off the table and onto the floor, a deep thud sounding as his head bashed the floorboards. Oliver stared for a moment, but the sailor remained motionless and everyone else carried on drinking.

He stepped back towards the bar and beckoned a word with the innkeeper, who seemed to be the only sober person around. The innkeeper was built like a warship, tall and broad and very strong, with a square jaw on a wide face. *Not a person you would argue with*, thought Oliver, *but a good person to have around in a bar full of drunks*. The man lent over the bar towards Oliver, resting on one elbow, and placed the other hand, which was the size of a dinner plate, next to Oliver's. Luckily, the rowdiness of the crowd drowned out Oliver's accent and the two of them managed a short conversation that enlightened him to the reason for the celebration. The sailors were rejoicing over the sinking of two British warships. However, he also found out that it was 1689, not 1699. He was in the right place, but not at the right time!

He decided to leave and left his beer on the bar. He made it to the door of the tavern without anyone paying him much attention, but as he stepped out he bumped into a group of marines. They greeted him in their native tongue, but when he replied he was rumbled.

Chapter 21

"So why do you want a compass and telescope?" enquired Laura again, as they carried their shopping up the path to Pegasus Ride.

"Well, Mum," Ben began, "the telescope is to go in the tree house and the compass, well, I just liked the look of it and thought it was interesting."

"I still can't believe you got them both for the five pounds I gave you."

Ben just smiled and shrugged his shoulders, grinning in the cutest way he could. Ben turned to Charlie who was clutching the tin of paint and raised both eyebrows a couple of times. He would have winked, but he had yet to master that.

After shopping, they returned home for lunch, which passed without any more awkward questions. The boys eagerly awaited George's arrival and, when the noise from the horse-brass front door knocker reverberated through the house, they were finally put out of their misery.

"He's here!" shouted Charlie. "It's George!" He scrambled off his kitchen chair and ran through the house to answer the door.

"Calm down, Charlie," shouted Laura, when the whirlwind raced past her.

Charlie wrenched the door open, banging it hard against the wall and the horse-brass did a knock of its own.

"Come in, George," Charlie said excitedly.

"Hi Charlie. Did you get them?"

"Yeah, yeah."

"What, both the…"

"Yep," Charlie interrupted with speed in his voice. "Ben's got 'em both in the kitchen."

When they got there, Ben called out a hello and waved to George. They then crossed the room together to the back door. On the way Ben picked up a cord-tie bag that he had brought down from his room, while Charlie collected the trophies from Emilie Brackets' Emporium and they ushered V out in front of them.

"We're off down the garden, Mum," Ben said, innocently, but deliberately failed to make eye contact with her as they piled out the door.

"Well, remember what I said this time," she said with a knowing look in the direction of the fast disappearing kids. "Don't go out of the garden without telling me."

"Of course not, Mum," Ben called back.

"Well, see you don't," she raised her voice to the empty space in the doorway.

The children weren't really listening, of course. Laura gazed out through the kitchen window and watched the four of them disappear down the garden. She briefly dried her hands and switched on the radio for company, twiddling the tuning knob to get rid of the background hiss. With music playing, she cleared up the lunchtime debris from the table and continued with the washing up.

By the time they got to the shed, V was trailing behind. Charlie and George had run on ahead, so Ben turned to offer her a hand, which she held as they entered the shed. Once inside, Ben cleared a space on one of the old tables and swung the bag that was over his shoulder onto it. George removed some old boxes off the end and Charlie put the telescope and compass down. Ben then released the cord around the top of his bag and emptied the contents on to the table.

He had brought the papers and books that he had been reading in order to learn about the previous owner of the house. The others stood by in silence while Ben arranged everything, laying it out like a military general would do with when studying the maps of a battle plan. Charlie and George looked on intently, like dogs waiting for a treat – almost panting with their tongues hanging out. V found a small box to sit on and clutched hold of Babbit, slipping her thumb into her mouth for comfort.

After a few moments, Ben felt happy at the layout and took a step back to survey to his work.

"Well?" asked Charlie, looking at his brother expectantly.

Ben put his arm around Charlie's shoulder. "From what I can make out about Oliver Bramley, he used the old aeroplane to take him to a place called Tortuga. It looks like he tried to be there in 1699, but something must have gone wrong with his plan. Look at all of this stuff in here."

Ben turned and gestured around the room with his other arm. "The pictures, the clothes; I reckon he's been coming and going all over the place in his aeroplane. However, he didn't come back from his last journey. We've seen the note Charlie found and I think that was meant for someone."

"Who?" asked George.

"I think it might be that postman."

"What, Mr. Hobbard?"

"Yeah, that's right. He seemed a bit concerned when I asked him the way to Emilie Brackets' Emporium and had lots of questions – and Mum said he was worried about what might have been left in the shed. Yeah, I reckon he knows something."

"Wow, Ben, I thought he just delivered letters and ran his shop," said George.

"No, he's in on it, I'm sure."

"Yeah, but we're still gonna find him, right?" blurted Charlie.

"Mum said we shouldn't leave the shed, Charlie," said V.

Charlie turned around to V on her seat. "Well, she won't know if you don't tell her and we won't be long, anyway. Remember last time."

"All we are going to do is find Oliver, give him the compass and help him get back. No mucking about this time, Charlie," said Ben, forcefully.

"Okay, okay," replied Charlie, wobbling his head

about like one of those nodding dogs in the back of a car.

"Right, this is the plan," explained Ben. "I give the orders and take the telescope; George, you grab the compass; and Charlie, you look after V."

"Ben!" complained Charlie.

"Charlie!"

"Okay," Charlie succumbed, taking hold of V's hand.

Ben gathered up most of the papers together and stacked them neatly on the table, taking the note Charlie had found, the map of Tortuga and the half treasure map. He tucked them in a small leather bag and slung it over his shoulder. He fastened the leather strap and buckle. The shed door creaked open and they all made their way to the aerodrome.

Ben slowly pulled open the large wooden hangar doors and there she was, the pristine looking bi-plane from another era. Her paintwork gleamed with a shine you could see your face in. While Ben finished opening the doors, Charlie and the other two walked around to the cabin door. With them all safely inside, Ben pulled on the flying helmet and spoke to Jenny.

"Can you please take us to the island of Tortuga in 1699?"

"Okay, captain," came the now familiar reply.

The engine spluttered into life and the aeroplane taxied out to the grass runway. Each of the children pressed their faces to a window as Jenny roared off into the sky. As they climbed higher into the clouds, they relaxed back into the wicker chairs. A gloomy darkness soon surrounded them, followed by a sudden flash of lightning and then another blinding flash, which pierced the darkness of the cabin. All covered their eyes with a hand.

Almost as soon as it had begun, it was over and they flew out of the cloud into a brilliant blue sky. The temperature in the cabin rose sharply. Jenny banked over to one side, dipped her nose down and descended towards a golden sandy beach. A light breeze lapped gentle waves onto the shore and the branches of nearby palm trees swayed silently as they landed. There was a little skip and a bounce before the plane slowed to a halt and the rumble of the engine gradually petered out.

The cabin door was flung open and the four children were disgorged from the aeroplane like a bag of apples being emptied on a table.

"We'll be back soon," said a confident Ben, before he slid the helmet off and threw it down on one of the chairs. He then ran his fingers through his hair to smooth it down and closed the door of the cabin.

They all gathered round as Ben unclipped the buckle on the small leather bag he was carrying and pulled out the map of the island. It was a page he had torn out of a book he'd found in the shed – a book with a number of maps of islands in the Caribbean.

"Hold that, Charlie," he instructed. "George, can I have the compass please?"

George handed him the wooden box containing the antique compass. Ben released the brass fastener and flipped open the lid. The compass sat in a pair of gimbals that, when released, allowed the compass to level itself independently of the movement of the box. The ornate and meticulous construction of the gimbals were obviously the work of a master instrument maker.

Ben knelt down in the sand and placed the compass box in front of him, carefully undid the two screws securing the gimbals and watched the compass level itself. The needle behind the glass eventually settled and stopped swinging about. He then twisted the box around in the sand to get the black end of the needle to line up with a little triangle with the letter N.

"Pass me the map, Charlie."

"What you doing, Ben?"

"Lining the map up with the compass. It's like the orienteering I did at school last year."

"Orien… what?" asked George.

"Orienteering. Finding your way using a map and a compass."

"Oh, I see," replied George, still very much confused.

"It's simple really, if you have a map with the direction of north drawn on it like this," said Ben, holding up the old map. "You simply line up the map north with the compass north and then you can start to work out where you are, using features that are nearby."

Ben shuffled the map around on the sand to line the north of the map with the north of the compass, which was pointing away from the sea and straight up the shore. He looked up the beach, and then to the left and right. To his left, at a distance of about a mile, he could see a small cottage on a ridge with what looked like a tower beside it.

"Pass me the telescope, Charlie."

Ben pulled out the telescope to its full length and placed the small end against his eye. He took a closer look at the structures on the ridge. He then picked up the map and squinted at it through narrow eyes.

V poked around in the sand with her fingers. "Are you going anywhere then, Ben?" she sighed.

"I'm just working out which way we should go."

"He's orienteering the map," blurted Charlie.

"I'm not orienteering the map, I'm orientating it," replied Ben, sounding rather frustrated. "Oh, never mind. Look, we've landed in a good place. I think that building over there is marked on the map and the town we want is round the other side of that ridge."

He pointed out on the map where he thought they should go. They could walk about halfway on the beach, then they would have to climb a grassy bank towards the top of the ridge. The map showed a track, or path, leading from a cottage (labelled as Jack's Warning Post) down the other side to the port of Tortuga. Ben re-secured the compass and closed the lid, handing it to George to look after. He then folded the map and returned it to his satchel, before taking hold of V's hand and started down the beach.

On their way, Ben viewed the cottage through the telescope several times, looking for signs of life. It was around midday and was very hot. There was not a cloud in the sky over them, but they could see large clouds looming on the horizon in the distance. Wildlife cackled and whistled in the undergrowth. Ben looked back at Jenny, her shape distorted by the heat haze radiating off the sand.

"Come on," he said, "we'll climb up here."

It wasn't so much of a climb, but more a steep walk up the grassy bank. At the top, they came across some goats grazing on the rough grass. One looked up, but the others weren't bothered. The interested one had large curly horns and lifted its nose high in the air, then nodded a couple of times and paced towards them. V hid behind Ben. George stepped forward and held his hand out for the goat to sniff.

"It's alright, V, he's quite harmless."

However, as George turned round to say it, the goat gave him an almighty whack in the backside with his horns and sent him sprawling to the ground. Charlie burst out laughing, until the goat looked at him. George picked himself up and watched the goat march towards Charlie, who by now was quickening his pace in the other direction.

"Give him that biscuit you've got, Charlie," he shouted, as both Charlie and the goat broke into a trot. Charlie dropped the telescope and buried both his hands into his pockets for the biscuit he had taken form home earlier. The goat was nearly within striking distance when Charlie finally managed to pull out a broken biscuit and lob it in the direction of the chasing animal. The other three, safe from the rampaging ruminant, were all giggling hysterically.

"Oh, very funny, you wait till you get chased," shouted Charlie. "Yeah, then I'll laugh at you."

The billy goat got stuck into the biscuit and wobbled his head in satisfaction of his successful intimidation.

The children then walked away from the goat herd, with V giving one final look over her shoulder. As they rounded a scrubby clump of bushes and small trees, the cottage and a small wooden lookout tower came into view. They paused for a moment and could see a tree that had been fashioned into a flag pole sticking out of the top of the tower. Due to the wind direction, they hadn't seen the flag from the beach, but now they could see the union jack flying. Only, it wasn't the union flag they were used to. This one had a strange crest of crossed cutlasses in the middle.

Ben stepped forward, telling the others to stay back. Slowly, he crept up to the cottage – which was really just a shack made from surrounding trees and with palm leaves on its roof. There were window openings, but no glass – just wooden shutters. A track led away from the shack in the direction they were headed in. It was then that Ben spotted a bearded old man who was fast asleep in a hammock. The unexpected sight made him jump. Springing backwards, his hand caught a splinter from the corner post and he let out an involuntary yelp of pain. Immediately, he slapped his other hand over his mouth to stop more noise coming out.

Cursing under his breath, he inspected the needle of wood projecting from the palm of his hand. The others looked on mystified at the figure of Ben jumping around, madly waving his hand. He studied the offending shard of Caribbean timber closely, then gripped the end tightly and gave it a slow tug. At first it resisted movement, but then, with a wiggle, it came out with some of Ben's flesh attached. A small pool of blood oozed onto the palm of his hand, which he thrashed up and down even more in an attempt to flick the pain away.

He wanted to scream, but did not want to wake the slumbering snorer in the hammock.

With his other hand, he waved a sign to the others that he was okay and pressed his 'good' thumb onto the weeping wound. The initial pain started to subside and Ben's grimacing face relaxed a little. He leant back on the wall and took a deep breath, before tilting his head around the corner again. The man was still in the land of nod and Ben decided it was time to risk creeping past. It seemed they could get away unnoticed, so he waved the others towards him, and they started along the track towards the town.

As they came out of earshot, Ben encouraged them to use a jogging pace until they were a long way down the track and properly obscured by the dense undergrowth that lined each side of it.

"What happened, Ben?" asked Charlie.

"I caught my hand on a splinter."

He showed them the weeping hole in his hand.

"Ow!" cried V, sympathetically cupping her hand over it.

"I'll be alright; it was more the shock of it."

Chapter 22

They continued about another hundred metres before they encountered a gap in the bushes, which gave them a view of the harbour. Ben extended the telescope and scanned the harbour and its surroundings.

"Wow, there's at least six cannons pointing at the harbour."

"Can you see it, Ben? Can you see the one we're looking for?" enquired Charlie, anxiously.

"Not from here, you dolt."

It was virtually a cloudless day, with just a few cotton-wool cumulus clouds slowly drifting by and the sun burning down on them from almost directly overhead. Birds tweeted loudly nearby and a lizard scampered across the track ahead and up a palm tree.

"Phew, it's hot," said George.

"What do you expect? We're in the Caribbean! Come on you lot, let's get on and get down there," said Ben, pointing to the harbour.

They passed by a number of shacks before approaching some more substantial buildings around the dock area. Most people seemed to stare a little as they passed by, but nothing was said. The kids just huddled together a bit more closely.

A long plank of wood fixed over a wide gateway

announced Porta Tortuga. The gates were opened up against the buildings on either side. Ben led V through first, with the other two not far behind. As they got to the end of the passageway, made by the two buildings either side of the gate, a stout little man with the shape of a wheelie bin approached them. His face had a very rugged complexion, like an old leather football that's been out in the rain too long and kicked about for many years. Cracks and grooves went in all directions when he smiled at them.

"Hey ye young 'uns, what ee doin' 'bout here den?"

Ben scratched his neck. "Err… um…" he stuttered as the others took stood behind him.

"Come on, lad, cat got yer tongue?"

"Err… well, we're looking for a ship."

"Ahh, well, ye be lookin' in de right place den. Yes, lots of dem 'ere."

Ben was gaining a bit of confidence, "Well, we are actually looking for the *Adventure Prize,* sir."

"Ah, de old *Adventure Prize*. Lovely ship. Yes, dat one is definitely a nice ship, one of the finer ships that comes in ere."

"So, you know it then?" asked Charlie.

"Oh yes I do." He nodded his head in confirmation, with a smile that revealed a mouth of either missing or dark brown teeth. "So you'd be looking for err, would ye?"

"Yes," said Ben with an exasperated expression.

"Well now, let me think. She's a tall ship she is, broad in der beam and not too short either."

"So it's a big ship then," said Charlie, eyes wide open in excitement.

"Oh yes, yes she's a big 'un, alright. Big as you'll see in 'ere."

"Well?" sighed Ben.

"Well what, lad?"

"Is the *Adventure Prize* here?"

"Oh, oh yes. No."

"What do you mean, yes, no?"

"Yes, the *Adventure Prize*; no, she's not ere."

"Not here?" puzzled Ben.

Football head continued, "Well no, not now. She was, now she ain't."

Ben was getting very frustrated by the drawl of the ancient mariner.

"But the ship should be here," replied Ben.

"Should she? Why's dat den?"

"Well, I read…" Ben started, but quickly corrected himself. "I mean, I was told it would be here."

"Ah well, between yous bein' told and yous getting ere, she's gone. Only just mind, she sailed the day before yesterday. There was a bit of arguing between the captains. Not good 'aving two captains on one ship. No, not good at all."

"Now what do we do?" asked Charlie.

"Why do you want that ship anyways?" asked football head.

"We were hoping to see…" Ben paused for a moment, "our uncle."

"Uncle?"

"Yes, our Uncle Oliver is the carpenter."

"Oh, the knife's assistant."

"What do you mean, the knife's assistant?" asked Charlie.

"The carpenter is de man who 'elps the surgeon cut off body bits dat git badly hurt in a battle."

V let out a shriek.

"Oh, tis usually for de best, young miss. Oh yes, often for de best."

Charlie and George looked at each other, stuck their fingers in their mouths and made vomiting faces.

"Anyways, as nice as it tis, I can't be standin' ere all day." He started to make off.

"Before you go," Ben said, "do you know where it is going?"

"Oh, yes, it was off to New York. Yes, dat Captain Kidd was heading for America. Mind you, if I knows 'im, he'll be stopping at Oyster Bay first."

"How long will it take?" Ben called out.

"Oh, about 3 months."

As football head walked further away, he raised a hand and waved without turning around, Ben had one more question.

"Where's Oyster Bay?"

"Nassau, of course," and then he disappeared round the corner of a large wharf.

"So now what do we do, Ben?" asked George.

The other two looked on with the same question in mind.

"We need to find out a bit more out this Oyster Bay. I'm sure, now I think about it, I read something about the place in Oliver's notes."

"Maybe there's someone here that could help?" suggested Charlie.

"You could be right. Let's have a bit more of a look around," said Ben.

They wandered a bit further along the quayside, admiring the ships that were there. It may have been the time of day and the heat, but there wasn't much activity going on.

Towards the end of a line of storage sheds, there was a smaller shed building with the roof projecting out over the entrance door. It was built out of stone with a timber roof. Attached to the roof over the entrance was a sign, saying 'Harbour Office and Chart Store'.

Ben eyed it first and led the group towards the office. Wooden shutters were hooked back either side of the window frames and the door was open. He stepped up onto the raised platform that spread across the entire front of the building. Standing in the doorway, Ben felt a light breeze brushing past him. Inside, a man stood behind a counter with small glasses perched on the end of his nose. On hearing them clattering in, he looked up from the counter and over the top of his glasses.

"Can I help you?" he asked in a more recognisable accent.

He was Mr Parsons, the harbour master and controller of everything that came and went through the Port of Tortuga. Ben approached the counter, holding V by the hand. Charlie and George lined up on either side. Ben cleared his throat with a small cough.

"I was wondering if you could help us with some information about a place called Oyster Bay in Nassau."

"What do you want to know?" he said, dipping his head slightly lower to obtain a fuller view of Ben.

"Well," he hesitated, "if you have a map of Oyster Bay or Nassau Island, that would be useful. And, um, do you know where the ship *Adventure Prize* is going?"

Parsons turned around and plucked a book from the shelf behind, opening it on the counter. He thumbed through some pages and then ran his finger down a line of entries.

"Here we are, the *Adventure Prize* is destined for…" his finger ran across an entry. "Ah, Oyster Bay indeed." He puckered his lips and pushed his glasses slightly up his nose. "Why would you be interested in where Captain Kidd is going?"

"It's our uncle," said Charlie

"What, Captain Kidd?" said Parsons with surprise.

"No, our uncle is on board. He's the carpenter," said Ben

"Oh, I see."

"We, err… were just interested in what sort of place he was sailing to. He talked a lot about the places he went and Oyster Bay sounded nice. Although, we weren't sure that's where he was going next."

"Oh right. Well, let me see."

Parsons walked over to a second counter where he rummaged around and pulled out a large scroll of paper. He unrolled it along the counter and held it open.

"Here you go, central part of Nassau Island with Oyster Bay. This will show you something of what's there. It's near New York, you know. I do believe it's quite nice there and I had heard that Captain Kidd was thinking of retiring from the sea and settling down there."

Parsons wiped a bead of sweat from his brow. The children all crowded over to see the map, although little Olivia could only just see over the counter.

"What will happen to our uncle then, do you think?" asked Olivia, innocently.

"Oh, they'll just appoint another captain, top up the provisions on the ship and set sail again. It is a British warship, after all. Although, I don't know when they'll be back here, so it could be some time before you see your uncle again, young miss."

Ben had been rubbing his hand gently over the chart and scanning the detail on it. He asked if they could take it to the table in the corner to take a closer look.

"Yes, of course, help yourself." Parsons rerolled it and handed it to Ben.

As he did so, he offered his other hand and said, "Parsons, Mr Parsons, young man."

"Oh, yes. Ben is my name, Ben Green." He shook the man's hand. "And this is Charlie, my brother; Olivia, my sister; and our friend, George."

Parsons smiled, nodded at each in turn, then returned to the book he had been working on when they came in. "Take your time."

Ben spread the map out on the table. Charlie held

one end down and George the other. Ben carefully read some of the place names on the chart and then opened the satchel hanging from his shoulder. He glanced over at Parsons, who had picked up his quill pen and was busy with some writing, before extracting the half map and placing on top of the Nassau chart.

There were no place names on the treasure map to reveal the location, but looking carefully at the north and south coast lines Ben reckoned they might be a good match. The scale was slightly different and the half map only had the minimum of detail, plus the riddle. Ben moved the half map up and down on top of the chart to compare the coast lines again – to him, they appeared very similar.

Ben slid the map to the top of the chart and then back down to line up the bottom again, checking twice over his shoulder that Parsons was not paying them any attention. In a whisper he explained to the others how the map they had found at home matched a small area in the middle of the chart. This news made Charlie start to excitedly drum his feet on the floor. Ben gave him a hard stare with eyes that said to stop and swivelled his head, yet again, to check on Parsons, who was fortunately still engrossed in his work. He refolded his half map and returned it to his satchel, and then rolled up the chart. He looked back at the others and held his right index finger to his lips. The chair noisily slid back as Ben stood up.

He approached Parsons, who still had his head in

his work. "I don't suppose we could borrow this for a while?" he asked, holding up the chart.

"Well, I don't know about that. I'll have to ask Mr. Tibbs – he's the one in charge of the maps and charts." Parsons stuck his head through a doorway behind the counter. "Stanley!" he shouted.

Stanley Tibbs was a wiry old man with a face like a chicken. He had a beaky nose and a pointed chin, which sat above a scrawny neck. His thin, wispy hair had a mind of its own and stuck out in all directions. His beady little eyes were set deep into his face.

"Yes?" he questioned, appearing at the doorway.

The sight made V hide behind Ben.

"These kids wondered if they could borrow a map."

"No," he squawked, bluntly.

"Well, it's the old one of Nassau. Didn't I see you with a new one recently?" asked Parsons.

"Oh, I see." He took the chart and partially unrolled it, then puffed air through his nose and handed it back to Ben. He reverse sniffed again. "In this case, yes, I suppose you can. It is a bit out of date now."

"Thanks, Stanley," said Parsons, as he winked at Ben.

"Thank you, sir," said Ben to Mr Tibbs.

"Was that all?"

"Yes, Stanley."

Stanley Tibbs disappeared down the passageway.

Ben thanked Mr Parsons, as did the others politely. They waved goodbye as they left the office.

"Come on, guys. We need to get back to Jenny."

Ben gave V a piggy-back up the hill and they all ran along the beach towards Jenny, who was sitting majestically on the sand. Ben was the last in; he gave Jenny instructions to take them to Oyster Bay and when they needed to be there.

Chapter 23

"Are we really going to find him here?" asked V.

"'Course we are, aren't we?" said Charlie, bobbing up and down on his chair.

Ben was preoccupied studying the compass with one eye, while the other looked out of the window as Jenny glided into a field some distance beyond the town. They bumped across the grass and rolled to a gentle stop before the engine noise cut out. The pasture was surrounded by woodland on three sides, which was mainly made up of tall pine trees. Although no cattle were in the field, there was plenty of evidence that they grazed there – as Charlie found out when he first jumped out of the aeroplane and straight into a great pile of fly-studded cow poo.

"Oh no! Urgh!" exclaimed Charlie, his face screwed up like an old dishcloth.

George just stopped himself in time at the door, bracing himself against either side, and watched Charlie hopping about and twisting his neck to try and see his poo-caked shoe for himself. Ben and V stuck their heads either side of George, blocking the doorway, to see the commotion. All three burst out laughing at the sight. Charlie wasn't very amused.

"Yeah, you just laugh."

"Well, it is a bit funny, Charlie."

"Not if it happened to you," he pointedly replied. He stopped hopping and started scraping the poo off on the grass.

George stepped out more cautiously and avoided the trap, followed by Ben. He then lifted V clear around the splatted pile of fly food. Charlie slid his foot one way and then the other, trying to scrape the poo off his shoe onto the grass. George, who was still giggling, gave Charlie a shove and they both started walking off.

"Hey, where are you two going?" called Ben.

Charlie and George stopped and turned round, "Err…"

"Exactly. You don't know where, do you? Wait." He opened the lid of the compass box and released the gimbals. After a few seconds, the pointer steadied. "Okay, guys, it's actually this way."

Ben pointed across the field to where there was an area of shorter trees. Holding V's hand, Ben made sure she didn't meet the same fate as Charlie. It happed to be a north-easterly direction, but it meant nothing to Charlie, George or V. Following in single file, Ben led them through the low canopy of woodland, but it wasn't long before they left the trees and were in open countryside again. About fifty metres from the last tree, Ben stopped.

"Here we are," he said.

"Here we are, what?" replied Charlie, as he looked all around him. All he could see was grass and a couple of pathways.

"The road I saw from the air as we came into land."

"This is a road?" asked V.

"Road!" exclaimed Charlie.

"It's not really what you would call a road, Ben," said George.

"Well, it is here. Remember where we are. It's not going to have tarmac and white lines, is it?"

"Suppose not."

"Anyway, by my reckoning, the town is this way."

All three followed Ben down the track as it curved with the line of trees gently to the left. After a few hundred metres they came across a dead tree, which was where another track joined from the right. It was a junction of three tracks, with the tree in the middle.

George was the first to spot something carved in the peeling bark and he walked over to investigate. Looking closer, he could see letters with an arrowhead carved into it. One spelled out the name 'Hempstead' and the other 'Oyster Bay'. George read them out to the others.

"Not much of a road sign," exclaimed Charlie.

"Not much of a road," laughed George.

"That confirms it then; it's this way." Ben started off again at the head of the troupe.

They hadn't gone far in the direction of Oyster Bay when Ben suddenly stopped. "Shh, I think I hear something." They all stood motionless, frozen to the spot, and listened hard. There was a clattering and rattling noise from around the bend behind them, and it was getting louder.

"What do we do, Ben?" cried V. She had grabbed hold of his hand tightly.

Ben froze for a moment, his head buzzing with nothingness. He was struggling for an answer. What should they do? Who would it be? Should they hide or should they stay where they are? What would they say to the noisy stranger? But before he had time to decide, a cloud of dust rushed into view. In front of the dust cloud was a single horse pulling a four-wheeled cart.

With no instructions from their leader, they all stood like statues in the grass as the cart rattled towards them.

"Woah, woah!" shouted the voice of the driver, pulling hard on the reins.

The cart drew up alongside the children and the dust cloud settled over them. The horse impatiently stamped its hooves while a strong, rough-looking man with a square face on top of a chiselled jaw gazed down on them. At first, he appeared rather intimidating and looked at them curiously. With a forefinger and the thumb of one hand, he raised the brim of his hat and pulled the brake lever with the other.

"My, my," he exclaimed, "what are you kids doin' out 'ere?"

The children were still motionless like wax models, and nothing came in reply.

"Hey, what's up? Don't be shy. I ain't gonna eat yer!" he laughed.

Ben waved the remaining dust away and replied, "Err... um... well."

"Spit it out, lad."

"It's… it's…" stuttered Ben, still trying to think what to say.

"Guess you're new about dese parts, as I ain't seen yous before. You off one of those two new ships in harbour? The ones dat bought more new settlers in from England?"

"Well…" Charlie started, but Ben grabbed his arm.

"The *Argenault* or *Beaumont*?" said the cart driver.

"Um… the *Argenault*," said Ben.

"Thought so," replied the man. "What yer doin' outa 'dis way den?"

"Err… looking for berries to pick," Ben replied in a questioning voice.

"Ha, ha! You won't find many down 'dis road, young fella. You need to go further to Hempstead to get anything. Why don't I give you a lift back into town? I'm goin' dat way."

They didn't need asking twice. Charlie was first in, climbing up onto the wagon, and found a seat on a sack of corn. Ben lifted V up and Charlie pulled her the rest of the way. George decided to sit up front with the driver.

"I'm sorry, I've 'aven't introduced meself. My name is Eddie Wheeler. I'm the blacksmith in town." He offered a massive hand to George to shake. It seemed that Eddie was a gentle giant of a man and a wide smile appeared on his big, square face.

"George, sir. Pleased to meet you."

"No 'sir' needed. Just Eddie will do fine."

"Okay, Eddie." George smiled.

Eddie next turned around to greet the other three in the back.

"Ben."

"Charlie."

"Olivia."

They all shook hands and smiled.

"Well you make yourselves comfy on doze sacks for der ride."

Eddie had just delivered some things he'd made to a merchant in Hempstead and was now returning with grain for a mill in Oyster Bay. With a sharp flick of the reins and a shout, they were on their way. Eddie's horse kept up a good trot until they were nearing the centre of town.

In the back, they stared at the sights they passed.

"It's just like the movies," said V.

There were men on horseback, carts, water troughs, wooden walkways and shops with poles set on posts outside for tying up horses. In the distance, above the buildings, they could see the tall skeletal masts of the ships in the harbour, their sails tied up like a neat row of sausages beneath the cross poles.

Oyster Bay was a growing port, partly due to buccaneers and privateers using it as a dropping-off point before going onto New York proper. At this time, New York was a hot bed of crime and full of undesirables. Even a ruthless pirate was at risk of losing his hard-won booty to a gang of cut-throats in the city. It seemed unlikely that Captain William Kidd would go to New York with a ship full of valuable treasure. Instead, he had planned to arrive with just enough to prove to the authorities that he had the gains expected of the average King's privateer on board. They would want to take the share owed to the British Crown for using a British Navy ship and crew.

Now at a walking pace, they approached a junction in the road. On a tree stump leaning at a precarious angle there was a sign, shaped like an arrow, with the words 'Farmingdale' on it. It pointed to a track that went off to the right, which was lined either side with tall pine trees. Eddie pulled gently on the reins and the cart came to a halt.

He turned around to Ben and said, "You bein' new round 'ere, you'll need to go and see Major Jones down dere at Stettin Brook. He controls pretty much everytin wat goes on round 'ere. He'll 'elp you and your folks find somewhere to stay, to 'elp you get started like. He's good like dat – for a fee, of course. But mind you don't cross 'im, cos he can be a real mean man if you does."

Eddie got the cart moving again. Ben looked at George and V and shrugged his shoulders. Soon after, they pulled up outside the blacksmiths. Eddie's name was painted on a long plank of wood that hung above the large double-door entrance. A lean-to roof was attached to one side and underneath was the fire hearth, which was surrounded by assorted tools for beating and bending metal into shape. In front of the hearth, in prime position, was an anvil mounted on top a small stump of a tree.

"Here we are," announced Eddie. "Back where yer started."

Well, not quite, thought Ben.

The kids climbed down from their dusty perch and thanked Eddie for the lift. He pointed the way to go and told them if they needed anything to come and see him. As far as Eddie knew, they had just arrived on a boat with their parents from England and would be looking for somewhere to live.

"What now then, Ben?" asked Charlie as they wandered between two large wooden storage wharfs towards the docks. Above the roofs of the sheds, the tall masts of several ships could be seen. Straight ahead, two other square riggers were at anchor out in the bay – one large ship and one much smaller schooner. A horse and cart trundled along the quayside loaded up with wooden barrels, and another was parked up to their left with bales of cotton.

"Look for the *Adventure Prize*," said Ben.

When they came out from between the sheds, the whole dock area came into view. There was a row of five ships, one to the left and four to the right. The one on the left was clearly a merchant ship that was being unloaded of cargo. There was lots shouting and what sounded like a song being chanted from below deck. A wooden jib stuck out over the side of the ship, acting like a crane, as a large bundle of sacks wrapped up in a rope net was being lowered on the quayside. Men were waiting to release the net and load the sacks onto a wooden handcart. It was a bit like a wheelbarrow, but with a long flat top for the sacks

236

to go on. A man in a straw hat was pushing another one towards the group. A sailor was leaning over the side of the ship and appeared to be supervising the lowering by much shouting.

To the right, two massive warships stood towering above the other two. They were moored back to back with the bow of the first facing them.

"Wowee!" exclaimed Charlie at the sight of the elaborately carved figure head protruding out with the bowsprit.

"Look at all the ropes," said V. This was the first time she'd been so close to a ship. Miles of rope were needed to rig this sort of vehicle and massive webs of rope stretched up from its sides to all places on the masts and sail booms. Charlie and George had been on a much smaller one when they had been taken on board Blackbeard's ship, so they were also impressed. For a moment, they stood there open-mouthed at the impressive sight. A gangway led from the side of the ship to the cobbled quay.

As they walked towards it, Ben said, "Don't even think about it, Charlie."

Charlie turned his head with a look of innocence spread all over it and then stepped past the gangway. Both the vessels were sixty-four-gun warships with three gun decks – two below and the main one on the top deck. Later, the British Navy would build even bigger ships with up to ninety guns on board, but these were still truly magnificent machines.

The rear, or stern, of the ships were even more ornately embellished than the bow. It was the highest part of the deck, with the poop deck sat on top of the captain's quarters and the officer's mess below. A row of windows illuminated the rear of the ship. The children paused to look at the works of art rising up from the water. Charlie started to wander, but Ben suddenly stopped him by grabbing hold of his shoulder.

Charlie nearly fell backwards. "Oi!" he shouted. "What d'you do that for?"

Ben ushered them all away from the ships and into the open-fronted wharf opposite. Pulling V's hand, he hurried them behind a stack of wooden barrels – each of which were nearly the height of Ben.

"What is it?" whispered George.

"Ssh."

"Ben?" Charlie pleaded.

Ben remained silent as he made sure they were all out of sight and well hidden behind the barrels. Positioned in a small circle, Ben wrapped his arms around Charlie and V.

"Didn't you see the name of that ship?"

A shaking of heads was all they could manage.

"It was the *Adventure Prize*."

"Is that the ship we're looking for, Ben?" asked V.

"Cor, it is, isn't it, Ben!" squeaked Charlie. Like a jack-in-a-box, he popped his head above their hiding place to look. With equal speed, Ben pulled him back down again.

"Get down, you twit."

"Oi, stop doing that!"

"What we going to do, Ben?" asked George.

"Nothing for a moment. Let me think."

Silence stung the air surrounding them. Excited anticipation screamed out of each of the little faces that looked at Ben. Charlie started twitching nervously and flicked his fingers on a barrel.

"Stop that," hissed Ben.

"Well, what we going to do?" protested Charlie in the quietest voice he could muster.

"Okay. Here's what we are gonna do."

Chapter 24

Standing before the French Captain, Oliver was introduced as a spy.

"A spy, you say?" said the captain, in a heavy French accent.

"I'm not a spy," retorted Oliver, sharply.

"We will hang you at sunrise. Take him away.'"

The captain turned his back on Oliver, preened his long black moustache and paced towards the rear of his elaborately decorated cabin. In front of a row of gently curving windows, which continued right across the back from one side to the other, was a large wooden desk. The French captain chose between a pair of flintlock pistols, picked it up from the desk and turned around.

"Or… I can shoot you now," he said with an evil smile. His eyes appeared to get closer together as he marched back to Oliver and put the pistol to his head.

"I'm not a spy," Oliver protested again. "I'm just a carpenter."

The captain sneered and rolled up his top lip, which made his huge moustache, which Oliver thought was rather comical, stick out even further. The smallest smile crept onto Oliver's face.

"You think this is funny. You stupid little Englishman."

The comment made it harder for Oliver not to smile even more, in addition to the fact that the Frenchman was barely five feet tall and was clearly wearing boots with large heels. The top of the French captain's head was still only just level with Oliver's chin!

"No, no, not this, but the fact you would even think I could be a spy. I… I… don't know the first thing about spying." Oliver pretended to stutter. "I… I can show you."

He went to get something out of his canvas bag, but one of the guards instantly grabbed his arm to stop him. "Look… I can prove it. My tools."

"We don't fall for that one. Loaded pistols in a bag, is it? Oh, very good; yes, very good, my friend." The captain stared Oliver in the eye and then looked down at the bag on the floor beside him. He then addressed the guards, "Have you not checked that bag?"

"Err…" the guards replied, looking blankly at each other.

"You fools," screamed the captain. He swiftly drew a cutlass out of his belt so that he now had two means of attack.

"Honestly," pleaded Oliver, "I do not have any weapons."

The captain pointed at one of the guards with his cutlass and told him to empty the contents of the bag. He went to hand Oliver his musket to hold, but before he could take it the captain had swung his cutlass, nearly taking off Oliver's hand. He was quick to withdraw his grasp and the musket fell on the floor. An almighty bang echoed around the cabin, accompanied by a bright flash of gunpowder. Oliver, still holding his arm, jumped back along with the other guard and crashed into the wall.

Luckily for the captain, the musket projectile just missed blowing off his foot and buried itself in the side of the ship. A plume of smoke rose from the deck, engulfing the guard that was halfway to reaching Oliver's bag on the floor. The captain rose, choking on the smell of cordite.

"You complete buffoon! You imbecile!" The captain was going mad – not at Oliver, but the incompetent guards!

Oliver really had a job not to laugh now, but thought better of it and tried hard to be serious. "If you'll just let me show you, you will see I'm telling the truth."

"The truth would be good. You couldn't be worse than these idiots." The captain took a couple of steps back and gestured to Oliver to show him the contents of his bag. "Alright then, show me."

He tapped the table beside him with his cutlass, tucked the one pistol he had into his jewel-studded belt and picked up the other.

Oliver carefully placed the bag on the table and slackened the cord that was secured around the top. Slowly, he reached in and withdrew an object wrapped in a linen cloth. The sneer returned and the captain took careful aim with his pistol, raising the cutlass in Oliver's direction.

Firstly, Oliver revealed a collection of woodworking chisels, each in their own leather holster to protect the blade. The captain leaned his head to one side and twitched the side of his mouth, which in turn raised one side of his moustache – the early stages of acceptance. Next, Oliver produced a small detailing plane, a tack hammer, a bradawl, a bevel marker.

"Okay," said the captain. "It seems that you are carpenter. Good for you. Come, sit down. We drink, eh?" He replaced his cutlass in his belt and placed the pistol on the table at the opposite end to Oliver. "What is your name, Englishman?"

Oliver had already prepared an alias – it was the name of his woodwork teacher from school.

"George Cotterell, sir," he replied, politely.

"Where have you come from, George?"

"I missed my ship a few years ago when they left port in a hurry and I've been working on the other side of the island, but now I want to return to sea."

"Ah, most fortunate for me then because we lost our good Monsieur Ballot to the pox recently. He had been my carpenter for five years. Perhaps you would like to replace him?"

Oliver had little option. He had learnt that the reason for the port being in French hands was that he had arrived in the year 1689 – not as he had planned in 1699! The British didn't retake control until 1695. A simple slip of the tongue to Jenny and he'd arrived in the wrong decade! And when Harry sent Jenny back, he would send her to 1699 as written in the note. Oliver was going to have to spend the next ten years waiting for history to catch up with him, so he thought he might as well sail the seas and try to find Captain Kidd that way.

"Okay I'll do it, but on one condition."

The captain laughed. "I was being polite, Mr Cotterell. You are not in a position to bargain, you are my prisoner."

"Yes, but I can only do my job properly if I am able to go ashore to source goods. So my condition is that I can come and go, to get supplies as I need."

"Oh, I see."

"You could, after all, send those two guards with me," Oliver said, smiling.

"Oh yes, I could really count on those two fools to make sure you came back."

"Well, where I am really going to go? I'm sure we can work together."

The captain smiled at Oliver. "Okay, you can have your wish, but I expect a good job to be done. Yes?"

"Yes."

"Let's drink to that."

The captain lifted a bottle from a rack mounted on the cabin wall and grabbed a couple of small glasses. He poured each of them a generous measure of dark red liquid and raised a toast. "Monsieur Cotterell!"

Oliver raised his glass too, but did not yet know the name of his captain, so paused and looked blankly at the little man in front of him.

"Oh, sorry, I am Captain Ricard of the magnificent ship the *Rouparelle*."

"Captain Ricard," Oliver replied.

★ ★ ★

Oliver sailed with the *Rouparelle* for many years, developing his skills as a ship's carpenter, and became very respected by Captain Ricard. They came across many ships in their travels, but it was not until 1698 that they came in close contact with a British man-o-war. The *Rouparelle* had taken a few smaller British merchant vessels and robbed them of their valuables, and had twice outrun larger pirate ships, but a British man o' war was a different story. They were very big ships by comparison, with several gun decks and well-disciplined crews – especially in the art of attack.

That day they had been traversing the Indian Ocean, when they were pursued and attacked by the *Adventure Prize*. The *Rouparelle* put up a small fight, but it was soon obvious that they were never going to be victorious against such a powerful ship.

The *Adventure Prize* drew up alongside and the two ships were lashed together. A plank was laid between the two and the victorious captain came aboard. Oliver had been below during the whole episode and was unaware that the very ship he'd been looking for all those years was so close.

A certain calm pervaded the ship and he ventured on deck, just as a group of British naval officers stepped on board. Their uniforms were adorned with gold braid, stripes and an assortment of swords. Their heads supported very impressive three-cornered hats.

Captain Ricard stood at the head of his senior crew and offered his cutlass. He wished for no further bloodshed and dipped his head in respect.

The victorious captain waved his hand at one of his subordinates to collect the offered cutlass and he addressed the assembled crowd.

"Good afternoon, gentlemen. My name is Captain William Kidd and all that is on this ship is now the property of the British Crown, including the crew."

There were cheers from the British among the crew. Oliver took a second or two to digest what he had just heard. *Was this actually true? William Kidd was standing on the deck of the Rouparelle – the very man he had been looking for?* A shiver shot through his spine.

Another fifteen minutes passed as Captain Kidd explained how things were going to be organised from now on. The officers of the *Rouparelle* were to be taken on board the *Adventure Prize* and put in the brig. They were to be replaced by some of his officers.

The two ships sailed as a pair to Madagascar where he liaised with a Captain Bartholomew Sharpe, who had also taken a French ship prisoner in the Indian Ocean. In Madagascar, Kidd's ship needed some major repairs and employed the services of George Cotterell to help. It did not take long for Kidd to recognise that George's, or rather Oliver's, skills were far superior to his own carpenter.

After two months in Madagascar, the ship was fit to put to sea again. While on shore, Kidd and Sharpe had decided to sail together for one last raiding trip through the southern seas to the Caribbean, before retiring to New York. The plan was to share any ill-gotten gains from piracy – though pirates aren't very good at keeping promises, so each would be watching the other like a hawk.

Before setting sail, Kidd insisted that Oliver join his crew. He also managed to convince a man named William Dampier to join him from Bartholomew Sharpe's crew. At first Sharpe had protested, but a promise of reward soon changed his mind. William Dampier was renowned for his journeys of exploration and, particularly, his recording of details of new lands and map-making. He had many books full of records of his travels, including illustrated maps of all the places he had been to. He was an expert navigator, too, which meant his maps were often more reliable than the ones that the British Admiralty provided – these could be out of date by many years.

Dampier had learnt his craft in his hometown of Bristol, England, which at the time was one of the most important naval yards in the country. It was also the birthplace of the infamous Long John Silver and housed one of the first naval colleges to teach the art of celestial navigation using a sextant. Before this, new recruits to the British Navy had had to learn the craft from the navigators on board ship. Dampier had learnt from a real master in Bristol before setting foot on board. He was also a fantastic natural artist and had taken with him all the materials he needed to make beautiful sketches of landforms, flora and fauna.

In the strict ranks of seniority, an officer would not normally converse with the lower ranks. However, Dampier did not hold the same feeling personally and Oliver had made his acquaintance before they left Madagascar. It seemed a mystery to Dampier that such a well-educated and well-spoken person could be a mere carpenter. Once on board and at sail, they would converse many times when the opportunity arose. Of course, Oliver could never reveal his secret.

During the journey to the Caribbean, Captain Kidd summoned Oliver to his cabin. Like the captain's cabin on the *Rouparelle,* it was an elaborately decorated room at the rear of the ship. It boasted ten windows and a large beautiful mahogany table surrounded by matching chairs. There was also a long couch to one side and a dresser on the other. Swinging lamps adorned the walls and on the table was a big leather-bound book and ink well, with two quill pens laid neatly at its side. Oliver was shown into the room by the senior shipmate, who then left. Kidd was staring out of one of the windows at the back and, without turning, welcomed Oliver and asked him to come forward.

A few moments of silence passed before Kidd turned around and walked towards Oliver. "Mr. Cotterell," he said, "I have an important task for you."

"Yes, Captain," replied an obedient Oliver.

Kidd approached him and uncharacteristically placed his arm around Oliver's shoulder. This might not be a good omen. Kidd was not known for being friendly. He was far better known for barking orders at men from the poop deck and pompously strutting around – not for giving a man hug! Oliver was immediately suspicious of his motives.

"I need you to make me a chest."

"A chest, sir?"

"Yes, a chest."

Oliver breathed a slight sigh of relief. He had made many of those before. Kidd, still with his arm around Oliver's shoulders, led him away from the door and towards the rear windows. One was open, which Kidd lent over and shut. He then turned to face Oliver, man to man.

"Not an ordinary chest. A special one."

Oliver's concerns returned. *'Special?' That makes me special*, he thought. *Not necessarily a good thing.* He had learnt that special people on pirate ships had a habit of mysteriously disappearing in the middle of the night, when their specialty was no longer needed.

"A special one?" Oliver queried, in the most innocent voice he could muster.

"Yes, a special one. I've heard, as well as seen, that you are a very accomplished carpenter and joiner. You are just the man for the job."

Do I have to be? thought Oliver.

Kidd guided Oliver to the side of the big table where the captain normally sat. "Come," he said, standing Oliver by the table while he locked the entrance door to the cabin. He smiled. "We don't want anybody disturbing us, do we, Cotterell?"

"No, sir," said Oliver, unconvincingly.

Kidd returned to where Oliver stood and lifted a key that was strung around his neck. He used it to unlock the drawer of his desk. Within the drawer were many papers and two loaded pistols, as well as what looked like a bag of coins. Kidd removed the bag, rummaged around the bottom of the pile of papers and withdrew one, then closed the drawer.

The piece of paper was folded in four, which Kidd now unfolded to reveal a sketch. At first Oliver couldn't make out what it was.

"There," said Kidd, "that's what I want you to make." His arm had returned to Oliver's shoulders, which now received an extra squeeze before being released.

Still far from understanding Kidd's primitive sketch, Oliver replied, "Oh, I see."

"I know you can make a very strong captain's chest, but this one is of my own design." He went on to explain the lines on the paper. It was actually a design of a chest that had secret compartments and secret locking mechanisms. He'd obviously spent much time on it.

"Now, Mr Cotterell, no one else is to know about it. Our little secret, yes?" Oliver nodded. "Of course, I can't expect you to do this without a little extra something, now, can I?"

He opened the bag and took out three gold

coins, equivalent to a year's salary as a carpenter, and handed them to him. "There, my man. Talk to no other about it, yes?"

There was a strong and forceful look in the captain's eyes. No one could misunderstand the meaning behind them.

Oliver left the cabin with a complete understanding of what was required and spent the next few weeks making the chest. It was made out of hard mahogany and was rectangular in shape, with a curved top. Each corner was reinforced with metal brackets overlaid with ornately carved strips of mahogany to cover the joints. The whole trunk had a double skin, within which items could be secreted away. The base had a double bottom that could only be accessed by removing concealed wooden and metal pins in the right order. Kidd had discovered the system in a much smaller box on a Chinese ship and had masterfully adapted it for use in his own trunk.

At times it had been difficult for Oliver to keep his work away from prying eyes, but he had managed it, and when the chest was completed, it looked no different from any other he had made. Although it had taken longer than Kidd wanted, he was very pleased with the result. It then resided in the corner of his cabin, and the main key to open its lid joined the desk-drawer key on a piece of leather around his neck.

They sailed into the South Atlantic Ocean in January 1699 and headed for the Caribbean. They would make landfall at several places before reaching Tortuga, their final stop before Oyster Bay and New York – where Captain Kidd planned to leave the Navy for retirement.

Chapter 25

In the year of 1699, the *Adventure Prize* sailed into Oyster Bay and moored up on the quayside. Captain Bartholomew Sharpe had decided to stay in the Caribbean. After securing the ship to the dockside, Kidd sent one of his crew to go ashore and find a man named Major Thomas Jones.

At one time, Jones himself had sailed as a privateer. Originally from Cork in Ireland, he had sailed as a fearless captain of the British Navy and was never one to spare the lash on members of his crew. It was rumoured that he had once cut off an ear of one of his crew members for not listening to orders, reasoning that if he wasn't going to listen then he didn't need his ears. Jones had commanded great respect from his officers. Nowadays, he was a respected member of New York society and had been made governor of the Island of Nassau, now known as Long Island.

He was, however, still one of the biggest crooks in the area and ran a mob of thugs in New York, as well as on Nassau Island, to keep things the way he wanted. It was best not to get on the wrong side of him or you might find yourself missing some fingers! Times were rough in New York then, with little or no law and order. Irish Jones, as he was also known as, knew how to deal with people who didn't play his game.

And so, Major Jones had been invited on board to dine with Captain Kidd in the luxury of his cabin. On a fine summer's evening, with the sweet smell of newly picked soft fruit on board, Jones joined Kidd for dinner. An act of party pleasantries was acted out between them over the dinner table.

"Oh, my dear William – if I can be so bold as to address you that way," said Jones. "Yes, of course we can find you somewhere to settle down, now you've had enough of the sea."

Kidd held up his wine glass and nodded in acknowledgement.

"No, there's no way the British military will find you here," continued Jones. "We can make sure of that." He could also arrange for them to find him if he wanted, too!

Major Jones invited Captain Kidd to stay for a while at his house, known as Stettin Brook. Stettin Brook was an impressive house by local standards, which were often no more than simple timber shacks. It stood in large grounds some way out of town, with a wide sweeping driveway that led to a porticoed entrance. It also had glass in the window openings, something that many houses did not.

Such a retreat was perfect, as Kidd had been informed that the Navy Board in England wanted him for questioning over the death of one of his crew members the previous year. He'd been overzealous in his punishment of the man and, as a consequence, he had died. The lashing of a man with a cat-o'-nine-tails was legal under the navy law, but not to a point of death. Although many men were lost to disease and malnutrition, which was accepted by the navy board, death by punishment was not.

Kidd had plenty of valuable gold, silver and jewellery in his possession to keep him in a very comfortable position for the rest of his life. However, he needed to find a safe place to live out such a life. He now feared England, a likely trial and the many enemies he had made throughout his career.

At this point, Jones was the only man likely to offer him sanctuary. The only other man Kidd trusted was William Dampier. In him, he saw a true gentleman, unlike himself. He was someone he knew he could trust – and he had to, for he was making a map of where he would bury his treasure! And Dampier wasn't like the normal self-centred officers he sailed with. He lived by a different code, one of true honesty. He would take what he was due and not a penny more. He was a man, the only man, that Captain William Kidd could trust with the whereabouts of his treasure trove. Anyway, Dampier would be sailing back to England soon in the *Argenault*. He was looking forward to returning home to Bristol, as he had a lot of his writings he wanted to collate and many more adventures to note down.

Over the next few days, under the disguise of exploring the region around Oyster Bay, Kidd and Dampier went off in search of a suitable burial site for some of his prized possessions. Unbeknown to Bartholomew Sharpe, some of the items in Kidd's haul were actually his! When they had divided them up in Tortuga, Kidd had been less than honest about what he actually had on board. Some were already secretly stashed away in his Aladdin's cave: the special chest.

It took the best part of a week to find a suitable site and Dampier set about mapping a route for Kidd, complete with cryptic clues that only they would understand. Meanwhile, as well as his special chest, Oliver had been asked to make a waterproof lining for one of Kidd's trunks. A normal officer's trunk was already fairly watertight due to the likelihood of getting a soaking on board ship.

Surrounded by a lawless society, he needed to be very careful about having a lot of valuables with him at one time. After all, many people were aware that he had been a successful privateer and would therefore be in possession of some serious treasure. He played it down, of course, saying that much of it had been distributed amongst his crew.

This was true to a certain extent, as some had to be shared out between the crown, the captain, the officers and the crew. However, the correct and fair amount relied on the calculations of the captain and some were fairer than others! Mutinies had occurred on ships where the crew had felt the captain was being dishonest about the total value of the haul on board. Kidd, in contrast, had always been clever and had revealed the total wealth of the ship's cargo; or at least nearly so.

Another problem was the map, as all someone had to do was get hold of it and they would be able to find the hiding place. So, as well as the cryptic clues, Kidd intended to tear the map in half. He would keep one half in his jerkin and hide the other half in the bottom of the special chest.

★ ★ ★

One afternoon Kidd and Dampier left the quayside in a cart, with the waterproof trunk on board. Most assumed he was bound for Stettin Brook, but he actually headed out of town on another road completely – not before stopping, unseen by any member of the crew, at a hardware store. There, they purchased a pick axe and shovel. They were gone all afternoon and only just arrived back in time before two of Jones' henchmen turned up to show them the way to Stettin Brook. Captain Kidd personally supervised the unloading of his personal effects onto a cart to go to Jones' place. Naturally, he took a particular interest in the special chest. He did not want that to be out of his sight for long and sat with it on the journey.

A large part of his wealth had been buried earlier and he had now hidden one half of the map in the false bottom of his special chest. The other half was hidden inside his jerkin. Neither made much sense on their own, but together they revealed a stash of valuables worth thousands, if not hundreds of thousands of pounds. He could certainly be able to buy his way into New York society with it.

However, it was not to be as within a few days, a group of Royal Navy Marines were at Jones' door with a warrant for Kidd's arrest. Thomas Jones had double-crossed him. His reward for the whereabouts of Captain Kidd was that he could keep Kidd's chest. Believing that the chest contained great wealth, Jones sought no further reward. Kidd, of course, was furious and threatened to return for revenge. The *Adventure Prize* would remain at Oyster Bay until a new captain was appointed, which would give Jones' mob time to search the ship as well. Of course, William Kidd was already one step ahead in that regard. Most of his fortune lay hidden somewhere that only he and Dampier knew about.

The Marines left with Kidd under guard. He knew that his fate was probably already sealed, returning to England as a prisoner. Some spoke in defence at his trial, but the evidence of the murder was overwhelming and he was sentenced to death by hanging.

Dampier, who by now was back in Bristol, visited his old captain in Newgate Gaol on the night before he was due to be hanged. Amazingly, Kidd still had half the treasure map hidden in his clothing and gave it to Dampier. As Kidd was now never going to be able to make use of it, he explained to his old confidant where and how to get the other half of the map. Dampier returned to Bristol and never made it back to Oyster Bay, but just in case he hid the half he did have in the spine of one of his journals.

Back in Oyster Bay, Jones managed to open the special chest, but found it contained nothing more than clothing and a few gold coins. Nothing of much value at all. Irish Jones was mad, really mad, as he had believed he was on an easy road to a fortune. He knew there must be some treasure trove somewhere and was sorely irritated by the fact he may have been tricked. He and his men searched the ship high and low, but could find nothing. Many of the crew were interrogated and several of Kidd's senior officers had even met with a grisly end, but none could enlighten Jones as to the whereabouts of a map. Irish Jones was getting impatient. Next in line was Oliver.

★ ★ ★

Back at Stettin Brook, Jones was discussing the situation with his best henchmen.

"There must be some sort of secret compartment we can't find on board that bloody hulk," moaned Jones.

Although he had the strength of an ox, he rarely used it in anger against another man; he was too clever for that. He got others to do his dirty work. If beatings were needed, he would send one of his gang to do what was required. Usually, only a warning visit was sufficient to strike fear into anyone, but occasionally a bit of softening up with their fist was required. Beyond that, they had plenty of unsavoury ways to make someone talk.

"The carpenter!" screamed Frank Ottawey, one of his thugs. "He'll know if there are any secret compartments on that damn ship."

Chapter 26

Cowering behind the storage barrels, Ben, Charlie, George and Olivia watched as sailors and dock workers moved on and off the various ships, loading and unloading cargoes and people. However, their attention was mainly on the activities associated with the *Adventure Prize*.

They suddenly noticed a smartly dressed young lad, of about Ben's age, walk down the boarding plank. With a spring in his step, as if pleased to be ashore, the boy cheerfully marched along the quayside. Ben decided it was time for action.

"You lot stay here; I'm going to speak to him."

Ben ran up to the cabin boy from behind and grabbed him by the arm. The lad nearly jumped out of his skin with fright, as his mind had been miles away. He was off the ship for the first time in weeks and then somebody grabs him from behind. The poor chap nearly wet himself. The other immediate scare, until he turned and saw Ben, was the ever-present danger of being kidnapped and pressed into service on board another ship. It was not uncommon for men and boys to be forced into service on a ship that was short of crew when it needed to leave port.

"Ahh!' screamed the boy, swivelling around to see his captor.

"Excuse me," said Ben, who was equally surprised by the boy's reaction.

"What is it?" squeaked the boy in a high-pitched voice, wriggling away from Ben's grip.

"What do you want?" He bent down and picked up the paper scroll he'd been holding before Ben pounced on him.

"I just wanted to ask you something."

"Well, what is it?" he said, impatiently. He brushed his arm where Ben had grabbed him, as if to remove something offensive – a commoner's touch. He had neat blond hair cut short and the face of a girl with a small button nose, which he was screwing up at the closeness of Ben. He took a step back to remove the stranger from his personal space.

"I'm sorry if I made you jump, but I wondered if you worked on that ship and knew who was on board?"

"Yes I do, but I don't know everyone."

"Do you know if there is a Mr Oliver Bramley?"

"'I'm sure I really don't know," squeaked the boy, as if it were beneath him to know anyone by name except an officer or other senior rank of sailor.

"He's the ship's carpenter," said Ben.

The boy straightened himself up and tried to stand a bit taller as he announced, "The ship's carpenter is Mr. George Cotterell. Sorry, I don't know a Mr Bramley."

Ben sighed a little and his stature slumped. He

felt deflated like popping a balloon. His face said it all.

"Now I must go, I've got to go and see Mr. Bailey in the harbour office."

Ben let the boy go and watched the vision in a blue uniform stride, rather than skip, away from him. He was no better informed than before, but then he had a thought and ran after the boy again.

"What is it now? I told you I don't know the man you're looking for."

Then, Ben described Oliver from the photographs he had seen.

"Well, yes," the boy replied crossly, "that could be him, but the carpenter's name is George Cotterell."

"Thanks," said Ben, and the boy went on his way again.

Back with the others, Charlie immediately asked, "Well?"

Ben shook his head in disappointment at first. "No, Oliver is not on the ship."

"Aw!" sighed Charlie and George together.

"He's not there, Ben?" enquired V.

Ben was deep in thought and stared blankly ahead as though hypnotised. He was churning over all of the documents and scraps of paper at Pegasus Ride.

"Ben?" V repeated.

"That's it. Yes, yes," he said quietly. "Of course it is."

"Of course what is, Ben?" asked Charlie.

"He's not here as Oliver Bramley, he's changed his name! It's George Cotterell." Ben's excitement made him feel like he'd just got the best birthday present ever. "I now remember seeing the name George Cotterell on one of the notes. He's not using his own name; he using the one he wrote down."

"Have we found him then, Ben?" squealed V in excitement."

He hugged her tightly. "Yes, V, I think we have."

Charlie and George started jumping up and down, thumping their fists together.

"Okay, you gotta calm down," laughed Ben. "We haven't actually found him yet."

"Us?" said Charlie. "It's you that's wetting yourself! Is he on board now?"

"The boy didn't say, but at least we know the right name to ask for."

They waited in their hiding place for the cabin boy to return, which he did carrying a small parcel. Ben dashed out and confronted him again.

"Oh, what do you want this time?" he squeaked, half talking through his nose.

"Mr. Cotterell, is he on board now?"

"No." The boy started to walk off.

"Wait, please."

"Look, there's no Mr Cotterell, no Captain Kidd, no senior officers. Just the quartermaster giving me orders – and if I take too long getting back, he'll take his whip to me."

"Oh, gosh, I'm sorry. It's just rather important I find him."

"Well, they've all gone off with Major Jones's men and they haven't come back yet."

"I see, thanks."

The boy was already running off towards the ship. He'd seen the figure of the quartermaster appear at the side of the poop deck, although fortunately he was actually looking in the other direction.

"Major Jones, remember what the blacksmith said? Not always a nice man," said Ben.

"At least we know where to go," said Charlie.

★★★

An hour or so later, they had completed the walk to Stettin Brook. Outside the grand house was a stone gateway, with an ornamental metal nameplate arching over two pillars.

"Now what do we do?" asked Charlie.

"Well, if he's in there, he may need our help – if what Mr Wheeler said is true."

"How can we help though, Ben?" asked George.

"Yes, what can we do?" squeaked V, timidly.

There was no actual gate in the gateway, just a track leading to the front door. It was set back under a portico which was supported on two stone pillars, similar to the gateway. Wooden shingles covered the roof and the porch. The house was mainly constructed of timber with a few stone walls randomly placed around the structure. It was quite different from the brick houses at home.

Ben led the way up the drive, with the others hiding in line behind him. They gingerly approached the wide front door under the porch. Pulses were rising in all of them and sweat bled out of their foreheads. V scratched at an insect bite on her arm. Ben crept quietly up the two steps onto the wooden deck of the porch, paused and turned around. The others were trying to hide behind the pillars, but were not doing a very good job of concealing themselves.

"Go on," hissed Charlie.

Ben faced the door, raised his hand and knocked twice. At first, nothing. Then, he heard heavy footsteps approaching the closed door. A huge ape-like man answered.

Towering over Ben, he asked, "Yeah, what you want?"

"I… I'm looking for my uncle."

"Yeah, what of it?"

"I… I mean we… were wondering if you might have seen him."

The ape stood in the doorway and shrugged his shoulders. "Why would I have seen 'im? Who is he? I don't know who yer bloomin' uncle is, do I?"

"His name is George Cotterell and he works on the *Adventure Prize,* sir. They said he might be here."

"Nope. Never 'eard of 'im."

"Oh, sorry," Ben replied, "but they did say we might find him here."

"Well you 'ain't and you won't. Now, 'oppit." The ape stepped back and slammed the door.

"That went well," said George with a sour expression.

Ben stepped forward and put his ear to the door. He could hear through it!

"Who was that?" asked a voice.

"Blooming kids looking for our friend."

"What?"

"Yep, 'im," replied Frank, the front-door ape.

The voices grew fainter as they walked back into another room. Ben turned around and directed the others to squat down as he rejoined them at the foot of the steps.

"What is it?" whispered Charlie.

"I think he's in there, guys. I'm sure of it."

Ben crowded them together and they moved to a position under one of the front windows. Slowly raising his head, he peered in. The room was empty – empty of people, at least. A picture hung over the fireplace opposite. It was a painting of a man in naval uniform. Otherwise, the room was sparsely furnished.

"Come on," said Ben. "Let's go round the back."

"Are you sure it's okay?" queried V.

"Come on, V, they're not going to hurt us," said Charlie

Charlie was up for it, but V was clutching Babbit even tighter and the thumb had taken residence in her mouth again. It was a sure sign of nerves or tiredness, or just needing comfort.

Having crept quietly around the back of the house, Ben checked several windows and saw nothing. However, the next made him dip back down like a dart. The figure seated in the chair, bound by his wrists, had a badly bruised face and was stood over by a second ape, who was rubbing his knuckles. A short, stocky man smoking a cigar entered the room with Frank. The room was bare of furniture except for the heavy wooden chair with the victim in it. There were red stains on the floor around the chair.

"Okay, Billy," said a gruff Irish voice. "We'd better get a move on. Some little tykes are lookin' for this git."

"So, come on, Mr. Cotterell. Why make this 'ard for yerself?" said Frank.

"Yeah, we don't likes doin' this anymore than you," laughed Billy, as another blow resonated through Oliver's jaw.

Oliver remained silent.

Major Jones threw down his cigar in a rage. "Christ, man! I said I would give you some of it! Where the hell is the map? You must know where he might have kept it. The loot's not on board, so where is it?"

He stormed across the room to where a thick lump of wood was resting against the wall. It was midday and the hot weather was getting to him as much as Oliver's silence. "Right, Billy, throw another pail of water over him and then you can use this on his legs."

Jones handed him the weapon. Billy smiled.

"Come on, Frank, I need a beer. This stinking heat is getting to me."

Before he left the room, he turned round and told Oliver that unless he'd got some information when he returned, he might find his piano-playing days would soon be over. Jones and Frank left the room, then the house and headed off on horseback for a tavern in town.

Ben had been crouching out of sight with the others while the shouting had been going on. Now it was quiet, he decided to have another peek through the window. He caught a further glimpse of the man slumped in a chair and another man the size of a fully grown bear, who was standing with his back to the window. Ben instinctively ducked down again, even though the bear wasn't looking in his direction.

"What did you see?" asked Charlie.

"Shh!"

Ben slid his fingers up the wall and gripped onto the window sill, then eased his head up to a position that meant his eyes were just above the bottom of the frame. He saw the bear walking towards a door, then pause and look back at the figure in the chair, saying, "I'm going out back to the bog. When I return, we'll carry on with our little chat."

He laid the leg bruiser down against the wall and opened the door to the backyard, which was right next to where the kids were crouching. Ben watched in horror as the door opened, instinctively throwing his arms around the others to protect them. Luckily, the door opened outwards and it momentarily sheltered them from view.

The bear never even looked around! He just slammed the door behind him and walked off down a path in the opposite direction. It led to a tiny shed about fifty yards away and he disappeared inside it.

Still crouching down, the kids simultaneously let out a sigh of relief.

"Phew, that was close."

"That's a funny little shed," said V

"It's the toilet, V."

"He's gone for a poo!" laughed Charlie.

"Yes, thank you, Charlie. We can see where he's gone," smiled Ben.

V stared curiously at the little shed. They didn't have loos at the bottom of the garden where she came from.

"Come on, you three. This is our chance," continued Ben, ushering them to the recently opened door.

"If he's like my granddad, he'll be in there for ages," joked George.

Charlie laughed.

"Oi, you two. Come on."

Ben opened the door cautiously and stuck his head around it. There was neither sight nor sound of anyone except the body slouched in the chair in the middle of the room. Aside from that, the room was bare except for a tall rectangular box, with handles on either side, which was leaning against the wall in the opposite corner. It looked very much like a coffin. In fact, many of the people that had had the pleasure of Major Jones's hospitality had wound up in the comfort of their own box!

Chapter 27

Oliver sat slumped in his chair, contemplating his fate. Is this what it has come to? His plan to send the native Indigenous Indian tribespeople of Long Island a legacy in the form of a treasure map would end in him being beaten to death. On principle, he would not give information to the wicked Major Jones. His old military training had taught him to do that. He'd had a good run, bringing hope and charity to many unfortunate souls in history, but soon he would meet his own end and not be able to help anymore.

He thought of what the old man in the desert had given him. Since that moment, he'd used his new powers to help others he thought deserved it. He hoped the old man would be proud of him.

He now had no way of getting back home, anyway. Something had gone very wrong. He also knew that Kidd was on his way back to England with one half of the map, because he had found it in Dampier's book – and that was back in the twenty-first century with his other findings and notes. As for the other half, he could only guess it was in the special chest in one of the secret compartments and he wasn't going to tell them that.

I'm done for, he thought. His head dropped lower

still in his partial consciousness. Blood dripped from his face into his lap. His legs had been kicked but the bashing from the beating stick had yet to start. He wished for the suicide pill the Royal Air Force had handed out when he was flying in the Middle East, where local tribes they were in combat with had definitely not been very hospitable to pilots who were shot down. However, he didn't have any pills and so he would have to wait for the end. He heard the door opening and feared the worst, but the door seemed to open more gently than before.

He waited for the bear to start shouting again. Instead, his ears were kissed by the sound of a quiet and friendly voice. *It's in my head,* he thought.

"Oliver, Oliver Bramley?" repeated the voice, followed by soft footsteps.

Oliver expected to see Saint Peter standing there, holding the gates open. No one knew him by that name here.

"Oliver? Oliver?" came the soft voice again. A gentle hand touched his shoulder. He opened the one eye he could – the other was too badly swollen and bloodied.

At first, he couldn't make out what he was seeing. *Was it one face? No, there's more. Where's Saint Peter? Is it children that welcome you to heaven? But surely the pain should go and I can just get up.* He leant slightly forward, but still felt restrained. He painfully blinked his good eye. He wasn't seeing double; there were four different faces staring at him.

"Mr. Bramley?" questioned the smallest.

"Er… yes." he mumbled.

"Come on, Charlie, help me untie him."

They struggled at first, but soon wiggled the knots undone and released his bond to the chair.

"You are Oliver, then?" asked Ben again.

"Yes, yes I am," he replied more clearly.

"But how… and… who are you? How do you know my name?"

Ben introduced them all and gave Oliver a brief story of how they had got there, while Charlie and George kept watch by the window for the bear's return. So far, there was no sign of him.

"Just like my granddad," said George to Charlie, staring at the shed.

Olivia held Oliver's arm lovingly, as if he were her real uncle, and Oliver's mind began to return its normal state with the compassion around him. He drew strength from it.

"It's dangerous for you here. We need to get out," Oliver said as Ben helped him up. "That Billy will be back soon expecting the pleasure of breaking my legs."

"Yeah, come on, guys. We'd better leave quickly," said Ben. "I don't think there's anyone else in the house, so we should go out the front way."

Charlie took one last look, "Still in the bog."

Oliver led the way through the house, opened the front door and they all quietly left. At the front were two horses tied up near to a water trough, who were busy flicking flies off themselves with their tails.

"Look," said Oliver, "we can use those to escape. Can any of you ride?"

"Yes, I can," said George, putting his hand up like he was answering a question at school.

The others remained silent apart from V, who said, "I'd like to."

Oliver took V with him on one and the two boys squeezed onto the other behind George. They initially rode the horses at a walking pace, staying on the grass to the side of the drive, so as to keep the noise to a minimum. Once in the lane they quickened their pace and broke into a trot, which sent the boys bouncing up and down like someone dribbling a basketball. Further up the lane, Oliver slowed back down to a walking pace – much to the delight of Ben and Charlie, whose backsides had been taking a bit of a pounding.

"Now, tell me a bit more about how you got here," requested Oliver.

"We worked out some things about you after we moved into your house."

"You've moved into my house?"

"Yes, our mum bought it."

"Oh, I see."

"Then, by accident really, we found your aeroplane," continued Ben.

The other three beamed smiles at Oliver.

"Yeah, Ben worked it all out," said Charlie

"So, you know why I'm here then."

"Reckon so," replied Ben.

They walked on a little further, exchanging stories.

"So, you found Dampier's half of the map then?"

"Yes, I've got it with me."

"You clever boy!" exclaimed Oliver. "I think the other half is in the chest I made for Captain Kidd, which, as it happens, is back at Jones's place."

Ben snapped a stare at the man. He knew what that was likely to mean.

"Where's Jenny?" asked Oliver.

"She's safe outside Oyster Bay in a field."

"Yeah, in a field of poo," added Charlie, sourly.

"Well, we've all come so far to get here. We must go back and get it," said Oliver. "Look, it will be alright. That pyscho will have found I'm missing by now and he'll be headed for the stables to get another horse, ready to ride into town to tell Jones. I don't envy him that! We need to get off the road before he catches us up."

Oliver led them into a small clearing and they hid behind some undergrowth. Surely enough, after a few minutes, Big Bear Billy galloped past in a cloud of dust, thrashing merry hell out of his horse.

"Obviously in a hurry to get somewhere!" joked Oliver. He then suggested that he and George take the horses and ride back to Stettin Brook to look for the map. George could keep lookout while Oliver went through the chest, as only he knew how. The others would wait in their hiding place for their return.

★ ★ ★

Oliver found the chest in Jones's study and set about removing the hidden pins and pegs to release the secret panels. There was one at each end, as well as a false bottom. George stood by the window on lookout duty, but he was also interested in watching the chest come apart. He was amazed at the ingenuity of the system Oliver had built, as he now gradually emptied the hidden pockets. Within them Kidd had stored some documents, gold coins, a small bag of diamonds and rubies, as well as the other half of the map.

"Geronimo!" he exclaimed, waving the piece of paper in the air.

George went wild with excitement and rushed over to Oliver to see what he had found.

Reach Penn's followers from the neck
latitude turn thy face the Hempstead way
tables full of nights to reach the beck
juice of mother earth over ye chest.

George had been expecting to see a complete map and was a little disappointed, but Oliver reminded him that they already had the other half. One part on its own was useless, but now they had both they could put them together.

Oliver studied it briefly, then folded it away and tucked it inside his shirt. It was more important than ever that they escaped, because if they were found with both parts of the map Jones would be able to find the treasure for himself.

"Keep looking out, George, while I put this back together."

Oliver reassembled the secret panels, but obviously took the two bags of treasure with him. He found it very satisfying to be depriving Jones of the loot. Even if now he decided to smash up the chest, he would find nothing but a few papers!

With the job finished, Oliver took George by the arm, saying, "Come on, kid, let's get out of here."

With fresh energy, they ran out of the house, jumped on the horses and rode to rejoin the others.

Chapter 28

"That's a sight for sore eyes," said Oliver, admiring Jenny.

"Why do you say that, Mr. Bramley?" asked V

"Oh, it's just a saying," he said, tousling her hair.

"Yeah, like one of Mum's," laughed Charlie.

Jenny stood before them as pristine and proud as ever. They had rested at Eddie Wheeler's place overnight and Oliver looked remarkably different today, although his eye was still very puffy.

Oliver climbed into the pilot's seat and the children took their places in the cabin. He pulled on his faithful flying helmet and reunited himself with his old friend.

"Welcome back, Oliver!" said Jenny.

"Good to hear you, too."

★ ★ ★

"I can't tell you how good it feels to be back home," said Oliver, as Jenny came into land over Rosemie Common. They swooped over Beryl and Harry's place just down the road from the garage and the pub. As they went over the garage, there was

Frankie tending to a car out on the front and Mrs Joice taking her dogs for a walk.

Approaching the airfield, the tattered windsock fluttered in the corner and Ted Tyrell's sheep were covering the grass. The crumbling control tower still defied nature's attempt to reclaim it, while the old wooden hangars stood on the edge of the airfield.

"Looking at the state of it, my house has missed me!" said Oliver.

"But it's our house now, Mr. Bramley," said V in a rather offended tone.

"Oh, oh yes. You've got a point, Olivia. I guess I'll have to find somewhere else to live! Harry and Beryl have got a spare room, so I'll stay with them for a while."

It would be difficult to explain this adventure to Mum easily; they couldn't just say: "We've just taken a ride back to 1699 and rescued the man who owned the house before us, and now he would like it back!" There would have to be another plan. Otherwise, she'd have a heart attack.

As they all helped to put Jenny away, Ben agreed with Oliver that they would meet up at the post office tomorrow and he would bring Dampier's half of the map. Together with the half Oliver retrieved from Kidd's travel chest, they would try to solve the puzzle. They closed the large hangar doors and waved goodbye. The kids ran back to the garden, through the broken gate and down through the elephant grass to the back door.

Oliver, with two bags of treasure in his hand,

walked more sedately across the airfield, breathing in the fresh summer air of the English countryside. Privet was in flower and the scent wafted past him as he left the airfield and walked down the lane towards the village. It really felt good to be back home and it was likely he could complete his original quest. He allowed a smile to stretch across his face, which no longer had any bruises, cuts, swollen eyes or pain.

★ ★ ★

Charlie, George and V chatted and laughed as they neared the house, but Ben followed a little behind them. For some unknown reason, he felt an urge to look up – not to the sky for an aeroplane, but to the attic window in the eaves of the house. For a moment, he thought he saw the face of a smiling woman, but he blinked and she was gone. He paused and took a second look, but no one was there. It definitely wasn't his mother, although he thought he recognised the face from somewhere. He looked away; his head was swimming with so many thoughts that he put the vision down to his imagination.

The kids trotted in through the back door very nonchalantly, as if they had just been in the garden playing games and mucking about.

"Had fun then, kids?" asked Laura.

They gathered around the table and, with bowed heads, looked furtively at each other. They'd all agreed not to say a thing about the trip.

"What's the matter? Cat got your tongue?"

The boys burst out laughing; the last time they had heard that was in 1699, from Football Head.

The reaction surprised Laura. "What have you lot been up to?"

"Oh nothing, Mum. Just messing about in the shed and garden."

"Well, so long as you haven't been out of the garden without telling me, eh?"

As if rehearsed, they responded in unison, "No, Mum, course not."

Laura made a suspicious face, her chin drawn into her neck and a frown on her brow.

"Honest," said Ben. "We didn't need to, because we've started making our den."

Laura shook her head. Somehow she didn't quite believe them; their eyes said different things to their mouths. "Well, anyway, wash your hands. It will be teatime soon."

The kids were already edging themselves out of the kitchen.

"Ben," said Laura, "before you go, please can you get me some more wood for the fire?"

"Of course, Mum."

The others disappeared upstairs, making the noise of a herd of elephants down the hallway. After bringing the wood in, Ben made his own way up the stairs. As he reached the small landing, he felt a chill breeze pass by him and heard a voice in his head. It was a voice he recognised, one he knew he would never forget. Although it sent a chill through him, it was a grateful voice – one of gratitude and thankfulness. He spun round on the landing in the direction of the disappearing chill.

"Sss… thank you, my dear. Sss… thank you so much."

There was nothing to see, only feel, and it disappeared as swiftly as it had arrived.

★ ★ ★

The sun came up on another beautiful summer's day in Rosemie Common. By ten o'clock, some small puffy white cumulus clouds drifted slowly on a breeze and a flock of starlings attacked some bread in the garden that Laura had thrown out.

As they left the house on their way to the post office, Ben looked up through the lower clouds and saw a holiday aeroplane, as V would call them, leaving a disappearing scar across the sky. He wondered for a moment where it might be going – though it wouldn't be as exciting a journey as Jenny could take them on. She was a truly magical machine; not just a bus ride in the sky. Over Ben's shoulder, he carried his leather satchel.

It was only a few minutes ride by bicycle for Ben and Charlie to reach the Hobbard's Post Office, where George was already waiting for them. "Ting a ling a ling," went the doorbell as they entered the shop and again as they closed it behind them. Out from behind the multicoloured plastic blind stepped a smiling Harry Hobbard. Shaking his head and grinning with a puffed out face, he rubbed his head with his hand.

"Come on, you best come through here." He lifted a section of the formica worktop and let them through.

He took them through the first room, which looked like a stock room cum post office sorting room, and out to a large kitchen in the rear. There, they found Oliver sipping a cup of tea, while Beryl was busy preparing some sort of baking.

"Morning, boys," said Oliver.

Beryl turned around, rubbing her hands down her apron. "Yes, yes, oh yes. Good morning, boys," she beamed, her cheeks displaying a bright rosy complexion. "Oh, we're so pleased to 'ave Mr Oliver back, so pleased."

She went over and put her arm around his shoulders, giving them a little squeeze and grinning even more. Harry and Beryl treated him more like a son than a friend.

It's going to be really lovely having him around, really lovely," she said, going back to her baking.

The three boys sat down opposite Oliver at the table, before Ben pulled out the treasure map and the old map of the Oyster Bay area he had got from Parsons in Tortuga. Oliver unfolded his half and placed it next to Ben's.

"So," said Harry, pulling up a chair, "there's a riddle that needs solving is there?"

"Yes," said Oliver, "this is the first time we've seen the complete map."

A day by cart on the seventh point to reach Penn's followers from the neck.

Take the sob road for three degrees of latitude turn thy face the Hempstead way.

A pace for a place of three round tables full of nights to reach the beck.

The crying tree shades the flowing juice of mother earth over ye chest.

Oliver ran his finger along the lines as he read them, then relaxed back in his chair. "Well, there it is. Where do we start?"

"Harry's quite good at those cryptic crosswords," said Beryl.

"Oh, go on with yer. Takes me a while sometimes," he smiled.

"Did you bring that map of Oyster Bay, Ben?" asked Oliver.

"Yes, here it is." Ben unfolded the map and handed it over.

"Good, let's see if this can help."

The two maps were placed alongside each other, then Oliver and Harry shuffled round to be on the same side of the table as the boys. They could all then study the maps from the same angle.

For what seemed like ages, yet was in fact only a few minutes, they stared at the table deep in thought. Harry scratched his chin, while Oliver looked sideways as if to solve a different problem, resting his face in his hand. Charlie used the opportunity to pick his nose and Ben gave him a dig in the ribs.

Harry broke the silence with, "Anyone got any

idea of a direction involving points? The seventh point – how many could there be?"

This somehow triggered Ben into thinking of the points of a compass. In his orienteering lessons, he had learnt that there were eighteen points on a compass, starting with north north east. The seventh point would be south south east.

"What if they're the points on a compass?" exclaimed Ben with pride.

"Good thinking, Ben," said Oliver.

"The seventh point would be south-southeast!"

"You're quite right, Ben. Well done, young man."

North was marked on the treasure map in the top right-hand corner with a diamond shaped pointer.

"That would mean this sort of direction." Oliver gesticulated over the map.

"What could 'from the neck' mean, Oliver?" Harry asked. "There's nothin' marked on the map."

Oliver suddenly remembered hearing a conversation about part of the harbour being called 'the neck', because of its shape.

"That is the neck," he exclaimed, pointing to the map. His finger then drew an imaginary line south-southeast from the area known as the neck, "But what is Penn's house?"

Silence surrounded them all again. Their faces strained in the search for the next answer, until Harry stamped his finger up and down on the map on the Quaker Meeting House.

"That's Penn's House – where it says the Quaker

Meeting House! William Penn was a well-known Quaker from England. I bet that's what it is."

Harry went on to explain how William Penn had sailed from England and founded Pennsylvania. There were Quaker meeting houses all over England and they spread over America, too. After his arrival in North America, he was effective in making good relations and successful treaties with the Lenape Indians. He was also instrumental in the foundation of what was to become the United States of America.

"Well done, Harry, that's the first line done," said Oliver, patting him on the back.

Charlie copied Oliver and patted George on the back. "First line, George! We've done the first line!"

"You've done the first line?" scoffed Ben.

Charlie smiled and wobbled his head from side to side.

Oliver tousled his fingers through Charlie's hair. "I'm sure there'll be something you'll do to help us solve the riddle, Charlie. What's the next line? Come on, you read it."

Charlie read the line out.

"What can 'sob' mean?" asked George.

"Is it short for something?" asked one of them.

Beryl opened a cupboard and removed a large circular baking tin, placing it on the worktop where she was mixing ingredients for a cake. "What if it is one of them anagram things? Or, what's the other ting?" She paused, then, "Oh, acronym."

"Acronym, yes of course," Oliver exclaimed.

"'S.O.B.', not 'sob'."

"Come on, boys. Where did you find me?"

"What do mean?"

"The town, the name of the town?" replied Oliver.

"Oyster Bay," Charlie blurted out.

"Yes, Charlie, that's right and there's also a South Oyster Bay. SOB!"

Oliver held out his hands as if to catch a very large ball, waiting for one of them to respond.

"Ah, the South Oyster Bay road," exclaimed Ben.

"But how far is a latitude mile?" asked George.

"Well," said Oliver, "that is not so well known. However, you are in the presence of a pilot that happens to know the answer. Aviation maps, like naval charts, have lines of latitude and longitude drawn on them."

He left them hanging on his words for a moment. They all turned and looked in Oliver's direction, waiting tensely for the explanation with anticipation.

Charlie's lips went to move into action and ask the question again, but Oliver smiled and beat him to it.

"It's a nautical mile."

"How long is that then, Oliver?" asked Harry.

"Oh, it's a bit longer than a normal land mile. I'll have to look up the conversion to be exact, but we'll be able to work it out easily enough. And Hempstead is to the west of there." He drew another finger line across the map, indicating where the town of Hempstead would be. Line two was complete.

"Okay," said Ben, "what about 'A pace for a place of three round tables full of nights'?"

"How does a night fill a table?" asked Charlie.

"It doesn't make sense."

"Have you got a piece of paper and a pencil, Mr Hobbard?" asked Ben.

"O'corse I 'ave, son." Harry poked around in a kitchen drawer full of odd bits and pieces, and found Ben a small pad of paper and a pencil.

"Thanks, Mr Hobbard." Ben started to doodle circles and the moon above. "What if the round table represents a full moon and there's three of them. Three full moons. And the days between are the paces?"

"Could be," mused Oliver. He rubbed his hand over his chin. "Why a pace, for a place, and how big is a round table?"

Ben continued to doodle on the pad.

"What if it is meant to be 'knights' not 'nights'," said Harry. "You knows, like them that had a round table."

"King Arthur, you mean?" piped up Charlie.

"Yes, them's the one. King Arthur and the Round Table wasn't it?"

"Yes!" shouted Oliver. "Of course, King Arthur's Knights of the Round Table, but how many places were—"

Before he could finish, Charlie jumped up excitedly and waved his hand about, "I know! I know!"

"Go on then," said Ben, slightly miffed that he might not have solved it. "How many were there?"

Charlie went on to explain that he'd been

learning about King Arthur and the Knights of the Round Table at school. According to the Round Table hanging in Winchester Cathedral, twenty-four knights sat at King Arthur's round table, plus a spare seat for the one who could achieve the finding of the Holy Grail. It made twenty-five in total. Therefore, they reasoned that three tables would give them seventy five paces.

A 'beck', Harry knew, was another name for a stream. It was Beryl placing another cup of tea in front of Oliver that inspired the idea that the 'juice of mother earth' may mean water, and George suggested that the crying tree might be a weeping willow.

Oliver slammed his hand down on the table in joy. Effervescent excitement spread around the room, and the boys thumped their fists and gave each other high fives. Oliver wasn't quite sure what this gesture was, but joined in anyway. Even Harry nervously held up an open palm to be slapped.

"Fantastic! Fantastic!" repeated Oliver.

"Who'd have thought anyone would bury their treasure underwater," remarked Harry.

"Clever, eh?" said Oliver.

"Will it still be alright, after all these years?" enquired George.

"I reckon it will," said Oliver. "I had to make a special waterproof box to go inside the trunk, which itself was built to keep out seawater. In any case, divers have been bringing up treasures like gold, silver and diamonds from sunken wrecks for years and it is always as good as the day the ship sunk."

As they all relaxed from their initial excitement, Charlie asked, "How do we know the treasure is still there?"

Oliver rubbed the top of Charlie's head in the way that adults do. "We don't, Charlie boy – but knowing no one else has had the maps, there's a good chance."

"But what about Mr Dampier?" asked Ben. "He had part of the map and probably drew it, and may even have helped write the riddle. He might have gone back for it himself."

"I don't think so," said Oliver. "I read in his diaries that he got a fair amount of payment from Captain Kidd for his work on the *Adventure Prize*. Kidd knew how to look after the people that were important to him. Also, as soon as he could, he boarded a ship out of Oyster Bay bound for England. In fact, he sailed around the same time as Kidd was taken a prisoner on board a Royal Navy ship of the line. He was lucky that Irish Jones never got hold of him."

By 1699 William Dampier had been desperate to return to England, as he had been away for many years – mainly at sea exploring new lands, including some of the coast of Australia and Philippine Islands, before he started sailing with the likes of Bartholomew Sharpe and William Kidd.

After his return, he settled in Bristol and never left England again. He travelled to London a few times to sell his work to the British Admiralty and advised on navigation and cartography, although the Navy Board weren't always receptive to his ideas. The members of the Navy Board were rather pompous and generally thought they did not need the help of someone who was now a civilian. He died alone without any family, and some of his work that he had stored in his loft was left undiscovered for years.

"What do we do now, Mr Bramley?" enquired Charlie.

"Well, the first thing is that you stop calling me Mr Bramley! That's far too formal. Oliver's my name, so please call me that."

"Okay, Mr Oliver," replied Charlie.

"How about just plain Oliver? I'm fine with that," he smiled. "Now, what we need to do is write out this riddle in plain English, so that anyone can find the resting place of this treasure."

"Why would we want to make it easy for someone else to find the treasure?" complained Charlie.

"Doh! That's the idea, Charlie," scoffed Ben. "Remember that Oliver wasn't going to get the treasure for himself. It was to go to the present-day native Indian community."

"That's right, Ben. Jenny isn't the way she is for personal gain, it's so that I can try and help others. Mind you, I've made some great friends and had some fantastic adventures along the way – although getting stuck in the seventeenth century wasn't part of my last plan!" Oliver laughed and gently slapped Ben on the back.

They all smiled and joined in the chuckle in agreement.

"If it wasn't for you lot, I'd still be there."

"You have Charlie to thank for that," said George. "It was his idea to get in the plane."

"It was me that worked out what you were doing, though," said Ben. "Charlie broke your plane to start with."

Oliver looked slightly disapprovingly at Charlie, but he was only jesting. The straight look lasted a few seconds, just enough time to worry the boy, before breaking out a big grin. "Don't worry, Charlie, you can't hurt Jenny. Remember, she is a very special aeroplane. She can look after herself. Did you not see the tree of life in the hieroglyph in the floor of the cabin?"

The three kids all shook their heads.

"It happened after I rescued the old man in the desert. Next time you get in, lift the carpet and have a close look at the floor."

Oliver went on to describe how the hieroglyph was embedded as if it had grown in the floor panel. He believed it to be connected with pre-Islamic Persian or Babylonian Mythology and the shape its branches took made it look like a cross. He couldn't really explain its presence; he only knew of its effect on his aeroplane and himself.

"Gosh, Mr Oliver," said Harry, "I've not seen it either."

"Well, no, Harry, I'd covered it with a carpet years ago. To save me getting any questions – should someone see it."

"So what do we do now, Oliver?" asked Ben.

"Well, we write out how to find the treasure and

send it anonymously to a respected local Native American Indian in the area."

"What's anonymous?" asked Charlie.

"Oh Charlie," sighed Ben, "it means they won't know who sent it."

"Oh I see."

Oliver, Harry and Beryl smiled.

Oliver asked Harry for some paper and a pen, and proceeded to write down a decoded message for their chosen beneficiary. He popped it in a brown paper envelope, along with the map and an explanation of how they should not reveal how they came about the information.

"Harry, could you get me the name and address of that person we found on the Internet last night?"

"Of course I can, Mr Oliver. No problem."

The boys looked at each other in surprise.

"You have a computer, Mr Hobbard?" asked Ben.

"Oh yes, we do. We do indeed, my love," answered Beryl.

Harry left the room.

"Of course, 'e don't how to use, mind. Oh no, not Harry – all smoke and mirrors to 'im, it is!"

They all laughed.

Moments later, Harry returned with a name and address to put on the envelope. The Chief of the Montaukett and a Long Island address. Once written out, the letter disappeared into the postal system sack.

"What shall we do now then, Ben?" asked Charlie

"Think you should be getting home, my lad," replied Harry.

"No, I mean where shall we go in the aeroplane? Can I fly it?" Charlie asked, with sparkling eyes.

"I think you've had quite enough excitement, young lad. We need to sort a few things out before letting you go on another trip – like telling your mum for a start," said Oliver.

"Good luck explaining that one," laughed Ben.

"Yes, I'm not sure how we'll do that either."

"We can fly again, though, can't we?" pleaded Charlie

"Oh, I'm sure we will."

"'Cause I've been learning about King Arthur and the Knights of the Round Table."

"Yes, you told us that, Charlie", retorted Ben.

"Well," Charlie continued, "Arthur was forced to fight and kill his best knight and friend Sir Lancelot, because he was told that Sir Lancelot had betrayed him – but it was untrue. Sir Lancelot was a true and good knight, and some of the others were jealous of him. We could go and put it right, Oliver, because after that King Arthur was never happy and he lost many of his knights, 'cause they stopped coming to his round table."

"Well, that's something we could look at," replied Oliver.

"It was your idea to go and find a pirate," protested Ben. "What about going where I would like? It doesn't have to be all about you, Charlie."

"Come on, boys, you don't have to have a fight over it. We can sit down and look at both ideas, and maybe George knows of more causes that need our help."

George nodded.

"Whatever it is, Charlie's bound to mess it up," said Ben.

Oliver put his arm around Ben's shoulder, "Now, Charlie obviously just gets a bit over-enthusiastic sometimes." He cast a glance in Charlie's direction, who gave a cheeky, squinting grin in return.

They left Harry and Beryl in the kitchen and went through to the shop.

"Now, boys, remember what I said: no more adventures without me," said Oliver.

The boys smiled at each other and headed for the door.

★ ★ ★

The following week, Oliver saw the news he had been waiting for. It was on the front page of a copy of the *New York Times*, which Harry had ordered in for him: 'Treasure Trove found in South Oyster Bay Park.'

According to the report, the chief's son had been playing in the park when his ball had fallen into a stream by a huge weeping willow tree. While poking around with a stick to find his ball, the boy had struck something hard. He had stabbed around in the water, hitting what he thought was a large object, before telling his father. The chief and his brother had then climbed into the stream and dug out an old wooden chest. Breaking it open on the banks of the steam, it had revealed another smaller box full of gold and silver coins, and bags of diamonds and rubies. The treasure trove had been found on sacred Native American Indian ground and would therefore belong to those that found it, not the state.

The value was estimated in the millions of dollars.

Oliver closed the paper and smiled.

Characters to Research and Places to Enjoy Visiting:

Blackbeard: His real name was believed to be Edward Teach and he was born in England. He sailed the Caribbean seas as a fearsome pirate and the ship he sailed, which he had captured from the French, was named the *Queen Anne's Revenge*. There are many books for all ages telling the story of Blackbeard's life.

Capt. William Kidd: Born in Scotland, he was a privateer and pirate. He started out on a voyage in 1696 as a pirate hunter and privateer, but soon switched sides and had a brief but moderately successful career as a pirate. A privateer was a ship's captain that was given permission by the King to plunder the vessels of foreign states at war with Great Britain. Eventually he was arrested, stood trial in England and was found guilty of various crimes. He was sentenced to death by hanging.

Capt. Bartholomew Sharpe: A buccaneer, ruthless thief and murderer, Sharpe was also an accomplished navigator. He was the first English sailor to make the treacherous voyage around Cape Horn from the west. He secured a book of charts of the South Americas from the Spanish, which assisted in his acquittal when put on trial for piracy in England.

William Dampier: Although at one time in his naval career he was made a captain, Dampier was not a successful one. As a crew member he circumnavigated the globe twice, at a time when few had any experience of such journeys. He collected a vast amount of navigational information about many of the seas he'd sailed and documented them for others to use.

Tortuga: A Caribbean island that forms part of Haiti. From around1630 onwards, the island of Tortuga was divided into French and English colonies, allowing buccaneers to use the island as their main base of operations. The island changed hands many times between the various occupiers over the centuries.

Man-o-WarSailing Ship: A term given to any large naval sailing fighting ship, normally equipped with many cannons on three-gun decks. The ship HMS *Victory*, preserved at Portsmouth Harbour (England), is an excellent example that Admiral Nelson used in the Battle of Trafalgar.

Long Island: An island located just off the northeast coast of the United States and a region within the US state of New York. It was originally known as Nassau Island. Nearby is Gardiners Island, where some of William Kidd's original treasure was recovered.

Native American Indian Tribes: There were many native Indian tribes on Long Island before the new settlers arrived. The Montauk, or Montaukett, were just one such tribe that sold their birthright to the British and other settlers. The Montauk people were one of hundreds of native tribes that existed in America before the arrival of the European settlers.

National Maritime Museum – Greenwich, London: The National Maritime Museum's manuscripts collection is the largest and most important archive of maritime history in the world. The collection occupies over four linear miles of shelf space and covers all aspects of British seafaring history from the fourteenth to the twentieth centuries. It also houses an amazing collection of naval artefacts and items of interest from hundreds of years of maritime history.

Portsmouth Historic Dockyard: The dockyard is home to many historic naval artefacts, including HMS *Victory*, HMS *Warrior* (the Royal Navy's first iron-hulled warship) and King Henry's warship the *Mary Rose*. The *Mary Rose* sank with the loss of many lives, but her recovery from the Solent in 1982 revealed a fantastic horde of sisteenth-century naval warfare.

Chatham Historic Dockyard: This is the shipyard that built the *Victory* and has many exciting exhibits like HMS *Gannet*, launched in 1872. It is also host to an array of interesting buildings, like the ropery, where the long and heavy-duty hemp rope required for sailing ships is made. It is the only ropery of its kind still in commercial operation.

De Havilland DH50: The aircraft used for the adventures of Charlie Green is a bi-plane from the 1920s. The only flying example is in Australia, where it was used by Qantas Airlines and was the first aeroplane used for the Royal Flying Doctor Service of Australia. The DH 50 was designed and built at the home of the De Havilland Aircraft Company, Stag Lane Aerodrome, England. It had a four-seat passenger cabin, with an open cockpit for the pilot above and behind the cabin.